ET

'Let *go*!' von Helsinore roared above the sounds of strangulation coming from his man and he waved the Luger in a threating fashion.

'Say *"please"*,' Rapido answered, keeping his thumb and fingers buried into the throat of his burly captive.

'*Gott in himmel!*' von Helsinore thundered and the pistol was shaking with a barely controlled fury as he was raising it to take aim. 'Let go, or I'll shoot you!

'Had such been your intent', you'd've done it, 'stead of talking,' Rapido asserted quietly and without relaxing his grip. 'Only I conclude you're all fired up to know how come a lil ole Texas boy like me can handle his-self so good. Happen I'm *wrong*, cut loose and *make* me leave go. Should I be *right*, say *"please"*!'

RAPIDO CLINT STRIKES BACK

J.T. Edson

CORGI BOOKS

RAPIDO CLINT STRIKES BACK
A CORGI BOOK 0 552 13623 9

First publication in Great Britain

PRINTING HISTORY
Corgi edition 1990

Copyright © J.T. Edson 1990

The right of J.T. Edson to be identified as author of this
work has been asserted in accordance with sections 77 and 78
of the Copyright Designs and Patents Act 1988.

This book is set in 10pt Times by
County Typesetters, Margate, Kent

Corgi Books are published by Transworld Publishers Ltd.,
61–63 Uxbridge Road, Ealing, London W5 5SA, in Australia
by Transworld Publishers (Australia) Pty. Ltd., 15–23 Helles
Avenue, Moorebank, NSW 2170, and in New Zealand by
Transworld Publishers (N.Z.) Ltd., Cnr. Moselle and
Waipareira Avenues, Henderson, Auckland.

Printed and bound in Great Britain by
Cox & Wyman Ltd., Reading, Berks.

*For Allan Barber, Les Marsh and Derek Woods
of Humbersome Heights Golf Club, Leicester,
who only put up with my lousy jokes and worse play
so they can be assured of one member in our
regular four-ball they all know they can beat*

Author's Note

When supplying us with the information from which we produce our books, one of the strictest rules imposed upon us by the present day members of what we call the 'Hardin, Fog and Blaze' clan and the 'Counter' family is that we *never* under any circumstances disclose their true identities, nor their present locations. Therefore, we are instructed to *always* employ sufficient inconsistencies to ensure neither can happen.

We would like to point out that the names of people who appear in this volume are those supplied to us by our informants in Texas and any resemblance with those of other persons, living or dead, is purely coincidental.

To save our 'old hands' repetition, but for the benefit of new readers, we have given a 'potted biography' of Alvin Dustine 'Cap' Fog and the formation of Company 'Z', Texas Rangers in the form of an Appendix.

We realize that, in our present 'permissive' society, we could use the actual profanities employed by various people in the narrative. However, we do not concede a spurious desire to create 'realism' is any excuse to do so.

Lastly as we refuse to pander to the current 'trendy' usage of the metric system, except when referring to the calibre of certain firearms traditionally measured in millimetres – i.e. Walther P-38, 9mm – we will continue to employ miles, yards, feet, inches, stones, pounds and ounces, when quoting distances or weights.

J.T. EDSON,
MELTON MOWBRAY,
Leicestershire,
England.

PROLOGUE

The Chance Of A – Um – Lifetime

'This is a fine state of affairs, I must say, Randy,'
commented Sir Howard Houghton-Rand, K.C.M.G.[1],
as he walked into a skimpily furnished room at a small
and seedy looking night club in Soho on the last
Wednesday in June. He spoke in jovial and somewhat
fruity tones which went well with his appearance. In his
middle fifties, tall, thickset, grey-haired, with rugged
and florid features, he contrived, despite holding the
post of Home Secretary in the Cabinet, to give the
impression of being no more than an amiable, none-too-
bright, albeit prosperous farmer. Although addressing
his companion, his gaze was directed at the man who had
risen to greet them as they came in. 'I can imagine the
headlines and stories in the Opposition newspapers if the
police should decide to raid this place while *we* are here.'

'So can I, Farmer,' admitted Sir Randolph Brandon,
K.C.,[2] in the dry voice he found an asset to his duties as
Director Of Public Prosecutions. Matching the Home
Secretary in height and age, he was lean and might have

----

*1. K.C.M.G.; Knight Commander of the Order of St Michael
and St George. Because it was so frequently awarded to officials
of the Foreign Office serving in Great – as it was then – Britain's
colonies around the world, the recipient of the lesser honour,
C.M.G. – Commander of the Order of St Michael & St George –
was jocularly referred to by his associates as having become a
'Colonial Made Gentleman'.*

*2. King's – Queen's while Her Majesty Queen Elizabeth is on
the throne – Counsel: a barrister designated as a counsel of the
crown and who cannot afterward plead against the crown – act
on behalf of a defendant in a case – without special permission.*

11

sat as model for a painting of a member of some exceptionally severe religious order which opposed all forms of amusement and had renounced the 'pleasures of the flesh'. He had absorbed this *persona* so thoroughly that he made his excellently cut dinner suit, clearly the product of the best tailor's establishment in Savile Row, look even more sombre and drab than the attire of a not too successful provincial undertaker. 'They would have a field day.'

'Have no fear, Sir Howard, there is *no* – um – danger of such an eventuality,' declared the third occupant of the room, whose acquaintance with the other two clearly did not extend to being on such close terms as to permit the employment of nicknames. What was more, despite the reassurance, his tone sounded hesitant and apologetic rather than certain in timbre. 'In fact, despite it's – um – name, there is no more respectable establishment in the whole of Soho than the – um – *Les Plaisirs des Paree.*'

'*Les Plaisirs des Paree,* huh,' Houghton-Rand grunted, glancing around the less than elegant room and thinking of the dingy stairs he had ascended to reach it. He made the comment to help him recover from the surprise caused by discovering who he had obviously been brought to meet. 'This place doesn't remind me of any of the pleasures of Paris I remember from my misspent youth.'

'Or me,' Brandon seconded, in a way which implied he too had sampled a number of the 'pleasures' offered by the French capital city at some time in the past and retained fonder recollections of them than might be expected from one of his apparently dour mien.

'There you gentlemen have the – um – advantage over me,' sighed the man who had obviously been awaiting the arrival of the illustrious pair. He spoke with the air of one saddened by his misfortune in the matter. 'Regrettably, having failed to – um – misspend my youth, if that is the correct term, I am not familiar with the – um – pleasures of that – or any other – um – city.'

Despite the light nature of the conversation, which in some way the apparently doleful comment of the last speaker had not made more serious, the Home Secretary continued to look at him in a speculative fashion. Like his companion, Houghton-Rand felt sure the man on the other side of the table had had more to do with the 'pleasures' offered by Paris and numerous other cities in Europe and throughout the United Kingdom than either of them. However, he was equally aware that the acquaintance had been in the line of duty and not while searching for hedonistic satisfaction.

Regardless of the conclusions drawn by the Home Secretary, the speaker, in addition to apparently being of a lower social status, showed none of the sartorial elegance of the men he was addressing. On the other hand, everything about him might have been intended to compliment perfectly his mode of speech.

Almost six foot in height, the man had a slender and seemingly fragile build which made Brandon look robust by comparison. He had sandy side-whiskers, rather outstanding ears, a mournful cast of features and a fairly prominent nose upon which, secured to his lapel by a silk cord, steel rimmed *pince-nez* perched so far down he must have found it very difficult to see through them. Nor did his garments – being of a style that was practically *de rigueur* for the bailiff of a County Court, or a Coroner's Officer, in an earlier decade – do anything to correct an impression of advanced middle age.[3] High and flat-crowned, the black hat – which lay alongside a neatly furled black umbrella in front of him on the table – had ceased to be fashionable several years ago. Nothing about him suggested why he should be meeting two such important personages. Yet it was obvious they regarded him as being something akin to a social equal.

3. *A more lengthy description of the attire worn by Mr Reeder is given in:* CAP FOG, TEXAS RANGER, MEET MR J.G. REEDER *and* THE RETURN OF RAPIDO CLINT AND MR J.G. REEDER.

Appearances notwithstanding, Houghton-Rand was aware that the archaic looking man was probably far better known to the general public than either himself or Brandon. Even before having been appointed Chief Investigative Officer for the Director of Public Prosecutions, Mr J.G. Reeder's picture had frequently appeared in newspapers which recorded his successful participation in solving a crime.

'Well, Mr Reeder,' Houghton-Rand said, after the three men had seated themselves at the table and his demeanour indicated he was ready to get down to the business of the evening. 'Why have you had me brought here?'

'The suggestion for the – um – meeting was Sir Randolph's, sir,' the elderly looking detective asserted, his demeanour seeming to imply he wished his subordinate status to the Director of Public Prosecutions to be established and whatever credit for the responsibility of the meeting should be placed where it belonged. 'Although I must confess that I selected the – um – rendezvous, to employ what is, I believe, a French – um – expression. I trust your journey here was pleasant and not too – um – uncomfortable?'

'I've had less *puzzling* rides,' Houghton-Rand claimed dryly. 'Usually when I've travelled by taxi, the driver took the *shortest* route to the destination instead of—!'

'Were we followed, Mr Reeder?' Brandon interrupted.

'Followed?' Houghton-Rand ejaculated in a brisker fashion than his usual mode of speech. 'Why should we be *followed*?'

'It was a – um – contingency I envisaged, Sir Howard,' Mr J.G. Reeder answered, making the words sound more like a shocking confession than a claim. 'You may not know it, but I am afflicted by a *most* distressing quirk of – um – nature—.'

'Your famous "criminal mind",' the Home Secretary suggested with a smile.

'My "criminal mind", as you so succinctly – um – put

14

it,' agreed the elderly looking detective, sounding almost sorrowful. 'Causing me to see evil in the most innocent things and reach unpleasant – um – conclusions as it does, it is a most – um – unfortunate malady and, I am afraid, it led me to consider you might be followed by – um – persons who would be most interested to discover where you were going and with whom you were to meet; also, if possible, to ascertain the reason for the – um – journey.'

'Hum!' Houghton-Rand said pensively, glancing at Sir Randolph Brandon and his own features assumed their most bovinely blank expression. 'I wondered why the taxi driver took such a roundabout route to get here. I couldn't believe he would have been doing it to push up the fare, not with *us* as his passengers.'

'Parker had his – um – instructions,' Mr Reeder claimed when his superior did not answer. 'And, I feel sure, he carried them out in a most – um – satisfactory fashion.'

Some of the things which had puzzled the Home Secretary since leaving his home were now becoming clear. Having been friends with Brandon since childhood, and being in close contact because of their official positions, he had seen nothing unusual in receiving an invitation to spend an evening with him. His surprise on being picked up in a taxi, especially one which looked so dingy and unkempt, had been explained as resulting from the Director's wife having taken their Rolls Royce and no other transport being available. However, he had been puzzled by the rapid pace at which the seemingly decrepit vehicle travelled through the streets while taking a very roundabout route to reach the night club in one of the less salubrious parts of Soho. Now he realized that equipping the taxi with an exceptionally powerful engine served a useful purpose. When being employed upon clandestine assignments, there would be times when a turn of speed far beyond normal was required.

Despite having cleared up part of his puzzlement, Houghton-Rand considered there were other matters of even greater importance demanding his attention!

'Then he was one of *your* men?' the Home Secretary asked, although the words were more of a statement than a question. 'But why should anybody want to follow us?'

'To find out where you are going and, if – um – possible, why,' Mr Reeder replied. 'There are those to whom this could be a matter of the greatest – um – importance.'

'Who, damn it?' Houghton-Rand demanded.

'You have heard of the – um – International Attainers?' the detective inquired, Brandon having sat back in a manner which indicated the proceedings would now be left in his hands.

'International Attainers?' the Home Secretary queried, but his tone did not show complete puzzlement.

'Each country where they are known, although "known" is hardly correct in its general – um – sense, has its own name for them,' Mr Reeder replied. 'I won't attempt to give the foreign – um – designations. However, amongst members of what is popularly called the um – underworld in this country, they are spoken of as the "Big 'N's".'

'I have *heard* of them,' Houghton-Rand admitted. 'But, to be frank, I never really believed that they exist.'

'I know the idea of an organization of that nature is more suited to the pages of a sensational novel,' Mr Reeder conceded. Then he went on with what, for him, was an unusually assured tone. 'But there is nothing more – um – certain than that they *do* exist and have for a number of – um – years.'

'Tell me all you know about them,' Houghton-Rand requested.

Losing all the hesitancy which had characterized his speech until then, the detective explained how the International Attainers came into being some time during the first decade of the 20th Century. They were a group of men from several countries, every one a millionaire many times over, who dabbled in collecting

16

objet d'art of various kinds. Each was sufficiently wealthy to obtain anything attainable for a high enough price, but this was not enough for them. They began to desire the unattainable and, being the kind of men they were, had set about achieving this.

As far as was known, the first subject of the Attainers' illicit operations was a Van Dyck painting held in trust by the reigning family of the Netherlands on behalf of the Dutch people. It was believed to have been destroyed in a fire while being taken to be cleaned. However, although no definite proof was forthcoming, Mr Reeder had been informed that a substitute was burned and the real painting was in the hands of one of the Attainers. On Houghton-Rand remarking that the man would never dare let anybody else see it, the detective replied that none of them intended to put the items they obtained on public display. Instead, each was kept in a secret hiding place and, while allowing his associates to see it, the ownership of the piece was all that counted with every one of them.

Having vast resources at their command, the Attainers were able to have the actual acquisition of each piece carried out by the criminal, or group of criminals, they considered best qualified for the task. When necessary, they would arrange for a perfect duplication to be produced and substituted for the desired object. However, to prevent the chance of blackmail by their employees, they had built up a secret organization with many of the attributes of an ordinary business. Each level of it knew only their immediate superior in the stratum above. Everything was arranged so that even the best and most astute criminal met only the person who hired him and never came into contact with what might be termed the 'Board of Directors'.

From the beginning, the Attainers had done everything they could to ensure the loyalty of those they employed. The criminals were rewarded more substantially than they might hope to be by their own efforts. What is more, should any of them be caught, the finest legal defence available was provided and, in the event of being imprisoned, the man, or men, would be reimbursed for all the time of incarceration and all dependants were generously cared for.

As an added precaution, the Attainers had established in no uncertain fashion just how serious the consequences of betraying their trust would be. About a year after they commenced operations, a cat-burglar was hired to steal a painting which did not require substitution. However, considering it would be marketable through his own sources, he had fled with it instead of handing it over. Some six months later, a number of other criminals who had 'worked' for the Attainers were gathered at a lonely property somewhere in France. The absconding cat-burglar was brought into their presence and the story of his perfidy and capture in another country when he tried to dispose of the painting was told. Then, after his wife and two children had been shot in front of him, he was skinned alive by a couple of Orientals specially imported for that purpose.

When Houghton-Rand had claimed the story sounded like something out of a blood-and-thunder novel of the most lurid kind, Mr Reeder had confessed there was no proof that it had happened. On the other hand, it was known that the cat-burglar and his family disappeared without a trace about the time the event was alleged to have taken place. What was more, many members of the underworld were convinced the retribution had occurred. One criminal, who had reason for feeling gratitude to the detective and who had supplied information on numerous occasions, had used it as an excuse for declining to make any statement regarding the activities of the Attainers.

Asked what else had been acquired by the group, Mr Reeder replied that he did not have a complete list. Nevertheless, he believed there was not a country in Europe which has not yielded at least one of its great and irreplaceable art treasures, be it a painting, piece of exclusive pottery, or item of extremely special jewellery, to them. Nor had their depredations been confined to Europe. They had carried out similar robberies throughout the world, but selected the objects with great care and the replacements were perfect copies of the originals. However, on those occasions when he or one of his associates in other countries were certain a substitution had been made, the fear of a political scandal which could rock, perhaps even overthrow, the Government concerned prevented the facts being made public.

'It *could* happen,' Houghton-Rand conceded, feeling sure that – although it was a closely guarded secret – the man he was addressing knew the situation had arisen many years ago in the United Kingdom.

Much to the Home Secretary's relief, Mr Reeder did not continue with the subject. Instead, he told of how – employing her maiden name 'Ollorby', to avoid having his organization known as being connected in the affair – Mrs Jane Amelia Grible succeeded in thwarting the attempt the Attainers had made to purloin the Crown Jewels from the Tower.[4]

'And a damned good piece of work it was,' Houghton-Rand praised. 'But I can't understand why a band of – well, let's not mince words and call them what they are,

---

4. *Because Edgar Wallace was not given all the facts, he made no reference to the involvement of the International Attainers when describing the incident, and referred to Jane Amelia Grible of Mr J.R. Reeder's organization as 'Mrs Jane Ollorby' and described her as holding a post at Scotland Yard, in the book he entitled:* THE TRAITOR'S GATE.

Edgar Wallace was allowed to pay an indirect tribute to the lady in question at first hand on Page 53 of RED ACES, *quote: 'This is Mrs Grible of my Department,' he – Mr Reeder – said gravely.*

We have been allowed to give Mrs Grible the credit she deserves by telling of her participation in the events we have recorded as: CAP FOG, TEXAS RANGER, MEET MR J.G. REEDER *and* THE RETURN OF RAPIDO CLINT AND MR J.G. REEDER.

no matter how rich – art thieves, who must all be getting on well in years, should want to have Sir Randolph and I followed.'

'Although some of the original group are still active, others have been replaced by younger – albeit equally wealthy – men,' the detective explained. 'What is more, from the beginning, desirable though they undoubtedly considered the – um – end result to be, the acquisition of such *objet d'art* was in all too many cases subsidiary to some more sinister business.'

'In what way?' the Home Secretary asked.

'Any way which would show them a substantial – um – profit,' Mr Reeder replied and elaborated.

One early example was the support the Attainers gave to Phillipe Jose Urrea when he took over as *Presidente* of Santa Carlos. In return for this, companies which they controlled – although none of their names were listed on the Board of Directors – were granted various concessions in that country which more than recompensed them for the costs they incurred. As a bonus, one of them was allowed to substitute an exact duplicate for the famous Cross Of Santa Carlos from the capital's cathedral. Since then, they had continued to sponsor minor insurrections, or ferment revolutions, wherever it would be to their benefit. However, while Mr Reeder admitted no legal proof against the Attainers had been obtained, he and his associates knew one of their efforts had not been minor in its effects. They had arranged for the assassination of Archduke Francis Ferdinand and Duchess Sophie of Austria at Sarajevo on 28 June 1914. This put the whole world in arms and, as they were prepared for the War which followed, increased their fortunes immensely.

Despite the evidence being insufficient to allow anybody to be brought to trial, Mr Reeder claimed that the Attainers had had a great many Russian art and other treasures – including the Lafcadio Loan Collection reported as destroyed in Moscow during 1918, but actually now in the possession of those Attainers who specialized in collecting paintings[5] – given to them as part of the recompense for the services they rendered to the revolutionaries in that country. They had not acted from any political ideals, their motivation being profit and the protection their own interests received against Bolshevik atrocities or interference. More had been forthcoming as a result of their being the greatest of assistance to the Russian Government, who as yet did not have outlets of their own, in supplying arms and explosives to anarchists and radicals elsewhere in the world.

'Most of what you've told me is pure conjecture,' the Home Secretary commented, as Mr Reeder stopped speaking. 'And, even when you are sure of something, you admit there isn't enough evidence to make it stand up in court.'

'Unfortunately, sir, that has been the – um – case – up to now,' the detective conceded.

'Then you have evidence at last?' Houghton-Rand asked hopefully.

'Not *yet*, sir,' Mr Reeder admitted, once again speaking with conviction. 'However, I might not be over-stating the – um – issue if I was to say we have the chance of a – um – lifetime to gravely curtail their future activities and perhaps even bring their reign of crime to an end.'

'And I agree, Farmer,' Sir Randolph declared.

'Tell me more,' Houghton-Rand requested, sitting up straighter.

'We have had communication with the man who might be considered the "Managing Director" of their "branch" in the United Kingdom,' the detective obliged and, somehow, he seemed to be much younger than was suggested by his archaic attire and general appearance. What was more, the hesitancy left his speech. 'He's sent us sufficient proof to establish his claim to that position and offers to give us evidence which will let us achieve

5. *For further information about John Sebastian Lafcadio, R.A., see:* DEATH OF A GHOST, *by Margery Allingham.*

our purpose. In return, he askes for immunity and that no attempt will be made to trace him after he has carried out his part of the bargain.'

'With so little time to make the arrangement, I took it upon myself to agree,' the Director of Public Prosecutions asserted.

'You did the right thing,' Houghton-Rand replied, nodding approval. 'Now what is going to happen?'

'We have been given a rendezvous, a password and countersign by which the informant and our collector of the information may recognize each other,' Mr Reeder explained, as once more his superior made it plain he was to continue. 'He will give us the means by which we can obtain all the documentary proof we require and, in return, we have agreed to take no action, other than checking it is all he claims, for two days. I feel nothing would have been gained by denying this period of grace as it will, in all probability, take us longer than that to check everything he has to offer.'

'Then everything is straightforward enough,' the Home Secretary suggested, wondering why he had been brought into the matter at this particular stage of its development.

'So far,' Mr Reeder agreed and reverted to his previous style of seemingly hesitant speech. 'Nevertheless, the affair is still a *long* way from being over and I admit I am – um – uneasy. For the past two days, we have all been kept under observation and we are at a loss to know *why*. Certainly it is not being done by any – um – criminals with whom we have had dealings, or who may expect us to do so in the not too distant future. In fact, every one we have questioned denies all knowledge of it.'

'And you think the Attainers may have learned what their man intends?' Houghton-Rand asked.

'He was still alive this morning, which makes me believe nothing – um – *certain* about his intentions is known,' the detective replied. 'However, my – um – criminal mind suggests it may be suspected that he is dissatisfied with his lot for some reason and seeks to sever his connections with them. In which case, even though he probably has accrued sufficient of their – um – money to make him financially independent of them, he would know he will never be safe while they are in their present position of power. Having drawn such a conclusion, they would probably consider he would approach *me* – if you will forgive the – um – immodesty of the assumption – as the one most suitable to help him attain his ends.'

'And that's why you thought we might be followed here?'

'It is. They would know I would need someone with greater authority to give final concurrence to the arrangement.'

'You have it,' Houghton-Rand stated. 'Can I ask where the rendezvous is?'

'Certainly, Sir Howard,' Mr Reeder assented.

'Good God, man!' the Home Secretary gasped, on being told the location of the meeting. 'It *can't* be there. *He* wouldn't allow it!'

'Nevertheless, that is where the – um – rendezvous is to take place,' the detective claimed with absolute conviction. However, he refrained from mentioning a theory which his 'criminal mind' – the more dramatic designation he gave to his penchant for producing theories which seemed too fantastic to be true, yet frequently proved correct – had suggested. 'I am so – um – sure of this, I have already made preparations for the – um – collection.'

'But from what you've said so far, I assume you won't be collecting whatever it is this chap, whoever he is, has to offer personally.'

'Regrettably, I will *not*. Nor, as I feel sure they are all marked, will any other member of our organization.'

'Then *who*—?'

'A young man of great courage and considerable initiative; but who, we hope for his sake, is not known to have any – um – connection with us. He is fully cognizant

23

with the risks, also that we have done as much as we can to try to minimize them. However, Sir Howard, should things go – um – amiss, we will need *your* assistance.'

'In what?' Houghton-Rand asked.

'Providing *adequate* support to ensure his safe departure from the rendezvous,' Mr Reeder answered and his face became grave. 'We are up against men of a ruthlessness far beyond any criminal in the United Kingdom and who will not hesitate before resorting to the use of *firearms* should the need arise.'

'And you want authority to have the local police armed,' the Home Secretary guessed.

'That would be a sensible – um – precaution, Sir Howard,' the detective conceded. 'However, I would also suggest you have *troops* standing by. What is more, I consider you would be – um – wise, to select those who have most recently returned from India, or some other area in the Empire, where they have had experience of being under – um – hostile fire.'

'You think it could be *that* serious,' Houghton-Rand said sombrely.

'I *know* it could,' Mr Reeder corrected grimly. 'In fact, sir, with that contingency in mind, I fear we must ask for your – um – *official* assistance in another matter.'

CHAPTER ONE

Rapido

'Well I've got us here without having a collision, running over somebody, or even so much as putting us into a ditch, much to your surprise,' said a cheerful young feminine voice, from outside the main dining-room of the Admiral Cornwallis Inn. The voice was of a kind which one might expect to hear at such an elegant establishment in Hampshire. The tones were indicative of good breeding and upbringing, but showed amusement rather than resentment over what had obviously been criticism of her ability as a driver. 'Now what do you think of this place, Rap – *Edward*?'

'I'd say it's mighty fine, way it looks, and going by the smell of cooking I'm getting,' came a masculine reply with a drawling and vastly different accent. 'I'll tell you, Beryl, you've got us beat to all get out over here when it comes to fancy saloons. We don't have *anything* like this back home to Texas, nor any other place I've been in the good old US of A.'

Listening to the second comment as he sat in a booth, Doctor Andrew Lachlan McCallister, MD, concluded that the still unseen second speaker's origins were on the other side of the Atlantic Ocean. However, the voice did not have the somewhat nasal twang generally associated with people from the United States due to it being most frequently parodied on the stage in England. Having spent three months in the United States shortly after becoming qualified, even without hearing the reference to 'back home to Texas', McCallister would have known enough to conclude the still unseen man had been born and raised somewhere south of the 'Mason-Dixon' line.

Considering the implications suggested by the two voices, McCallister darted a worried glance at the only other three occupants of the large and comfortably furnished dining-room. Unkept in dress, all were tall, two being lanky and the other built on massive lines. It was obvious from their appearance and what they had been saying that they were all in a very bad humour and he suspected that they would not be averse to finding somebody upon whom they could vent their spleen.

The doctor did not recognize any of the trio, but could guess what they were. Since settling in London, he had come across a number of people looking, speaking and behaving as they did among the pseudo-intellectual set which based itself, dabbling in what they called 'art' and espousing politics of a communistic persuasion, in and around the Bloomsbury district. Although he had been surprised to see them so far from their usual haunts, the remarks passed between them had supplied a reason. He was aware that their kind, despite professing a hatred of capitalism and those who benefited from it, never hesitated to batten on to anybody who was wealthy – and stupid – enough to keep them in better circumstances than were usually their lot.

It seemed the trio had been fortunate enough to find such a person. A middle-aged spinster had developed a taste for what she believed to be the Bohemian style of life and had invited a group of their kind to stay in the grounds of a nearby mansion where she lived as a permanent house-guest of her wealthy family. Far from being grateful, they had encouraged her to demean herself by acting in ways most unsuitable for one of her years. This behaviour had come to a head that morning. Having been induced to dance in a diaphanous gown most unsuitable for a woman of her years and less than slender build, she had suffered a stroke. Apparently, what they had not realized was that, in the interests of keeping the peace with their hostess – who had a penchant for hysterics, or highly dramatic, ear-splitting and prolonged vocal protests, which made everybody else's life a misery, when her desires were thwarted – the family had allowed them to remain on suffrance. Using the incident as an excuse, the owner had ordered the entire party to leave the property. The rest had gone straight back to London, but they had elected to break their journey at the Inn.

Despite finding the frequent and gratuitous profanities with which the trio interspersed their conversation annoying, being afraid of the possible consequences to himself was not the reason McCallister had refrained from stating his objections. Nor did he doubt he could hold his own if they started to take out their spite on him. While not as tall as any of them, he had a sturdy build and, living an active life outside his profession, was much fitter. Therefore, he did not doubt his ability to render a good account of himself if there should be a rough-and-tumble. But having been imbued since childhood with a respect for law and order, he had also developed a strong sense of responsibility to his profession since graduating as a doctor and all this prevented him from following his inclination.

Neatly dressed in a tweed three-piece suit, with a white shirt and his old school tie, there was an air of mildness about McCallister's pleasantly good looking, clean shaven face which was far from being his true nature. At school and while a medical student, he had established a reputation for being willing to indulge in any kind of rough horseplay or any reckless escapade his fellows thought up. On qualifying three years ago and being accepted as assistant to his uncle, Sir James Bannister, MD – plus numerous other initials – he had elected to live in a more sedate fashion as required by his changed circumstances. Nevertheless, the old spirit still remained and showed itself on such occasions as Burns' Night, or Hogmanay, which Scots living outside their native land tended to celebrate with even greater gusto than when at home. However, it was neither of these days and he was willing to remain in the background as long as the truculent trio continued to ignore him.

Until the arrival of the trio, whose names appeared to be Giles, Ben and Leonard, McCallister had been as relaxed and at ease as was possible under the circumstances. It was the last Friday in June, the weather was pleasantly warm rather than oppressively hot and he had been deriving satisfaction from the thought that he was going to be far removed from his routine professional duties until the following Tuesday. Realizing that he was making better time on the journey than he had anticipated and having no desire to arrive at his destination too early, despite the interest he had in the weekend house-party he had been invited to attend at Mansfield Manor, he had decided to stop and have lunch at the Admiral Cornwallis Inn. He had just been finishing his meal when the untidy trio put in their appearance.

On coming in, the three had remained at the bar instead of taking seats at a table. Looking somewhat grudging, McCallister had concluded, Giles, the tallest, had bought drinks for them and, showing even more reluctance, supplied cigarettes from a tarnished silver case. Studying the slender brown tubes, the doctor felt sure he had come across a similar type in the course of his specialized professional duties. He had also noticed that, having served them with drinks and cast a glance in his direction which took in his still half finished pint of beer, the elderly combined barman and waiter had withdrawn from the room and had not returned.

In an attempt to put the three from his mind, McCallister has set about dealing with the second reason he had had for breaking his journey. He had been beyond the suburbs of London before remembering he had not passed on certain instructions to another of his uncle's assistants. Nor, to his relief, had he seen a telephone box from which he might rectify the situation. Removing one of the already stamped blank postcards which he invariably carried in his wallet, he had laid it before him on the table. However, on taking the fountain pen from the left breast pocket of his jacket, a low hiss of annoyance had broken from his lips. It was not his own, but one he had bought from the Magic Supplies' counter at Selfridges as a birthday present for a nephew. While it looked normal, he had known there was no point in writing the message with it.

Returning the pen to the pocket from which it had come and deciding he would borrow one from the Inn, having no desire to contact his colleague by telephone as this was sure to entail an unnecessary, long and tedious discussion which he wanted to avoid, McCallister found his dislike for the behaviour of the trio increasing. He also conceded the situation could have been worse. There was nobody else present who might have taken umbrage at their loudly spoken remarks and, if they had arrived earlier, their foul language would have spoiled his enjoyment of an excellent meal of the kind for which the Admiral Cornwallis Inn was famous.

Now that situation seemed likely to change!

Noticing the three men by the bar were looking towards the doorway, McCallister turned his gaze in the same direction and studied the couple who entered. In view of his assumptions regarding the unkempt trio, particularly where the masculine newcomer was concerned, he was disappointed by what he saw. Unless he was mistaken, by virtue of her obvious 'county' background and the nationality of her companion, both would be regarded as suitable should the other occupants of the room wish to take out their spite upon somebody.

If it had not been for his misgivings where the trio were concerned, McCallister would have found the female newcomer a most pleasing sight. In fact, as he did not share their prejudices against members of the upper class, she was the kind of woman he regarded as being most attractive. Not quite five foot four inches in height, she looked to be in her early twenties at most. Even being clad in a thick white woollen polo-neck pullover, jodhpurs and suede chukka boots could not conceal the shapely contours of a body fast ripening into womanhood. Partially concealed by a rakishly tilted black beret, her boyishly short and shingled platinum blonde hair framed a radiantly beautiful golden tanned face which showed breeding, strength of will and intelligence in its lines. Despite her youth and small size, there was about her the undefinable aura of one long accustomed to making decisions and having them carried out. She moved with a free-stepping and straight backed grace which neither sought to emphasize, nor distract from, her femininity and everything about her suggested she indulged in a healthy outdoors existence.

Under different circumstances, apart from the way he was dressed, the man with the blonde would not have struck McCallister as being worth a second glance. There was nothing either striking or imposing about his appearance, rather the opposite in fact. He had curly black hair and, except for having a darker tan than one might expect to acquire in the British Isles, his moderately handsome face was not eye-catching or even especially noticeable. Bare headed, he was hardly more than three inches taller than his companion and perhaps five years older. His attire was not what one would expect to see in Hampshire, nor anywhere else on this side of the Atlantic, come to that. In his right hand was a broad-brimmed, low-crowned white hat. He had on a slightly loose fitting waist-long brown leather jacket, its fastenings being open all the way down to display an open necked dark blue shirt with an attached collar. Around his throat was knotted a large, albeit tightly rolled, dark red silk handkerchief of the kind known in the United States as a 'bandana'. Held up by a wide brown leather belt with a floral pattern carved into it and a large silver buckle embossed by the initials, 'R.C.', his peculiar looking trousers were dark blue in colour. Their fairly narrow legs were turned up at the bottoms to form lighter-hued cuffs almost three inches deep which hung outside black riding boots with higher heels than was customary and uppers which were not so tightly fitting as those worn in Europe. The sharp toes of the unusual footwear were protected by silver guards about an inch and a half in length. The buckle and toe-guards were obviously costly. However, although the jacket, shirt and 'muffler' – as McCallister thought of it – were clearly of excellent quality, their wearer gave them the appearance of having been handed down to him from somebody better favoured in physique.

Before McCallister could continue his scrutiny of the strangely dressed young American, he saw and heard enough to warn him that his misgivings over the possible reaction of the trio to the arrival of the couple were justified.

Even in normal circumstances, being so obviously a member of a higher class of society than their own and possessing material benefits which aroused their envy, everything about the girl was calculated to provoke the trio's hostility. Under the prevailing conditions, although no mention had been made of them, this was even more the case. Despite what had been said earlier, the expulsion from the property which the group had hoped would provide them with a luxurious standard of living for a long period, had been brought about by a young woman who might have been her slightly older sister and not the senior male member of her undoubtedly upper class and 'County' family. Therefore, the combination of seeing a girl so obviously from the same class as the one who had evicted them and an American – having the close to paranoid hatred their kind always expressed about the United States and its people, despite being all too eager to follow the worst 'liberal' trends to arise in that country – and given an added inducement from the insignificant appearance of the man, provoked a reaction from them.

Exchanging glances with the other two, Giles spat aside the butt of his cigarette and began to describe in a loud voice, supplying great detail and much profanity, a sexual encounter he claimed to have had with a 'county' debutante. Also speaking in equally carrying tones and employing just as much bad language, his companions interspersed the story with derogatory comments implying all members of that class were equally forth-coming and promiscuous. Although the blonde neither spoke nor moved, as the scurrilous conversation continued, McCallister saw her lips tighten and a slight tinge of red came to her cheeks. However, there was an interruption before he could make one himself.

'*Gentlemen*!' the small American said in what seemed a mild tone, just as the doctor was about to rise and intervene. 'I'd be real *obliged* happen you'd clean up your talk, or hold it down so the lady here doesn't have to hear it.'

Such a response was clearly what the trio wanted. Throwing a satisfied glance at his companions, who remained at the bar, the tallest of them swaggered towards the couple. As he had been doing ever since he received the drink of brandy he ordered for himself – although the other two had had to content themselves with half a pint of bitter apiece – he was holding a small glass goblet by its base in the palm of his left hand.

'And who the hell do you think you are to tell us what to do, you god-damned Yankee?' Giles demanded in a menacing fashion.

'*What* did you call me?' the American inquired, instead of answering the question.

'A god-damned *Yankee*!' Giles supplied.

'That's what I *thought* you said,' the small American admitted. Despite there being no change in his tone, nor any other indication of his intentions, he rose as he was speaking. He seemed to be behaving in the same leisurely fashion which had characterized his speech and actions ever since he came into view. Nevertheless, before anybody else could say a word or make a movement, he was on his feet and his right hand rose to close around Giles' left. Moving away from the table, he continued to talk without relinquishing his grip. Instead, it was obvious to at least two of the onlookers that he was tightening it. '*Hombre*, I was born in *Texas* and there's *nothing* in this whole wide world rankles me more than to be called a *Yankee*. Fact being, when somebody

32

does *that,* it's like stick-teasing a diamondback rattler. I get all riled up, mean and ornery.'

Being so startled by the response that he remained in his seat, McCallister watched what was happening with a mixture of concern and curiosity!

When Giles felt his hand grasped, his proclivities in such matters being directed at other men and not women, regardless of the story he had been telling, an expression of interest came to his face. This emotion remained only momentarily before it was replaced by surprise. Then alarm was registered and was followed by pain. Letting out gasps redolent of agony, he made no attempt to either draw free his captured hand or to use the other as an aid to escaping from the suffering being inflicted as the base of the goblet began to dig into the fleshy portions of his palm.

Beating Ben to a similar deduction, Leonard became aware that all was far from being well with Giles. While uncertain what was happening, but taking into account the small size and general air of insignificance which the American presented, he lunged forward to effect a rescue. However, even as McCallister was about to yell a warning and get up to render assistance, he discovered it was not required where the would-be recipient of the attack was concerned.

Before the reaching hands could be laid upon him, the Texan took most effective counter-measures. Without releasing the hold on his captive, who was emitting a succession of agony-filled 'Agh's!' instead of trying to extract himself from the grip, he snapped his right leg in a sideways kick. Nor, McCallister concluded, was it a reaction provoked by panic and desperation. Propelled with great accuracy, especially when taking into account the speed of delivery, the high heel of the boot struck the front of Leonard's shin with considerable force. Knowing just how painful even a much less gentle impact could be upon that poorly protected region, the doctor was not surprised by the response which the attack elicited. A howl of agony burst from Leonard and, twisting aside, he stumbled away to collapse against a table with his hands flying down to close about the assailed limb.

Even though the small Texan had dealt so successfully with Leonard, McCallister realized the danger was not at an end. Slower to think and react, the much more massive third man was now moving forward. What was more, he was approaching from behind and he opened his arms to enfold his intended victim in them. Paying no attention to the clatter made by the doctor shoving away the table and rising hurriedly, the Texan once again proved capable of supplying his own solution. Giving Ben no chance to put the scheme into effect, but continuing to retain his grip on Giles, he pivoted at the waist and, letting out an exclamation which sounded like 'Kiai!', he propelled his left elbow backwards. It smashed into the massive artist's *solar plexus* and the result proved as adequate for his needs as had the kick.

In spite of the disparity in the sizes and weighs of the participants, the result of the Texan's latest means of defence proved just as effective as its predecessor had been. Any man following a sedentary life-style like that of Ben – which entailed frequently over-eating, drinking to excess and taking as little exercise as possible – was ill-prepared physically, or mentally, to resist such treatment. Although he had never suffered such an experience, he felt as if he had been smashed in the vulnerable region by a battering ram. All the air gushed from his lungs. Clasping at his midsection, he turned aside to blunder away a few steps before dropping to his knees and crouching huddled over to croak in breathless torment.

'You're not what even your momma would call *pretty* and you don't look to me like you've got the brains of a knobhead mule, *hombre*,' the Texan informed his captive, still in that almost caressingly gentle voice which somehow now sounded as if underlaid with a steely and menacing timbre. All the time he was speaking, the fingers and thumb of his right hand worked to keep up the constriction he was applying to the hand he was grasping. 'But you should try showing the sense of a *louse*. Which I reckon you'll surely be wishing you had when I get throu—!'

Staring at the scene before him, suddenly McCallister started to appreciate all its ramifications. First he became aware that, although the clothing tended to obscure the fact, the small Texan had the build of a Hercules in miniature. Confirmation of this came from the sheer agony which played on Giles' face and the gasping cries of suffering he was uttering, while doing nothing positive to try to bring about his release. It was obvious that his hand was being crushed with an exceptional strength. What was more, although considering the treatment was justified, the doctor could envisage what would happen if the pressure was continued. However, before he could make up his mind upon how best to intervene, the matter was taken out of his hands.

'*Rapido!*'

The girl had come to her feet and she spoke just one word, but it proved sufficient!

Glancing around, the Texan gave a nod. Then, reaching to take hold of the top of the goblet with his left hand, he removed his encircling fingers and thumb. Giving a sobbing gurgle, Giles reeled backwards a few steps. Even at the distance separating them, although no blood had been drawn, McCallister could see the livid red groove where the base had been grinding ever deeper into the soft flesh of his palm. What was more – showing how close had been the margin before a worse injury was inflicted – as the Texan set the goblet down on the table, the glass of its bottom snapped. If the release had been delayed for even a couple of seconds, the breakage would have occurred in the artist's hand and he was certain to have sustained a serious cut.

'All right, you three muggle-smoking knobheads,' the Texan said, swinging his gaze from one to another of his intended attackers and all trace of gentleness had left his drawl. Balancing lightly on slightly spread apart feet, he crouched a little and his hands, balled into fists, were raised in a position of readiness. Instead of seeming insignificant, he now exuded an aura of one who was completely confident in his ability to control any eventuality. 'Get the hell out of here *pronto*, which means faster than just *fast*, or we'll go on with this ring-around.'

Staring at the speaker, an expression of something like awe mingled with alarm came to each man's face. Watching them, McCallister was reminded of the way in which a visitor to his home in Scotland had behaved when his mother's apparently docile and harmless Pekinese had showed a most unexpectedly aggressive resistance to being picked up and petted. Being an astute judge of human nature, even though it was a trait he rarely found a need to exercise in his professional duties, he felt sure none of them would be willing to defy the small Texan, who had proved to be so devastatingly competent when dealing with them.

Confirming the supposition, blubbering like a child, Giles clasped his left hand in the right and led the rush for the doorway. He was closely followed by Leonard, who – not unexpectedly – was limping badly, yet contrived to make almost as good speed. Hoisting himself upright laboriously to the accompaniment of wheezing gasps, although remaining bent forward and clutching at his midsection, Ben stumbled after his companions with an alacrity which was not his usual mode of progression.

'Sorry to have made fuss that ways, sir,' the Texan drawled after the trio had disappeared from view, reverting to his soft mode of speech and once more looking insignificantly harmless.

'Think nothing of it, you'd every right to do as you did,' McCallister replied, with only a slight hint of a Scottish burr in his voice. During his time in the United States, he had become acquainted with the term 'muggle' and decided he was not alone in having deduced the trio were smoking *marijuana*. However, since making his home in London, he had developed the reticence of the typical middle to upper class Englishman where engaging in conversation with strangers was concerned. Therefore, despite being consumed by curiosity, he did not attempt to satisfy it. Instead, he resumed his seat while continuing, 'And I wouldn't have missed seeing it for the world.'

'Looks like I owe you for a busted glass, friend,' the Texan remarked, turning his attention to where the wizened barman-cum-waiter had come through a door behind the counter. Taking a wallet from the right hip pocket of his unusual looking trousers, he removed a ten shilling note and walked forward. 'Here, I reckon this'll cover it.'

'Sure and there's no need for *that* at all, sir,' the man replied, employing a rich brogue which left no doubt as to his origins. 'I was just going to fetch the Mister to have them throwed out, but you saved me the need and, faith, 'twas very pretty the way you did it. It's having Irish blood I'm thinking you must be.'

Watching the open admiration with which the barman was regarding the small Texan, McCallister felt it was well merited. What was more, he concluded that appearances were most certainly deceptive and there was *much* more to the seemingly insignificant American than met the eye.

Then the doctor recollected something. About six months earlier, he had attended a dinner at the Japanese Embassy in London. Part of the entertainment after the meal had been a most impressive exhibition of the types of unarmed combat developed by that nation. Among other feats, he remembered, was a man giving a demonstration of what had been called '*karate*'. After breaking planks of wood and bricks with a bare hand or foot, the expert had displayed methods of launching attacks by kicking and striking in various fashions not practised in Occidental countries, including using the elbow to deliver a blow at an assailant coming from behind. On performing each of the feats, he had given a cry similar to that employed when the Texan dealt with the massive artist. However, McCallister decided this was nothing more than a coincidence. It struck him as being highly unlikely that the small visitor from America could have learned similar methods of unarmed self defence.

Asking the barman for the loan of a pen and ink, as the girl and her companon began to talk quietly together, McCallister regretfully told himself they did not appear to want his company and, being too well bred to try to force it upon them, decided in all probability he would never be able to satisfy his curiosity about the small, yet *very* efficient young Texan.

CHAPTER TWO

David Versus Goliath

'Impressive, isn't it?' asked an attractive feminine voice.

'Very,' Doctor Andrew McCallister agreed.

'And what a tragedy,' the same speaker continued.

Knowing what was meant, the young doctor was in complete accord with the sentiment!

Everything McCallister had seen since his arrival at Mansfield Manor had interested him, or aroused his unstinted admiration!

Still determined to avoid arriving early, after leaving the Admiral Cornwallis Inn, McCallister had taken advantage of being in the vicinity by making a detour to look at a stretch of a chalk stream owned by a friend of his family. He had a standing invitation to fish it and, provided conditions were suitable, intended to do so before returning to London on Sunday. Satisfied that all would be well, as long as the weather did not change too drastically in the meantime, he had continued to his original destination.

Approached through massive wrought iron gates – which were by tradition never closed – in an equally high fence of the same material, then along a wide gravel path traversing an expanse of excellently kept gardens, with flower beds and quite large clumps of dense decorative bushes scattered across the open areas of lush green turf, the magnificent mansion looked just as it had when built early in the Georgian era. Because the outside walls were kept clear of the ivy which all too often was allowed to grow practically unchecked over other buildings of its kind, the excellent state of preservation could be seen to its best advantage. However, this also tended to cause the iron bars which were fitted to every window on the first floor to be even more noticeable.

On knocking at the massive front door and being admitted by the butler, who had intimated disapproval by remarking all the other guests had arrived *much* earlier, McCallister had been even more impressed. While the interior also retained the luxurious style and furnishings of the era in which it originated, the present owner had not hesitated to take advantage of modern developments designed to make life easier and more pleasant. He had been in similar establishments which, on account of rising costs, were dimly lit by day and night and, even in summer, tended to be cold and draughty. Being extremely wealthy, clearly Commodore Sir Granville Delamont, VC, DSO and two Bars, RN Rtd., had not skimped when catering for the creature comforts of himself and his guests. Not only was there electric lighting of much greater brilliance than was frequently offered but also, although not in use due to the clement weather, what would be most adequate central heating had been installed.

The domestic arrangements matched the appearance of the property. At the head of the indoors staff, tall, heavily built and of a most distinguished appearance, was Guerney, the butler. Supporting him on the distaff side, also large, massively bulky and having an extremely grim visage which aroused awe in trades-people and others with whom it was her duty to deal, was the housekeeper, Mrs Blount. Between them, they ruled with what McCallister sensed was a despotic hand over a dozen or so footmen, a similar number of maids – which seemed a large number for one person's needs, but Sir Granville had established a tradition that the guests at his house-parties did not bring their own servants – and others of lower status with more menial tasks to perform.

From what McCallister had seen of the footmen, despite all being big and with more rugged and harder faces than was usual amongst their class – in fact, he would have thought them more suitable to the rougher elements of the crowd at a race meeting – they were competent in their duties. Certainly he had had nothing to complain about the one who had carried his bags and acted as guide to the room he had been allocated on the first floor. In spite of highly spiced stories he had heard about their kind elsewhere, judging by what he had seen of them, he could not imagine any of the distaff side of the domestic servants being the object of amatory attentions from the male guests unaccompanied by female companions. None could be described by even the most charitable observer as being good looking and, beneath uniforms designed to conceal rather than titillate, their figures were either skinny or lumpy rather than attractive and eye catching.

A wide staircase led to the first floor and, at the top, a balcony on either side overlooked the entrance hall. Ascending it, McCallister arrived at a wide passage. To the left and right of the balcony were eight doors bearing numbers, although those which faced them across the passage did not. While being guided to the quarters allocated to him, he was informed in a pointed fashion that the gentlemen's accommodation was to the right of the stairs and the ladies at the left.

'And you *all* keeps to your own sides, sir,' the servant had continued, his harsh voice suggesting he had been born in one of the less salubrious parts of London within the sound of Bow Bells. 'The Guv – *Commodore* don't go for no hanky-panky like ladies and gents sharing a room when they're not married.'

'I'll keep it in mind,' McCallister had promised with a smile, having heard of the high moral tone required by his host. Studying the somewhat military bearing of the man, he elected to change the subject and asked, 'You're an ex-serviceman aren't you?'

'21st Lancers,' the footman answered. 'All of us blokes're ex-service. You wouldn't reckon it to look at him, but old – *Mister* – Guerney was a Regulating Chief Petty Officer in the Navy.'

'The lady with him looks as if she could have been one, too,' McCallister commented, remembering having heard that Sir Granville had retired all the domestic staff employed in his wife's time – with a more substantial sum of money than was often the case in similar circumstances – after her death. It was obvious he had elected to supply employment for ex-servicemen when replacing them.

'That she does,' the footman had agreed, also grinning. 'Fact is, she was a head screw at Holloway before she come here as housekeeper and still thinks she is, 'cording to the maids.'

Declining an offer to help him unpack and giving a tip calculated to dispel the age-old stories about Scots being parsimonious, McCallister, while leisurely settling into the luxurious room to which he had been conducted, studied his surroundings with satisfaction. Except for one part of the fittings, it compared most favourably with any accommodation he had previously occupied. The exception was the discovery that the window, which overlooked the front of the building, could be opened inwards. However, even if he should have wished to do so, leaving through it was rendered impossible by the bars attached to the outside of the wall. Being inquisitive by nature, as well as by professional inclination, he had decided to try to find out why they were fitted provided he could do so without giving offence to his host.

Having changed into the semi-formal attire required by convention, McCallister left with the intention of meeting his host and the other guests. He had been told dinner would be served at half past eight and guessed they would be assembling somewhere on the ground floor about half an hour earlier. On leaving his room and looking over the protective rail of the balcony, he had seen that the double doors of what was obviously the library were open. Going down, he had found himself to be the first to arrive. Having accepted a glass of whiskey from a footman with an accent redolent of the rougher part of Glasgow, he had studied his surroundings. In addition to the numerous leather bound books which filled glass fronted cabinets on the walls, there were a number of up-to-date magazines covering various subjects laid on stands. Several comfortable looking armchairs, each supplied with a reading lamp, were available and, for those of a less studious bent, there was a full sized billiard table at one end of the room.

Several paintings graced the walls and, although McCallister was no expert, he sensed that – with two exceptions, each by a present day artist of great renown – they were worthy of being classed 'old masters'. The first exception was what was termed a 'narrative' subject showing a small cruiser flying the British 'White Ensign' attacking a much larger warship with the banner of the Imperial German Navy. At the bottom of the frame, a well polished brass plate was inscribed with, '*DAVID VERSUS GOLIATH*'.

Facing the 'narrative' illustration, being above the fireplace and clearly in the place of honour, was a large portrait. It depicted a man wearing the full dress uniform of a senior officer serving in the Royal Navy during the Great War. There was one incongruous note, yet understandable to everybody who knew the legend of Commodore Sir Granville Delamont. Despite the formal nature of his attire being correct in every detail, the artist had him wearing a large pair of motorist's goggles. While he would be of no more than medium height, if the fittings on the bridge of the vessel which formed the background were in their true perspective, he was sturdily build. It was his face, however, which caught and held a viewer's attention. Undoubtedly handsome, there was an air of authority about it which suggested – as had been the case, according to all McCallister had heard – he was a natural-born leader capable of commanding respect and obedience from those who served under him without needing the assistance of the Articles of War, or the powers vested in him by the Admiralty.

Like every boy of his background and generation,

McCallister knew the story of the epic battle which gained Sir Granville the Victoria Cross and yet also ended in a personal tragedy. He was, in fact, the kind of officer which cropped up at fairly regular intervals in the Royal Navy. Born into a long established naval family, he had taken to that career as a duck takes to water. Following a period as an outstanding Cadet, from the time he was appointed Midshipman, dramatic incidents and action seemed to occur wherever the exigencies of the Service took him. However, from the beginning, he had shown a brilliance in handling every emergency which gained him rapid promotion. Furthermore, no matter how dangerous the assignment upon which he was engaged, he had carried it out with a planning and forethought calculated to reduce the risks involved and keep his own casualties to the minimum. It was this trait more than any other which those who served under him valued most highly. Therefore, only a very few junior officers and ratings who came under his command ever hesitated before volunteering – demanding almost – to do so again.

Such had been Sir Granville's's high standing with his superiors that, despite still being somewhat younger and lower in rank than was generally considered acceptable in those days, he had met with no rebuke on announcing his intention to get married. Of course, Lady Anne Mansfield had been regarded as such a 'good catch' that it helped stifle any possible objections or criticism. By a long established family tradition, being the only offspring, she had inherited Mansfield Manor and a fortune on the death of her parents. Financial considerations apart, possessing an upbringing and personality ideal for the purpose, she had always been a great asset to his career and never more so than in the aftermath of his greatest achievement.

Already a legend in his own time, due to a most successful participation in numerous actions against 'enemies of the Crown' throughout the world ever since he was a Midshipman, Sir Granville had attained his greatest glory from a battle which far surpassed the rest in its achievements. During the summer of 1917, serving in command of a small squadron comprised of the *David*, an *Active* Class light-cruiser, and two K-Class torpedo-boat destroyers, he had come across the German heavy cruiser, *Osnabrucken*. Despite his own vessel being armed only with ten four-inch guns and the K's three of the same calibre – plus four paired 21-inch torpedo tubes – apiece, against the German's eight 8-inch main armament, he had given the order to carry out a type of attack he had rehearsed with them on several occasions.

The ensuing fight had been in the finest traditions of the Royal Navy, worthy of ranking with the exploits of Commander Cochrane and his *Speedy* sloop,[1] or Captain Ramage's actions with the frigate, *Calypso*.[2] Conditions were ideal for the tactics employed by Sir Granville. Discoveries made after the War indicated they were also helped by the commanding officer of the *Osnabrucken* who was annoyed at having failed to participate in the Battle of Jutland – which the Germans were claiming to have been a resounding victory for their naval forces. The *Osnabrucken* had been brought to sea before her crew were fully worked up and, therefore, they were still far from being at the peak of efficiency required by a vessel engaged in a war. Having laid a smoke screen, the small British ships darted in and out of it to repeatedly inflict damage with their much lighter weapons, retreating into concealment before the German eight-inch guns could be trained with equal effect upon any of them.

1. While serving in the Mediterranean during the first Napoleonic War, amongst numerous other actions, Commander Lord Thomas Cochrane captured a Spanish frigate with twice the number of guns and more than double the crew of the Speedy.
2. Details of the career of Captain Lord Nicholas Ramage – later Admiral of the Fleet, the Earl of Blazey – can be found in the Ramage *series of biographies by Dudley Pope.*

Although casualties were suffered by the British from near misses, these were far from as many as would otherwise have been the case under less auspicious circumstances and if suffering poorer leadership.

The climax of the fight had come when, appearing simultaneously on each side of the enemy while the *David* contrived to hold its crew's attention, the K's each launched all of their ready loaded torpedoes at the optimum range. Directed by skilled aiming, with a backing of good luck, every one had struck home and not even the excellently designed protection given to the *Osnabrucken* could fend off eight such smashing blows spread below the waterline along its sides. Then at the moment when victory was assured, the tragedy occurred which prevented the British participants from experiencing the exhilaration and pleasure they would otherwise have felt. The last shot fired by the rapidly sinking vessel had exploded just short of the *David's* bridge.

By the unfathomable vagaries of such things, there was only one casualty. Caught by the searing blast of the explosion, Sir Granville's face was very badly burned and he was thrown backwards against the superstructure with a force which broke his lower spine. Prompt and skilful attention by the *David's* Principal Medical Officer had kept him alive. However, even ashore nothing could be done to restore mobility to his legs, or repair the damage left by the burns. In one respect, he had been fortunate. A keen participant in motor racing and winner of several prestigious events, he had the habit of always wearing his motor goggles when either training for or going into action. Showing such a blatantly cheerful disregard for stuffy and hide-bound regulations was the kind of behaviour much admired and enjoyed by those under his command. In fact, the 'lower deck' in particular considered his remarkable good fortune – which had always kept down casualties – stemmed from the adornment. Certainly they had proved *very* lucky for him that day. By protecting his eyes against the ball of flame from the shell, they had prevented him from being blinded as well as grossly disfigured for life.

Much as McCallister had always admired Sir Granville's career in the Navy, as a medical man, he considered what followed was of even greater merit in many respects. Left with a ruined face and the prospect of spending the rest of his life confined to a wheelchair, aided by his wife's devotion and support, he had had the strength of will to continue living. Although offered promotion to the rank of rear admiral, along with the award of his country's greatest honour for valour and performance of duty under conditions of gravest peril, he had declined the former on the grounds that he would be taking up a place on the seniority list which could be filled by an active officer. Resigning from the Navy, he had come to spend the remainder of his days at Mansfield Manor. The only concession he had made to his dreadful injuries was to request that, having no desire for them to see him so reduced from the good looking, virile and active man he had always been, none of his former colleagues should visit him. Backed by a strong hint from the Lords of the Admirality that his wishes were respected, along with their own understanding of his motives and the good manners which so character-ized their kind, even those who had been his closest friends had respected his request.

Such had been Sir Granville's indomitable spirit that, in addition to having helped the estate to flourish, he had survived the trauma caused by the death of his wife in a hunting accident. What was more, he continued to reside at the Manor and run the property as efficiently as he had done with her help. He was allowed to do this, despite the custom which had not only given her control of the inheritance but also decreed it must revert to the most closely related of the Mansfield family in the event of her demise. Defying the convention, she had stated in her will that her husband must be allowed to continue in his present capacity as 'lord of the Manor' until his demise. Rumour had it that the closest relative had sought to contest the will and was warned by 'learned counsel' that to do so would be most ill-advised as any attempt to go against wishes intended to provide for a seriously injured national hero – who was still proving to be an asset to the affairs of the estate and who in addition treated him with considerable generosity – would be doomed to failure in the courts.

Perhaps to relieve his loneliness after the death of his wife, although they had never felt the need while she was alive, Sir Granville had started to entertain visitors by giving weekend house-parties. However, they were not selected from his old colleagues and friends in the Navy. At infrequent intervals, as the only duty he was expected to perform in return for the very generous allowance he received and which allowed him to live in reasonably affluent comfort in London, Michael Mansfield – the next in line of succession for ownership of the Manor – was required to perform the task of providing guests from amongst his associates. The parties did not rate as an essential element of Society's functions, or part of the 'Season', and rarely attracted guests of any special importance. What was more, a number of the invariably young people selected to attend claimed they were far from being wildly exciting. On the other hand, everybody agreed the standard of hospitality could not be faulted and Mansfield never found great difficulty in persuading the small number required to come.

Although McCallister was not a socializer by inclination, he had had a good reason for contriving to receive an invitation when Mansfield – an acquaintance, rather than a close friend, from his days as a medical student – had mentioned the latest party was to take place during a meeting at the Ritz earlier in the week. Now he was waiting for it to commence and, until his examination of Sir Granville's portrait had been interrupted by the comment, he had been wondering how it would develop.

'Very tragic,' the doctor agreed and turned.

Having decided views where women were concerned,

48

McCallister considered the one who had addressed him was as attractive as she had sounded. She was about his age and height, with black hair cut tightly around her head and a pallidly beautiful face. Decorous in style though it undoubtedly was, the simple black evening gown she wore still showed off her figure to its best advantage. The few pieces of jewellery she had on were far from ostentatious and there was an air of quietly competent charm about her which he found met with his approval. With something like satisfaction, he noticed she wore neither a wedding or engagement ring. Then he decided with some disappointment that, although alone at that moment, she must be accompanied by one of the other male guests.

'I'm sorry I butted in on your reverie,' the young woman apologized. 'But nobody else is down yet. Perhaps I'd better introduce myself. I'm Billie Oakroyd.'

'Andrew McCallister,' the doctor responded, wondering whether the name was supposed to mean something to him.

'Have you brought your wife, or fiancé, down, Mr McCallister?' Billie inquired, her manner suggesting nothing more than polite interest.

'I don't have either, I'm afraid,' McCallister replied.

Before any more could be said, the sound of male and female voices and footsteps came from the hall.

'Ah, here comes out assistant host and his fiancé, the Dragon Lady,' Billie remarked, glancing through the open doorway. 'He looks even more grumpy than usual. I suppose it's only natural, though. It must be extremely annoying for him – and her – to know that, by the strict letter of the law, all this should belong to him; but, as things stand, he can't lay hands on it until after Uncle Granville dies and he looks likely to go on for a long time yet.'

'Uncle Granville?' McCallister queried, despite being in agreement with what the girl had said about the way Michael Mansfield looked and probably felt.

'I'm by way of being one of our main host's poor

relations who's been invited to make up the numbers and supply a dinner partner for any gentleman guest who's come alone,' Billie said frankly, then a look of contrition came to her face. 'Oh Lord!' Don't tell me—!'

'Well, I've come alone,' McCallister admitted, smiling to prove he had not taken offence at the explanation. 'And, if you don't mind me saying so, I hope I'm the only one as I'd be delighted and honoured to have you as my dinner partner.'

Glancing through the door while making the declaration, the doctor received a surprise. Coming down the stairs were the beautiful blonde girl and the small Texan who had aroused his interest in the dining-room of the Admiral Cornwallis Inn.

CHAPTER THREE

He's Nobody In Particular

'Is something wrong?' Billie Oakroyd inquired.

'Not really,' Doctor Andrew McCallister replied, realizing that he must have been staring very pointedly at the couple who he had found so interesting on their first brief – yet action-packed – meeting. Nodding towards the other guests descending from the first floor, he continued, 'It's just that I turned up too late to meet anybody else.'

'Don't you know *any* of them?' the attractive young woman asked.

'I know Michael Mansfield and Miss Gore-Kauphin, of course,' the Scottish doctor answered. 'Although I'll admit we don't move in the same circles as a rule.'

'That's nothing to be ashamed of, neither do I,' Billie declared, then she shrugged and smiled. 'But I musn't be *catty*, I suppose.'

Deciding the young woman disliked the couple in the forefront of the guests, McCallister quickly turned over in his mind what he knew about them!

Except for having the good fortune to be the nearest surviving relative of Lady Anne Delamont, McCallister did not think there was anything notable or distinguished about Michael Mansfield. Rather the opposite, in fact. Certainly the next in line of succession for ownership of Mansfield Manor was nowhere near as fine a physical specimen as the portrait showed Sir Granville Delamont to have been.

Thirty-five years of age, five foot ten in height, Mansfield's evening clothes hung baggily on his sparse frame and – his attire generally being an open-necked shirt, an unfastened woollen waistcoast, unpressed slacks and cheap brown shoes intended to indicate his connection with the 'arts' – he looked far from comfortable wearing them. However, his longish yellow-brown hair was for once plastered down neatly. His plain and invariably surly pallid features seemed even more so and it was obvious he was far from happy. McCallister decided either he did not relish the idea of the weekend festivities, or – more likely – he resented having to occupy a subordinate position in the house which, but for a legal technicality, he considered he should be able to call his own.

Lazy by inclination and far from as intelligent as he imagined himself to be, Mansfield had barely scraped through graduation at university. Having been left with moderately independent means, he had gravitated to London. Being too incompetent to secure employment which he considered worthy of his talents, like many of his kind, he had elected to follow a course a later generation would refer to as 'drop out'. Declaring an abhorence of Capitalism and the employment it offered to those willing to work, he hovered around the fringes of the theatrical and artistic circles where anybody with sufficient money to make them a target for sponging upon was welcome.

Having squandered the majority of the inheritance which had come from his parents, the death of Mansfield's aunt could not have come at a better time for him. He was finding it difficult to make ends meet and, shortly after her demise, Sir Granville had granted him a most welcome and generous allowance. In addition to wanting to maintain his circle of sycophantic acquaintances, which had shown signs of dwindling as his money ran out, he had become engaged and he found that his dire financial straits was not conducive to a congenial relationship with his fiancée. In fact, it had been at her instigation that he had sought to contest the will which kept him from ownership of the estate he – and she – coveted.

There was much in the appearance of the woman walking alongside Mansfield, and according to rumour, now dominated his life, to suggest why Billie had referred to her as 'the Dragon Lady'. Almost matching him in height, but some ten years younger, her bearing augmented the suggestion of self-willed arrogance about her whole demeanour. Her tawny hair somewhat longer than the current dictates of fashion decreed, hung lankly about her face and did nothing to soften its supercilious expression. Her brown eyes were cold, her nose sharp and her unsmiling mouth was tight lipped. The long-sleeved Chinese-style black gown she wore did nothing to flatter a figure so slender – her enemies, and they were many, designated it 'skinny' with some justification – it seemed in danger of being bowed over by the large silver cross and chain hanging around her neck. The rest of the jewellery she wore was just as bulky and ostentatious. Although it was not required by the dictates of convention under the circumstances, she carried a somewhat larger than was usual black vanity bag in her right hand.

Born of a wealthy theatrical family long known as much for its liberal to radical affiliations as its acting ability,[1] Wanda Gore-Kauphin had been completely spoiled from early childhood. She had grown up wilful and, as she was never subjected to discipline in her formative years, with a temper which had been allowed to flourish without control. She had taken to the stage with the assumption that gaining immediate 'stardom' was her inalienable right. However, her ambitions far outstripped her competence. The position held by her father as a prominent actor-manager ensured parts came her way, although he never allowed her to appear in one of his productions. However, she had not showed to

1. *Information regarding the activities of an earlier member of the family, Vera Gore-Kauphin, during an ill-fated visit to the United States is given in:* THE REMITTANCE KID *and* THE WHIP AND THE WAR LANCE.

advantage in any role she played. The most charitable review she had ever received had said, 'She speaks and acts as if she has trained at the Academy Of Dramatic Snapping, Snarling And Shouting.' Disgruntled by her lack of success, which she blamed upon everything except her lack of talent, she had followed the course adopted by numerous other equally unsuccessful performers. Preaching Socialistic beliefs which grew more radical with each failure, she had been reduced to appearing in plays by writers with similar ideals. While these were rated highly as having 'great merit and social conscience' by some critics – the word 'message' not yet having come into usage for such works – the mass of the theatre-going public regarded them as being too boring and uninteresting to be worth attending.

Although McCallister had not specialized as an alienist,[2] based upon his knowledge of Wanda's background, he considered that her failure to win the acclaim as an actress which she felt she deserved had done nothing to improve her never too amiable disposition. What was more, it was rumoured that her feelings were further soured by her father – having become disenchanted by paying increasing sums of money to prevent her incurring a well deserved penalty for her behaviour – declining to keep supporting her. Even before this happened, McCallister had wondered whether she had taken up with Mansfield in the hope of improving her financial position.

'How about the others?' Billie inquired, breaking in on the train of thought her comment had started.

'I've met Roz Brampton and Jimmy Brocklehurst fairly often in London,' McCallister admitted. 'But I can't place the other two.'

'The girl is Beryl Snowhill,' Billie supplied. 'Her people run one of the biggest and, from what the

---

2. 'Alienist': name given at that period to a specialist in the study and treatment of mental disorders. The term is now, 'psychiatrist'.

servants have been saying since they heard she was coming, the most successful of the training stables in Wiltshire. They're trying to buy a piece of property Uncle Granville owns adjacent to their's and I think she's been sent to try and sweeten him up a little, in the *nicest* possible way, towards the deal.'

'Who's the man with her?' McCallister asked, noticing the small Texan still wore the same high heeled black riding boots in spite of the rest of his attire – which tended to make him seem just a little less insignificant – being in keeping with the dictates of British convention for such an occasion.

'His name is Edward Marsden, I *think*, but she calls him "*Rapido*",' Billie explained and her tone implied she did not consider the Texan was of any importance. 'But don't ask me *why*. There isn't anything *rapid* about the way he moves, or speaks. Perhaps he's an American jockey. At least, she says he's going over there with her – and a maiden aunt as chaperone, of course – to help her to buy some racehorses. Apart from that, as far as I can gather, he's nobody in particular. By the way, how well do you know the love birds?'

'I haven't met Miss Gore-Kauphin socially, although I've heard about her of course,' McCallister answered, keeping a neutral timbre in his voice so his less than flattering feelings about the woman he had named did not show. 'But I've known Mansfield since I was a student.'

'Good heavens, you don't look old enough to have been at university with him.'

'I'm not. He was often around the pubs we used while I was at Bart's.'

'Oh,' Billie said. 'Anyway, I didn't mean him, but the *other* pair of love birds.'

'We've bumped into each other at various places and I was at their engagement party,' McCallister explained, glancing at the second couple on the stairs. The man was about his age, red-haired, jovial-featured, gangling in build and about five foot ten. Perhaps a year younger

55

and an inch shorter, the woman was statuesque. Framed by close cropped black hair, her good looking face had an air of authority about it. In fact, her whole bearing gave the same impression and, despite wearing a stylish evening dress, her gait was closer to a purposeful stride than a mere walk. 'Jimmy's something at the Home Office and Roz is a sister at Guys. In fact, she's how I first got to know them. We often went to the same dances, dinners and other inter-hospital functions while I was at Barts and we still see one another occasionally.'

'So you're a doctor then,' Billie guessed.

'I qualified some time ago, unlikely as it may seem,' McCallister replied and was pleased to see something which would allow him to change the subject before it could be taken further. Past experience had taught him that to mention his specialization aroused either revulsion, or what he considered to be a morbid and sensation-seeking interest. 'I say, isn't that—!'

'It is,' Billie confirmed. 'I'll give him his due, Michael has made quite a catch getting *her* here – and *him*, if it comes to that.'

'I hope we have a chance to see her sing and dance,' McCallister remarked, still looking up the stairs beyond the rest of the party.

'I'd like to see anybody stop her,' Billie said dryly. 'Unless I'm sadly mistaken, she's set her cap on our flying wonder.'

As if wishing to emphasize that they were the most impressive looking people present, the couple who had been the subject of the remarks were coming down the stairs a short distance behind the others. If it was the intention to make an impact, the doctor was willing to bet it was the woman who sought to produce the effect although each was a celebrity in a different field.

By design and the aid of a particularly bountiful nature, everything about Joan Darling – she never used her actual name 'Lady Honoria Darlington-Travers' for professional purposes – was intended to catch the eye. Only five foot five inches in height, she seemed taller and the effect was only partly the result of a mass of fiery red curls and shoes with very high heels. Radiantly beautiful, she had a genuine zest for life which reached to the back rows of the largest theatre and yet was not overpowering at closer range. Taken with her undeniable talent, this had made her currently the most sought after leading lady for musical comedies and farces in London. With a decolleté cut to an extent none of the other female guests could equal, although somehow she made it appear decorous, the bodice of her flame-red gown clung like a second skin to the well endowed torso of her close to buxom, yet firmly fleshed, figure. However, below the waist, the practically diaphanous long skirt flared in a way which would allow her to display her talent as a dancer if she should be asked to entertain with a number from one of her numerous hit shows.

Also in his early twenties, the man was six foot tall and had a good physical development which the excellently cut mess dress of a Flying Officer in the Royal Air Force set off admirably. His black hair was sleeked back from ruggedly pleasant, well tanned features. The suggestion of fitness and health he exuded was real enough. It went beyond the need to keep in top condition for his duties as a fighter pilot, a field in which he excelled to the extent of having for the past two years been selected for a solo aerobatic exhibition at the prestigious Hendon Air Display and numerous other venues. He played rugby and cricket for the RAF with such prowess he was expected to be selected to represent England in both sports and his reputation as a cross-country runner was equally high.

'Look after *them*!' Wanda ordered rather than suggested, jerking her head imperiously towards the couples to her rear as she and her fiancé reached the hall. 'I'll go and make sure those idiots in the kitchen don't make a worse mess of the meal than usual.'

'Another illusion shattered,' Billie hissed. 'I thought she had such a great love and respect for the working class.'

'About as much as all her kind do,' McCallister replied just as quietly, watching the other guests approaching.

'Hello, McCallister,' Mansfield greeted on entering the library. 'I see you've met Billie. Do you know everybody else?'

'Not everybody,' the doctor answered, then glanced at his two acquaintances. 'Hello, Roz, Jimmy.'

After McCallister had been greeted in return by the engaged couple, Mansfield introduced him to the remainder of the party. With that done, the surly featured young man clearly considered he had fulfilled his duty and left them to their own devices. On being presented to them, McCallister had noticed neither Beryl nor the Texan mentioned their meeting that afternoon and he refrained from referring to it.

Having been formally introduced, without which essential ceremony no social intercourse between English people could be conducted, the group gathered in the centre of the library. For a few seconds, while the footmen circulated with drinks under the watchful eye of the butler, the conversation was commenced on typically British lines. After the inevitable exchange of comments about the weather and a discussion to discover mutual acquaintances, Billie asked the fighter pilot if he was on leave.

'Not exactly,' Flying Officer Allan Morningford replied cheerfully. 'I was tossing Game Little Gertie around the sky on Thursday morning when I realized I was near Poppy Bushnell's place. Her father's a General, but we can't hold *that* against her. Anyway, I toodled over there and saw Poppy, Jenny Glossop and Dinky Davenport by the swimming pool. So, as I know she's keen on flying and, thinking the old boy would be at the War House generalling, or whatever they do there, I decided to give her and the other girls a treat. I did a couple of low runs right side up, then I went by again upside down.'

'Did they enjoy it?,' Joan inquired, making no attempt to conceal her pleasure at having heard that Morningford

58

had named his Gloster Gauntlet fighter after the character which had brought her greatest acclaim from the public.

'*They* did, judging from the way they were waving,' the Flying Officer answered, his tone more wry than gratified. 'The trouble is, the General had been at some regimental reunion on Wednesday and, having celebrated not wisely but too well, came home instead of going back to Town. It seems he took umbrage to being woken up by a dashed great Jupiter VI nine-cylinder radial blaring outside his bedroom. When I landed back at Middle Wallop, Wings[3] was waiting and he was more than a trifle *miffed*. It seems the General had made a note of my Squadron number and been on the telephone breathing fire and smoke about some damned young idiot flying around his house at about ten foot off the ground. Well, that wasn't *right*; but I couldn't very well tell Wings.'

'Why not?' the red head asked.

'Dash it all, old girl,' Morningford replied in an aggrieved tone. 'I wasn't an inch higher than *six* feet on any of the runs.' He paused before going on with the air of wanting to put the record absolutely straight, 'Well, to be truthful, probably I was nearer *seven* feet on the last.'

'And so you're in dire trouble?' Joan guessed.

'Not *entirely*,' Morningford denied cheerfully. Possessing such a breezy and enthusiastic nature, as well as having what was obviously a genuine love of his work as a pilot, he had imbued the whole story with a sense of fun which avoided any suggestion of boasting, even when he was clarifying the matter of the extremely low level at which he had been flying. 'Poppy called Wings and said she'd just about been able to stop the steam coming out of Daddy's ears before he did anything too dire, but she wasn't able to talk him out of driving over

3. '*Wings*', *the Royal Air Force's term for a Wing Commander.*

to see the Station Commander. She and Wings considered, under the circumstances, that I would be better off *anywhere* except Middle Wallop for a few days, so I beetled up to town. I thought of putting up at the RAF Club, but decided to look for somewhere that I couldn't be contacted. So, when I heard Mansfield saying his uncle was giving a house-party for the weekend and *you'd* be here, Joan, I wangled myself an invitation.' The red head seemed about to make some response, but – having decided he had talked enough about himself – he went on before she could do so, 'I say, Jimmy, how's the Farmer keeping, still looking as if he wished he was down on his estate prodding pigs in the back?'

'He's in the peak of condition,' Brocklehurst replied and continued to discuss the Home Secretary in a manner implying he was imparting a vitally important State secret. 'But I have heard him say that he hates *everything* to do with agriculture and only goes to have a few days at his farm when he can't think of a reason to stay away.'

'I know just *how* he feels,' Joan asserted with feeling, having been diverted from what she had been on the point of saying.

'I don't think you'd be any happier prodding pigs, dear,' Morningford claimed sympathetically, being aware that the red head's parents were landowners in a large way. Then he swung his gaze to the small Texan, who was standing by Beryl and had not taken any part in the conversation after having commented, in response to being introduced as 'Edward Marsden', that he preferred the nickname she used. 'I say, Rapido, If you don't mind my asking, what brings a Yankee to our shores?'

'Where-at's the Yankee?' inquired the Texan, his voice still the lazy drawl.

'Why *you* are, aren't you?' Morningford asked.

Remembering what had happened the last time he had heard somebody call the small and seemingly harmless Texan a Yankee, McCallister felt alarmed!

CHAPTER FOUR

Do You Shoot?

'No, sir, I'm *not* a *Yankee*, I'm a *Texan*,' Rapido answered, still looking and sounding as slothfully innocuous as he had just before he had begun to deal so effectively with the three offensive artists at the Admiral Cornwallis Inn. 'Fact being, I was raising seventeen summers before I found out that god-da—*gosh-dashed* Yankees wasn't all one word.'

'*Gosh-dashed*?' Joan Darling queried, her beautiful face alive with merriment. She had appeared in a show on New York's Broadway and had heard in full the words which were interrupted.

'Well now, ma'am,' the small Texan drawled, giving the impression of being a child caught in a piece of mischief. 'I'll have to come right out and 'fess up that I wouldn't have said it *quite* that way was only us menfolks here. But momma would've rightly taken a hickory switch to my hide had I said the *real* thing with you beautiful ladies standing 'round to hear it.'

'Having seen what had happened when the three artists at the Admiral Cornwallis Inn had suggested that Rapido was a Yankee had made Doctor Andrew McCallister tense, ready to intervene and prevent something similar taking place. However, realizing that the Texan had not taken offence at the Flying Officer's words, he relaxed and began to enjoy the ensuing comments as much as everyone else.

Until that moment – Michael Mansfield having done nothing beyond introducing the guests to one another – there had threatened to be a hiatus. All the usual topics permissible between people with few interests in common had been nearly exhausted when Flying Officer Allan Morningford had addressed Rapido. The ensuing conversation had served to break the ice and, accepting drinks from the footmen who were being supervised by the butler, the guests had changed into a cheerful group. However, McCallister noticed Mansfield did not join them. Instead, he had wandered off and was standing looking at a copy of *Country Life* in a distracted fashion which implied his attention was neither on the magazine or the people he had invited to the party.

'I've been admiring your shoes, Mr Marsden,' Rosalind Brampton remarked. 'They're rather unusual.'

'Not back to home, ma'am,' the Texan denied, elevating the legs of his trousers to show the almost knee-high uppers of footwear which was unconventional in every respect by British standards, especially as an adjunct to evening wear. Rising from ankle level on the black leather was a curling white pattern like the so-called 'Austrian knot' which had once graced the sleeves of officers in the Confederate States' Army and was still used as decoration, or an insignia of rank, by other troops when in dress uniform. 'Cowhands found this sort of boot was best suited for their work. The sharp toes can find, then go into and slip out of a stirrup real fast should it be needed, and the high heels dig into the ground better than low ones would, so's you can hang on easier when you're roping critters on foot.'

'Are you a – cowhand?' Morningford asked.

'No sir, they have to work *way* too hard for me,' Rapido replied, having allowed the legs of his trousers to fall back. 'But I've been wearing this kind of boot, 'cepting they wasn't so fancy most times, since I got to be fifteen and they tied up my leg to get the first pair on.'

'Why did they have to tie your leg up?' Billie Oakroyd inquired.

'Well, ma'am,' Rapido answered. 'In the back country down to home, kids run around kind of wild, woodsy and barefoot while they're growing up. Then, comes them being old enough to start working cattle, their folks need to throw a rope over them and tie up their legs one at a time, 'cause that's the only way they can get boots of any kind on 'em.'

'I hope you don't mind me asking,' Joan put in. 'But how did you get the nickname, "Rapido"?' She paused, wondering if she had gone beyond the bounds of polite conversation. However, seeing the Texan seemed amused rather than offended, she went on, 'It sounds Spanish.'

'It's Border-Mex, the kind of Spanish that's talked along the Rio Grande, ma'am, and means *real* fast,' Rapido explained with a grin. 'Which I can see you're trying to figure out how come they called me *that*. Well, cowhands've got a mighty strange sense of humour. One of my *amigos'* grandpappy had him a big white stallion and he called it "Nigger" and, down to home, there's a feller who stands six foot fifteen and three-quarter inches tall, who's four foot twelve and a half across the shoulders and got a chest like a big beer barrel. He's known as "Tiny".'

'Are you *sure* about his size?' the red head queried.

'Would I *lie*?' the Texan challenged, but with an air of injured innocence rather than annoyance. 'Only I've got to admit I don't reckon he's more than six foot *fifteen* at most.'

'That is quite a *difference*,' Joan admitted, recognizing an excellent raconteur and willing to help keep him going. 'So they call you "Rapido" because you *don't* do anything in a hurry?'

'That's about the size of it, ma'am, like that owlhoot of yours, Robin Hood, said when somebody asked him if he was using .45 calibre arrows,' the Texan confirmed. 'You see, where I was born and raised, I was sort of made to grow out of the notion of hurrying. It's kind of *extra* hot down to home most times. Fact being, they do tell – though I've never seen him, mind – that's where the Devil comes when he wants to warm up. Why it's real common after early spring's gone to see a hound dog chasing a jack-rabbit and they'll both be *walking* slow and easy.'

'Oh come on now!' Billie Oakroyd protested. 'Surely you don't expect us to fall for *that*?'

'Like I said before, ma'am,' Rapido drawled, still exuding a guileless air which seemed genuine. 'Would I *lie*?'

'I think it's only fair to warn you,' Beryl Snowhill put in, delighted by the impression her companion was making. 'Every time Rapido says that and looks like butter wouldn't melt in his mouth, take whatever he tells you with a pinch of salt. I've heard about that Tiny chap and he wasn't an inch taller than six foot *thirteen*.' Then she looked shocked and her hand fluttered to her mouth as she continued, 'There now! He's got *me* at it!'

'Do you do much riding at home, Rapido?' James Brocklehurst inquired, concluding – as McCallister had earlier in the day – that there was more to the small and insignificant looking visitor from America than met the eye.

'I've thrown a leg across a saddle on occasion,' Rapido admitted, although the words sounded more of a confession. 'Roads still being sort of scarce and none too good down to home, there wasn't any other way of getting most places when I was growing up. Trouble was, as time rolled by and things got better, I got 'round to concluding a horse was dangerous at both ends and uncomfortable in the middle. So now I'd sooner do my riding in a Cadillac limousine.'

'I saw some cowboys in a Wild West Show at Madison Square Garden while I was in New York,' Joan remarked. She was to play an American girl in her next show and, wanting to get away from the usual accent employed by British performers in such circumstances, she sought to keep the Texan talking so she could learn to imitate his way of speech. 'They all wore spurs with the most *enormous* rowels which I thought looked very cruel. Is that the kind you use, Rapido?'

'Why sure, ma'am, I did when I had to ride,' Rapido confirmed in an unabashed fashion. 'But only one.'

'Why just *one*?' the red head queried.

'Well, ma'am,' the Texan drawled. 'They're sort of heavy and drag hard on your legs, so I reckoned just the one would be enough. I always found that, once I got one side of the horse going, the other side just natural' had to come along with us.'

'Have you done any riding over here?' Brocklehurst asked.

'Not a heap,' the Texan replied. 'I don't take kind to those dinner plates you call saddles.'

'We found you an American range saddle and so I could take you out with the hunt,' Beryl protested, as if wishing to have it known the English tradition of hospitality had been upheld.

'I'm not gainsaying it,' Rapido admitted. 'Only, seeing as how it was a *Cheyenne roll* rig,[1] I hope that word doesn't get to the folks down to home about me sitting it, else my name'll be a by-word and a hissing.'

'What's wrong with that kind of saddle?' Rosalind Brampton wanted to know, being as keen as her fiancé on all matters equestrian.

'It wasn't made in *Texas*, ma'am, which's *bad* enough,' Rapido explained. 'But on top of that, it's only got *one* girth and isn't fitten for anybody 'cept a *dally man*.'

'A *what*?' Roz queried and the rest of the group showed a similar interest.

'A feller who takes a half hitch around the saddlehorn after he's caught something with his rope, then holds the short end in his hand so's he can turn it loose real fast should he reckon things are getting just a lil mite risky,' Rapido elaborated. 'When a Texan ropes something, he

---

1. *'Cheyenne roll': a type of saddle devised around 1870 by Frank Meanea, a saddlemaker of Cheyenne, with the intention of producing something different from the other rigs of the day. He achieved this by fitting a leather flange extending over and to the rear of the cantle board. It became very popular over the next twenty years in the northern cattle raising States, especially those east of the Rocky Mountains. However, it never found much favour in Texas.*

65

figures to hang on to it comes he – the *Hot Place* – and high water. Which being, he *ties* his rope to the horn and does just that.'

'I hope you didn't try to rope the fox while you were out with the hunt,' Joan remarked, amused – as were the others – by the changing of what obviously should have been 'hell' to something more innocuous. 'How did you like it?'

'It's 'most as good *fun* as chasing range-raised cattle out of thorn-bush country,' the Texan declared. 'And, what with those stirrup-cups afore starting out, a whole heap more pleasant.'

'So you enjoyed the stirrup-cups?' Billie asked, having noticed the level in Rapido's glass had not gone down very far.

'Well, not 'specially, ma'am,' the Texan admitted. 'I've never took over kind to the notion of drinking something some jaspers've walked around barefoot in to make. Way I see it, that wine stuff'll *never* replace cold beer. Not everybody feels that way, mind. There was one old gent at that fancy hunt who'd been taking the stirrup cups so copious he lost a stirrup-iron, and his horse, which was a mite frisky, shoved a hoof in it. Well, that old gent looked down and said—' Then he lost his drawl and his voice took on the timbre of a somewhat drunken elderly English gentleman. '"I say there, old thing, it's no good you trying to get on. There's hardly enough room for *me* up here."'

'How did you get on with the hunt itself?' Brocklehurst wanted to know, after the laughter had died down.

'Well, I *reckoned* I'd done pretty good one way and another, seeing's as how I'd come home still safe in the saddle and with all my buttons fastened,' Rapido answered, reverting to his normal accent. 'Only, when we got back, the head he-hooper – what you call "the Master", Beryl tells me – came over and said, "I say, old chap, as you're new to this business, I thought I'd better tell you that when you see the fox, you call, 'View halloo, tally ho, yoicks!', not 'there goes the furry lil red son-of-a-bit – *gun*!'"'

'Did I tell you about the time I was stooging along at about seven thousand feet in a Siskin?' Morningford inquired, when the amused reaction to the Texan's latest anecdote was concluded, feeling British prestige demanded some form of response in kind. 'Suddenly the kite went into a completely *uncontrollable* dive. *Nothing* I could do would pull it out. In fact, I was just thinking I'd be trading in my parachute for a harp—!'

'Whee dogie!' Rapido ejaculated, looking suitably impressed. 'Sounds sort of *dangerous*. What happened?'

'Luckily I ran out of petrol a hundred feet from the ground,' the Flying Officer asserted with a straight face. 'Of course, the engine stalled and the kite stopped and there I was for two hours before they got some more juice up to me and I could land.'

'Oh *Allan*!' Joan chided. 'Surely you don't expect us to believe *that*?'

'Would I *lie*?' Morningford challenged in a fair imitation of the way Rapido posed the same question.

'Good heavens!' Beryl groaned, as the Texan joined in the chuckling at the reply. 'It *is* catching!'

Before any more could be said, Wanda Gore-Kauphin returned from her self-appointed mission to the kitchen. Her carriage was never too graceful, but the way she stalked through the door and the expression on her never too amiable face suggested something was seriously wrong. In fact, studying her expression and demeanour, McCallister decided she was in the same kind of temper that had made it necessary for her father to pay sums of money to save her from being charged with assault when her habit of lashing out with her hands had caused trouble with victims of her temper.

'Damn it, Michael!' the unsuccessful actress snarled, paying not the slightest attention to the other occupants of the library. 'Those bloody idiots in the kitchen have cocked things up. Dinner will be at least half an hour late. When I found out what was happening, I tried to sort things out; but that Mrs Blount as good as told me it was none of my bloody affair. Tell your uncle I want her *sacked!*'

'He won't do it, dear,' Mansfield replied worriedly, being all too aware of how violently his fiancée could react when thwarted in anything she wanted. 'I've hinted at it before, but he says he's quite satisfied with her.'

'Well she'll be the *first* of them to go when I – *we* take charge!' Wanda asserted.

In her annoyance, the actress failed to see – although McCallister did – the cold look which the butler directed her way. At that moment, so great was the change in his expression, he ceased to be the usually impassive and dignified senior male domestic servant in a very well run country house. In fact, it was easy to imagine him as the Regulating Chief Petty Officer in the Royal Navy responsible for maintaining discipline over frequently less than amenable sailors, using physical means should the necessity arise as well as through the powers granted by his rank.

'I say, Rapido,' Morningford remarked in a slightly louder tone than was necessary, seeking to lessen the embarassment he felt sure the other guests shared with him. Glancing out of the French windows, across which the drapes were still undrawn to let in the daylight which still remained flood into the library, he continued, 'Do you know a chap called Alvin Fog?'

'Do you mean him that's a sergeant in the Texas Rangers?' the Texan inquired.

'That's the one,' the Flying Officer confirmed.

'Well, I've heard tell about him,' Rapido drawled, his tone neutral yet somehow implying he had no liking for the man in question. 'They do say he's a real *big* jasper, 'though not *quite* so big as Tiny back to home, and a regular snake when it comes to fetching out and using a gun. But I can't say's how I've ever met him face to face, 'though I've heard tell he's over here on a John Law chore of some kind. Have you crossed his trail?'

'No,' Morningford denied. 'But he was a guest at 28 Squadron and he pulled a neat trick on them. It seems he wanted to have a go at flying one of their kites and, having heard about how fast he could draw and shoot a revolver he'd been carrying when some chap try to kill J.G. Reeder, the Squadron Leader said he could fly a plane if he could hit a clay pigeon with his revolver. He agreed, but when the time came, it was some peculiar sort of shotgun he brought from under his jacket and not the revolver.'[2]

'What I've heard tell,' Rapido declared, 'that's just the sort of sneaky trick he'd pull.'

'It must have been most impressive, though,' Joan commented.

'It was, by all accounts,' Morningford confirmed, then returned his gaze to the Texan. 'Do you shoot?'

'Allan means with a shotgun, Rapido,' Beryl elaborated.

'Wouldn't say's I'm any *good* with one,' the Texan answered. 'But I've popped a cap on occasion and sometimes brought down a duck, was it close enough and flying *real* slow.'

'Do you feel like "popping" some "caps" now?' the Flying Officer inquired. 'I've heard that Sir Granville has a clay pigeon range behind the house and I thought we might be able to have a go on it while we're waiting for dinner. How about it, Guerney, can we?'

'Well, yes, that will be possible, sir,' the butler replied, reverting to his usual impassive demeanour. 'I saw you had your gun case in the car when you arrived and had everything made ready. The gardener who usually attends has gone home for the night, but I will have Henry and William do so.'

'That's jolly decent of you,' Morningford praised.

'Not at all, sir,' Guerney claimed. However, it was obvious the remark made by Wanda still rankled and, just for an instant, the baleful look came back to his face

2. *The incident is described in:* THE RETURN OF RAPIDO CLINT AND MR J.G. REEDER.

as he darted a brief glance at where she was standing with Mansfield. Then his features became blandly impassive once more and he continued, 'We *all* attempt to give Sir Granville *every* satisfaction, sir.'

CHAPTER FIVE

I'd Hate For My Life To Hang On The Difference

'The light won't hold out for much longer,' Flying Officer Allan Morningford assessed, glancing to where the sun was sinking towards the western horizon. 'So why don't we just try a couple of birds apiece "down the line", on the special thrower Sir Granville has had installed and see how it goes, Rapido?'

'I'm sitting in on your game, *amigo*,' the small Texan answered, having learned since his arrival that 'down the line' was the British equivalent of what was known as 'trap shooting' in the United States.[1] 'Which being, I'll leave you call the play.'

As if wishing to provide proof of how eager the whole staff were to give satisfaction to Sir Granville Delamont, Guerney had wasted no time in fulfilling the wishes of the guests. Having described the piece of equipment to which the fighter pilot had referred and receiving his orders, two of the footmen went to make ready the clay pigeon shooting facilities which had been requested. A third footman was dispatched upstairs to Morningford's room and returned carrying his well polished tan pigskin

---

1. Being intended primarily as training for long range, fairly deliberate, aiming and firing, in 'trap' or 'down the line' shooting, the clay pigeons are sent away from the competitor in a straight, or slightly angled line. On the other hand, 'skeet' shooting is carried out to simulate the kind of conditions which might be met when hunting grouse, partridge, quail, or pheasants. To achieve this, the targets are dispatched from various angles and generally at shorter range.

gun-case. However, when another was told to fetch shotguns and shells owned by their host for the visitors who had not brought their own, Doctor Andrew McCallister and Jimmy Brocklehurst had declined the loan on the grounds that there would not be sufficient time for everybody to shoot before the light faded to an unacceptable degree. Nor, as the Flying Officer had offered the loan of one of his guns, had there been any need for Rapido to be supplied from those kept on the premises.

Leaving the butler to attend to the rest of the arrangements, the visitors went around to the rear of the building, with the exception of Wanda Gore-Kauphin and Michael Mansfield – who had remained glowering and muttering quietly to themselves in the background throughout the preparations. A question asked by Joan Darling before leaving the library had elicited the reply that, as the area around Mansfield Manor was free from all other human habitation for at least four miles, with nobody working any closer in the fields at that hour, there was no danger posed by shooting at clay pigeons on the premises. On arriving at the site, in addition to discovering that the grounds at the back were just as impressive and well maintained as those in front, they had concluded the safety claim was valid. A good two hundred yards away, the high fence continued to mark the boundary of the property and was lined from top to bottom for a considerable distance with sheet metal which was pock-marked by the flying pellets.

Giving his attention to the area equipped for the sport of clay pigeon shooting, McCallister decided that they came up to the standard of the rest of Mansfield Manor's appointments. Known as 'stands', the firing positions for those involved were laid out as required by the type of competition being engaged upon. While the other members of the party were standing engaged in conversation with those who were to take part in firing 'down the line', McCallister went forward to discover that – despite being confined to a wheelchair – Sir Granville had sought to keep up with the times by having had a special type of automatic angling trap thrower installed. It differed from those which, having been developed in the United States during 1923, were now manfuctured under licence in the British Isles by being able to discharge two clay pigeons in quick succession and on divergent courses,[2] instead of the single target generally used for such shooting.

As with the more conventional type, the device was situated in a small open-fronted 'house' some sixteen yards ahead of the centre firing point. Unlike the houses for skeet shooting, which were protected at the front, the operator was shielded from badly aimed shots by the sides, back and roof having a lining of metal sheeting. McCallister found it was already being set up for use by the burly footman who had escorted him to his room. As was the case with other trap-throwers, a further precaution against accidental hits on the building was provided by it being inclined so that the targets flew out of the doorway in an upwards arc calculated to let them cover between fifty and fifty-five yards before returning to the ground.

On their way to the range, Morningford had ascertained that the Texan was familiar with the basis of clay pigeon shooting and had suggested they take advantage of the rules before starting to shoot. Because the clays were always sent away from the shooter at a predictable height in 'down the line', although the angle of flight was unpredictable, the competitors were allowed to watch a couple discharged by the man in the trap-house without being required to shoot. Having seen this aid to aiming put into action, Rapido requested that the pilot showed him how it was done in England.

2. *For some unaccountable reason, possibly because it was difficult to maintain in operating condition, this type of automatic angling trap-thrower did not gain favour in the British Isles or the United States and the company manufacturing them went out of business.*

Opening his case, which also contained cleaning materials and a box of shells, Morningford disclosed a brace of magnificent double barrelled Purdey twelve bore shotguns. Each was nestling on the dark red velvet lining in carefully shaped depressions. Lifting one up, he opened the breech and, having fed in a couple of shells, kept it broken. Not until he had strolled in a nonchalant fashion to the centre of the five shooting stands did he close the action. Then he adopted the somewhat akward looking classic British shooting stance with an ease which implied considerable training.

'Pull two!' Morningford called loudly.

On the command, there was a double clang from the trap-house and two circular black clay pigeons, about four and a quarter inches across and one-and-an-eighth-inches deep, appeared in rapid succession and flew forward, albeit on a diverging course. Bringing the butt of the shotgun to his right shoulder in a smoothly flowing motion, with his right elbow halting parallel to the ground, Morningford inclined his torso forward so as to set his weight upon the advanced right foot. At the same time, he sighted down the rib and fired the right hand barrel in a continuation of the move. Then, swiftly altering the alignment, he sent off the second charge of shot. There was applause from the onlookers as the nearest and then the furthest of the rapidly flying targets – made from a mixture of lime and pitch – burst into a cloud of dust. It was an excellent display of how to deal with the situation posed when shooting down the line.

'Your turn, old boy,' Morningford declared, turning around after he had broken open the shotgun to eject the empty cases. Gesturing towards the second Purdey as he returned, he continued, 'Use Jemima. You'll find she's the same as Hortense here. The right barrel is half choke and the other quarter.'

Lifting the indicated shotgun from the case, Rapido guessed he was being granted a rarely offered privilege in being allowed to use it. As he checked it was unloaded, his actions, leisurely though they were, showed

74

he too realized he was handling a superlative example of the gunsmith's art. What was more, he took the basic – yet essential – precaution without needing to be told. In fact, it and all his subsequent actions were carried out as if long experience with firearms had made them second nature. Satisfied upon what the most of the watchers appreciated was a vitally important point, he hefted the Purdey in his hands to test its balance. Still moving in a most leisurely fashion, he stepped to the firing point and, keeping the muzzles pointing over the trap-house, brought it up into the firing position a couple of times.

'Man, this's what I call a *gun!*' the Texan stated, having opened the breech once more before turning towards its owner and there was no doubt about his sincerity. 'It handles as sweet as my old Winchester '97 cornsheller[3] back home.'

Having made the pronouncement and turned forward again, Rapido loaded the two shells passed to him by Morningford. However, apart from carrying out the precaution of keeping his right forefinger outside the triggerguard, he did not duplicate the other's actions beyond closing the breech. Instead, he stood facing the trap-house with his feet opened to about the width of his shoulders and his body apparently relaxed. Nor did he offer to raise the shotgun into the British position of readiness, but allowed it to dangle in his hands before him at arms' length.

If any of the other guests and the man in the trap-house had been able to see the Texan from the front,

---

3. *'Cornsheller'; nickname given to the Winchester Model of 1897 pump action shotgun. It became famous for its simple, rugged construction and unfailing reliability. In fact, one enthusiast is reputed to have claimed, quote: 'It would stand any sort of minor abuse such as being run over by the old farm wagon or being dropped in the creek and rescued a few days later with never even a stutter when called on to speak.' see;* WINCHESTER, The Won That Won The West, *by Harold F. Williamson.*

they would have been surprised by the change which had come over him. His face had taken on a look denoting complete concentration upon what he was doing. Furthermore, what appeared to the group to his rear to be a casually slouching posture was anything but that. Rather, his small yet Herculean frame – slightly but not much more noticeable in the well fitting black dinner jacket – gave the impression of being a coil spring made from the finest steel and held under compression. He looked, in fact, like some kind of very dangerous predatory creature which was alert for prey and ready to launch an immediate attack when it appeared.

'Pull two!' Rapido ordered, speaking more briskly than usual, before anybody could comment about his apparent lack of preparedness.

Responding immediately, the man in the trap-house discharged the targets!

By chance, the black discs diverged at an even more acture angle than previously!

It was, as those spectators familiar with shooting down the line knew, a far from easy situation!

At the first warning clang of the trap-thrower being operated, even when seen from behind, all the seeming relaxation left Rapido. Bending his knees slightly, he thrust his torso forward and the magnificent Purdey flashed to his right shoulder at a pace vastly different from his normal leisurely movements. If anything, it rose even more swiftly than its mate had in Morningford's hands. Even while he was making the motions, he watched the clay pigeons leaving the trap-house and he gave rapid thought to dealing with the problem posed by their divergence. Halting in a somewhat crouching posture – which made him appear even smaller – he remembered what he had been told about the way the barrels were given 'choke', meaning a short distance at the muzzle end of the barrel narrowed to produce a tighter pattern of the cloud of shot when discharged. He had learned enough about British nomemclature to be aware of how this compared with the American system

76

of designating the means of increasing the chances of making a hit at various distances. Therefore, he knew what to expect when he started to shoot.

Aware that the right side barrel had the tighter choke, the Texan chose it to take the first of the rapidly departing targets. With the alignment made to his satisfaction, which took only a split second, he squeezed the forward trigger. With a solid crack, one-and-one-eighth of an ounce of tiny Number 7 size lead balls were thrust through the unrifled tube. On emerging, as they sped after the departing disc, they began to spread apart. Nevertheless, sufficient of them struck it and caused it to disintegrate. However, its mate was still moving away.

Showing no greater difficulty than Morningford had in controlling the recoil kick of the shotgun, Rapido was just as fluid in turning it until he was lining the twin barrels to the required direction. On the rearmost trigger being operated, the charge in the left side chamber was expelled. Having to pass through a smaller aperture than those from the right hand barrel, the shot were held closer together on emergence and did not separate so quickly. In this way, their spreading was delayed a vital trifle and, although the second target was further away, it too was shattered.

'Well done!' Morningford praised, as the Texan ejected the spent cases and blew smoke through the barrels. 'Although I hope you don't mind me saying that your shooting stance would have made old Cowdrey, the chappy who taught me to shoot, go pale.'

'It wouldn't do for everybody, I'll admit,' Rapido answered, having reverted to his more usual behaviour and mode of speech. 'But it works for me.'

'So I noticed,' the Flying Officer said. 'And how does Jemima handle compared with your old cornsheller, whatever that may be?'

'She comes *real* close,' the Texan assessed. 'Fact being, I'd hate for my life to hang on the difference between them.'

'Give her another go, old boy,' suggested Morningford,

77

taking two more shells from the gun-case and holding them out.

The eagerness with which the Texan accepted the offer gave even greater proof of how highly he regarded the Purdey and how delighted he was by the chance to continue using it. Adopting the same crouching posture, he proved just as successful against the second pair of clays. However, probably because the fading light was making the targets increasingly difficult to see, he missed the second target on the next flight.

'And about *time*!' Rapido grunted, as expressions of sympathy arose from the spectators. 'I just knew I'd get it *right* was I to try long enough.'

'*Right*?' Joan queried. 'But you *missed* one!'

'No, ma'am,' Rapido corrected, walking from the firing point with the Purdey – its breach open to show both chambers were empty – on the crook of his left arm. 'I finally did what I've been trying to do all along.'

'How do you mean?' the beautiful red head inquired, having done a lot of clay pigeon shooting and, in fact, being quite competent at it.

'Well, ma'am,' the Texan drawled, looking very serious. 'It's not generally known, but right spang in the middle of each cloud of shot's leaves a scattergun, there's a hole just a smidgin bigger than the clay pigeon. 'Most anybody can *hit* the danged things, but the *real* test is to put it through that hole without the lead touching it.'

'But how do you know whether you've put it through the hole, or—!' Joan began before she could give the explanation sufficient thought. Then she realized the impracticality of the suggestion and brought her protest to an end. Glaring with mock indignation as laughter came from the rest of the party, she spluttered, 'Oh you – you *gosh-danged Yank – Texan* you. That's another of your, "Would I lie's"!'

Before Rapido could confirm or deny the assertion, the butler came from the rear entrance of the Manor and announced that dinner was ready to be served.

'I hope there'll be time for me to clean Jemima, Guerney,' Morningford asked, having cleaned the other gun while the Texan was firing at the other clay pigeons.

'Not *you*,' Rapido corrected, deftly separating the Purdey he was holding into its three main components. 'When I ride a horse, I *always* do the grooming myself and it's the same when I shoot a gun.'

'Go ahead then, old boy,' the Flying Officer authorized and it was obvious that the small, seemingly insignificant, Texan had risen even higher in his estimation.

79

CHAPTER SIX

I Am Your Host, Sir Granville Delamont

'Ladies and gentlemen!' announced the butler of Mansfield Manor, his booming and cultured voice bringing the guests to a halt as they were commencing the traditional formality of the women leaving the men in the party to themselves for a short while at the end of the meal. 'Sir Granville asks if you will all be so kind as to come into the library and make his acquaintance?'

The delay caused by the problems in the kitchen had been of sufficient duration to allow the cleaning of the second shotgun to be completed and the two participants in the 'down the line' shooting to have a wash before the guests were seated in the elegant and magnificently furnished dining-room. The food had been excellent and there had been a lively conversation to make the time pass even more enjoyably. However, regardless of their aspirations to become the owners of the property, neither Wanda Gore-Kauphin nor Michael Mansfield had done anything to help maintain the festive spirit. Instead, they had sat at opposite ends of the long table and only speaking when addressed. Even then, they said no more than was absolutely necessary and were, for the most part, left to themselves.

To Doctor Andrew McCallister in particular, it had seemed that the couple were determined to be less sociable than they had been in the library. In fact, if anything, they had both appeared more preoccupied and even a trifle nervous. He wondered if the latter emotion was caused by concern over whether the selection of guests would meet with the approval of Sir Granville Delamont. While the inheritance of the estate could not be changed, its present owner would be at liberty to reduce – or even stop – paying Mansfield an allowance should he be so minded. It was not a prospect either would regard with equanimity in their less than affluent financial straits.

Leaving the dining-room, with Wanda and Mansfield bringing up the rear, the party made their way to the library. On entering, they found that all the moveable furniture had been taken away to leave the centure of the floor clear. However, it was doubtful whether any of them gave the matter a second thought. With the exception of Billie Oakroyd, who knew what to expect, they all gave the small group – particularly the man at the forefront of it – in the middle of the room their complete attention. It was the first sight they had had of their host and, although they knew of his affliction, his appearance came as something of a surprise and shock.

Despite being seated in a high-backed wheelchair, there was still the proud carriage of the head and shoulders which the artist had shown in the portrait which could be seen behind Sir Granville Delamont. As far as the waist, he was clad in an excellently tailored black dinner jacket, stiff-bosomed white dress shirt and black bow tie. Taking into account his age and physical condition, he had as fine a figure as any man present. However, from the waist down, he was covered by a thin grey blanket which was folded over something at the level a cummerbund would have reached to hold it in position. Being aware that he was incapacitated by the damage to his spine sustained in the *David Versus Goliath* battle, the fact that he was in such a conveyance had been expected by his visitors. However, not even any remembrance they might have had of his other injuries had prepared them for the most striking thing about him. A black silk hood covered his head and hung loosely down until being tucked inside the wing collar of his shirt. There was no aperture for either his nose or mouth, but his eyes gleamed through two slits which allowed nothing more than them to be seen.

Even though they had never met, of all the guests,

McCallister was best able to envisage what lay beneath the hood and he knew there was an excellent reason for it, even after so many years had elapsed. Having retained his hero worship for Sir Granville, shortly after having become a medical student, he had sought out an article which was written for the *Lancet* by the Principal Medical Officer of the *David*. In addition to recording the extent of the injury to his spine and its treatment while still at sea, there had been a professionally vivid description of the other terrible damage caused by the last shell fired from the stricken *Osnabrucken* exploding close to him. The face had been so badly burned that not even the finest plastic surgeons could rebuild it. As well as leaving the skin marred by deep scars with barely more than the holes of the nostrils remaining, all his hair had been burned off by the searing blast and would never grow again.

Realizing he was staring at his hero in a way which might be misconstrued and give offence, McCallister turned his gaze to the other three members of the group. With one possible exception, they did not strike him as being the kind to be on close terms with his host. However, before he could give the matter any thought, his curiosity about them was satisfied.

'Good evening, ladies and gentlemen,' the man in the wheelchair greeted, his voice having a hearty and surprisingly robust timbre to its upper class accent. 'Allow me to introduce myself and my friends. As you will probably have guessed, I am your host, Sir Granville Delamont.' He paused, then gestured with a hand in the appropriate directions as he continued, 'Please let me present: Baron Ludwig von Helsinore, who – despite being *Danish* – was Commander of the *Osnabrucken* when we had our little difference of opinion. My personal physician, Doctor Christophe Dubarry – by the way, he is *not*, he assures me, related in any way to a certain *Comtesse* with the same surname of whom you *may* have heard. Lastly, but by no means *least*, a man who deserves every sympathy for putting up with a cantankerous codger like me for as long as he has, my

82

constant attendant, without whose care I would be left like a stranded whale, William Brown.'

On his name being mentioned, the man to the right of the chair clicked his heels and gave a stiff-backed, yet seemingly indifferent, bow. In his late forties, tall, lean and ramrod straight, he wore his immaculate evening attire as if the garments were a uniform. His close-cropped gun metal grey hair and iron hard face, its cheeks bearing the kind of scars acquired – especially by students at Heidelberg University – in duels with a sabre, gave him more the appearance of being a Prussian Army officer than a former Commander even in the German Navy.

There was a distinctly Gallic look about Doctor Dubarry, but it was not the jovial peasant variety. Rather his somewhat porcine features looked surly and humourless. Nor were they improved by a heavy black moustache drooping over his full lipped mouth. Instead of smiling at the way he was introduced, he acknowledged the words with a brief inclination of his almost completely bald head. Matching von Helsinore in height and about the same age, he was much more heavily built, and yet his evening wear seemed to hang baggily upon him.

Looking at the man standing behind the wheelchair, McCallister decided he had never seen anybody more suited to the very common – by virtue of the large number who bore it in the British Isles alone – name, 'William Brown'. While he was fairly tall and must be reasonably strong, else he would be unable to carry out the various duties entailed by the position for which he was employed, he was not sufficiently physically well developed to attract attention. His neatly trimmed hair was the ordinary brown shade which defied exact classification and, except that his clean shaven features were suggestive of Anglo-Saxon origins, there was nothing especially noticeable about them. In fact, apart from the white tunic style jacket of a male nurse he wore, he would have been totally indistinguishable amongst a crowd anywhere in England.

'Now then, Michael lad,' Sir Granville went on.

'Come on over and present our guests to me.'

Trying, none too successfully, to look pleasant, the next in line of succession for ownership of Mansfield Manor left his fiancée where they had been standing beyond the other visitors and advanced to carry out the request. Halting just in front of his uncle, he commenced what was clearly a well established ritual by calling forward the guests in what he regarded as the order of their importance. Despite his frequently stated dislike of members of the Armed Forces, he began with Flying Officer Allan Morningford. Then he introduced Joan Darling. They were followed by Jimmy Brocklehurst and Rosalind Brampton. McCallister was next, but – by virtue of the reason she had given for her presence – Billie Oakroyd remained where she was. Beryl Snowhill and, making the presentation in what was clearly an afterthought, Rapido – who was introduced formally as Edward Marsden – completed the ceremony.

With the exception of the Texan, in each case, Sir Granville showed he either knew already or had been primed in advance by his nephew about the status of each guest. He praised Morningford's ability as a pilot and claimed to have seen and been most impressed by the last aerobatic display at Hendon. Telling Joan how much he enjoyed hearing her sing on the wireless, he apologized for never having seen her on the stage and hoped she would dance for him some time over the weekend. Having had a joke with Brocklehurst about civil servants, he congratulated them on their engagement and Roz upon her recent promotion to sister. Learning that McCallister was a nephew of a now retired Surgeon Commander of the same name, he told how they had once a memorable run ashore in Hong Kong and promised further details when there were no ladies present. Greeted warmly, Beryl was assured that they would talk about the property in which her family were interested on Sunday morning.

'So you're an American, Edward?' Sir Granville inquired, after having shaken hands with the last guest to be brought forward.

'A *Texan*, sir,' Rapido corrected. 'We let the rest of the United States join us back in '48.'[1]

'So I've heard,' the man in the wheelchair claimed in a tone which suggested he was smiling behind the hood. Then, as if wishing to make up for the way his nephew had behaved, he continued, 'And what do you think of our country?'

'It's choicely fine, sir,' the Texan declared. 'And, sure as night follows day, I've *never* seen such a fancy place as yours. We've *nothing* like it anywheres back to home. I'm sure looking forward to the party.'

'I think I should warn you that there won't be any of the wild high jinks – I think you call them in your country – that you hear about happening at house-parties elsewhere,' Sir Granville said.

'I should think not, for shame,' Rapido replied. 'Being raised an churched all right and proper.'

'Are you a Catholic?' Sir Granville asked.

'No sir,' the Texan denied. 'My folks've been Baptists as far back as we know.'

'Baptists, huh?' the man in the wheelchair said, nodding with what might have been approval. 'Of course, in the Andrew – Royal Navy to you,[2] Edward – we only acknowledge the Church of England and Catholic faiths, which can make things somewhat difficult for those who follow other denominations.'

'Here we go with the jolly jack tar nonsense!' Wanda Gore-Kauphin muttered to her fiancé, who had with-

---

1. *Although Texas attained freedom from Mexican rule after the Battle of San Jacinto on Thursday, 21 April 1836, it did not become accepted as part of the United States of America until 16 February 1848. Information about the struggle by the people of Texas to attain independence from Mexico is given in the* Ole Devil Hardin *series.*

2. *'The Andrew': British sailors' nickname for the Royal Navy. It originates from the memory of a legendary member of the press-gang service, Andrew Miller, who was said to have claimed ownership of the Navy because of the hundreds of men he had forcibly enrolled into it.*

drawn to her side when his uncle started to talk to the Texan. 'And then it will be the *funny* stories!'

'I hope he doesn't take long with them,' Mansfield replied, just as quietly.

'So do I,' the unsuccessful actress supported, gripping the vanity bag tightly. 'This is one night I'm looking forward to his stupid game.'

'Mr Guerney!' Sir Granville called, while the *sotto voce* exchange of comments was taking place. 'Are we running a long ship here?'[3]

'I would hope not, sir,' the butler intoned, but he had adopted a posture more in keeping with the rank he had held in the Navy than his present position as the senior male servant in the household.

'Then,' Sir Granville went on. 'As the sun is well over the foreyard,[4] splice the main brace[5] and we'll celebate the Siege of Gibraltar.'[6]

3. *'Long ship': in the parlance of the Royal Navy's wardrooms, a derogatory term for one which is lacking in the traditional hospitality to its guests and where a long time is allowed to elapse between serving them drinks.*

4. *By convention, one did not drink in a Royal Navy's wardroom before noon. However, in the days of sailing ships, when the sun had risen so it could be seen above the foreyard – the lowest yard on the foremast of the vessel – the officers considered the morning was sufficiently far advanced for the taking of a 'nooner' drink to be acceptable. The term is often changed to, 'the sun is over the yard arm'.*

5. *In the days of sailing ships, the main brace was the thickest and strongest rope of the rigging. When it was damaged, a great number of men were needed to effect the repairs and, in most cases, the completion of the task was rewarded by an extra issue of rum. As time went by, the traditional announcement when there was a task or event of sufficient merit to justify a similar award came to be, 'Splice the main brace'.*

6. *'Celebrate the Siege of Gibraltar': a traditional excuse used in the Royal Navy's wardrooms to give a guest a drink. The fourteen sieges sustained by the garrison at Gibraltar covered such a lengthy period of time that one could celebrate the event on any day of the year.*

'Aye aye, sir!' Guerney assented in the traditional naval fashion and turned to wave forward the footmen bearing trays of drinks.

'As I was saying,' Sir Granville remarked, after his guests had been supplied with the means to 'splice the main brace'. 'The Andrew only recognizes two denominations. Which reminds me of an ordinary seaman I had under me when I was a divisional officer in the old *Princess Royal* just after she was commissioned. His name was Knobby Clark and he was something of a skate, which means, ladies, he was a scrounger and always on the lookout for ways to avoid his duties. One thing he hated was church parade. One Sunday, as usual, the pipe was given for C. of E.'s to form up to starboard and Catholics to port for divine service. Everybody went one way or the other, except Knobby. "Are you deaf, Clark?" the Master at Arms demanded. "No, sir," Knobby replied. "I'm a Primitive Methodist." "Very well," said the Master, who knew him *very* well. "But we don't have a service for you lot, so go and clean all the heads" – that's lavatories, ladies – "instead." Anyway, next Sunday, the pipe was given and there were just two groups of men. Looking around the Master saw Knobby with the C. of E.'s. "Clark," he said. "I thought you said you're a Primitive Methodist?" "I *was,* Master," Knobby replied. "But I've become C. of E. because I didn't like their place of worship".'

CHAPTER SEVEN

A Simple Little Game

'Well, Allan,' said Sir Granville Delamont, after the guests grouped in front of his wheelchair had stopped laughing at the punch-line to the anecdote. 'Do you have one of what the chaps in the Royal Naval Air Service used to call, "There I was, upside down, nothing on the clock, and still *diving*!" stories for us?'

'Yes, sir, one does come to mind,' Flying Officer Allan Morningford admitted, considering the honour of the Royal Air Force was at stake and being determined to uphold it. However, he had already told his favourite 'mixed company' joke and needed to think for a moment before selecting another which came into that category. 'A couple of years ago, I was sent to Salisbury Plain to watch a new idea being tried out. It was to drop soldiers by parachute behind the enemy lines. However, it seemed the pongoes who'd been chosen weren't too happy about the idea.[1] So their padre said he would make the first jump. He was told he would be landing about five miles away, but there would be a car waiting to pick him up. Unfortunately, when he jumped, the parachute didn't open. As he was hurtling down, he said, "Just like the crab-fats.[2] I expect the car won't be there when I land either".'

'Well, sir,' Jimmy Brocklehurst said, as amused

1. 'Pongo': *derogatory name given by British airmen and sailors to a soldier. Said to be derived from certain tribes in West Africa calling the gorilla a* 'pongo'.
2. 'Crab-fats': *derogatory name given by British soldiers and sailors to members of the Royal Air Force.*

groans arose from the other guests and their host looked his way in what – even while wearing the hood – was clearly an interrogative manner. 'I was walking along the corridor of a train one day and thought I saw the Archbishop of Canterbury in a compartment. Deciding to find out if I was right, I opened the door and asked, "Excuse me, sir, but are you the Archbishop of Canterbury?" The man replied, "Urinate off and shut the something-or-other door, you something-else nosy young something-even-worse!" – you'll understand I can't use the *exact* words with ladies present – So I still don't know whether it was the Archbishop of Canterbury or not.'

'I mind one time a Sassenach was boasting about his heritage to the minister of our kirk,' Doctor Andrew McCallister declared, deducing it was his turn to entertain the company. Like the pilot, he had at his dispoal a selection of jokes which were much enjoyed at such purely masculine affairs as rugby club suppers and bachelor 'stag-nights', so had to choose one suitable for the ears of the female guests. Then he changed from the broad Scottish accent he had adopted into an exaggerated upper class English tone, "I'll have you know that my family have been entitled to bear arms since the time of William the Conqueror," he said.' The Scottish burr returned as he concluded, '"Oh aye," the minister replied. "And my family have been entitled to bare legs since the time of Adam".'

'Lord, I don't reckon I can top *that*,' Rapido drawled. 'But there was this priest and a rabbi lived opposite each other down to Fort Worth and they got on 'bout as well as that Yankee, General Custer, did with the Sioux Indians on the Little Bighorn. Fact being, no matter what one did, or got, the other tried to do better. Well, one day, they both drove up to their houses in the latest model Cadillac limousine fitted with all the fancy do-dads's could be got for 'em. Figuring to show he'd got something the rabbi didn't, the priest rushed inside his house and came out with a bottle of holy water which he yelled was blessed by the Pope in Rome and starts sprinkling it on his car. Would you believe the rabbi got him a hacksaw and cut a couple of inches off his car's exhaust pipe?'

'I wish somebody would *explain* that to me,' Rosalind Brampton asserted with an air of what might have been innocence, when the laughing ended. 'But it reminds me of the alienist who went into business with a rabbi. That way, they could deal with odds and ends.'

'And *this* is the woman I'm going to marry!' Brockle-hurst ejaculated, making a wry face. 'How about *you*, Billie?'

'I don't know any "parson" jokes,' Billie Oakroyd confessed. Then she darted a mocking glance at Baron Ludwig von Helsinore. Like Doctor Christophe Dubarry, he clearly did not consider the jokes as amusing as did the rest of the guests. 'But I found out how you greet a group of German alienists at Christmas. You say, "God rest ye Jerry mental-men".'

'Oh dear!' Beryl Snowhill groaned, as the others looked her way. 'It's *my* turn, is it? Well, I remember my uncle, the Bishop of Darnley, took me to Doncaster races one day. We were in the paddock and saw Mick Mulcay give something to his horse, Bonny Legs. So did one of the Stewards for the meeting and, knowing he isn't called "Micky the Shopper" because he spends a lot of time and money in shops,[3] asked what it was. "Sure and it's only just a chocolate sweetie as the little darling's so fond of, your honour," Micky replied. Taking a couple more of the things from his pocket, he popped one into his mouth and swallowed it. However, as the Steward wasn't satisfied, he grabbed the other and did the same. After they had walked away, Uncle said to me, "Come on, dear. I want to have a fiver on Bonny

3. For more information about the dishonest behaviour of Mick Mulcay, see, Part VI, 'Micky The Shopper', EDU-CATED EVANS, *by Edgar Wallace*.

Legs to win. If anything is in front of her at the post, it will either be the Steward or Micky".'

'After *that*, I think you all deserve a *change*,' Sir Granville declared, following the laughter evoked by the beautiful little blonde's story. He did not ask either of the men flanking his wheelchair, or Wanda Gore-Kauphin and Michael Mansfield, to participate. Instead, he went on, 'And I hope that you'll indulge an old man's whims by joining in a simple little game.'

'You're boss of this range, sir,' Rapido drawled and if the glances which passed between the English members of the party were any indication, they knew what was coming. 'So I'm ready, willing and able to go along whichever way you point.'

'Very well,' Sir Granville said, reaching into his jacket's inside pocket to bring out a bright red leather wallet which was decorated by a dragon made of rolled gold. It was about the size of a tobacco pouch, thin and most distinctive in appearance. 'There's a little prize in here I think the winner might like. All you have to do to win is be the one who's holding it when game ends. You might say you'll be playing a cross between hunt the thimble and blindman's-buff, except that nobody needs have a blindfold. Instead, we have the lights switched off for fifteen minutes and the rest have to find which one has the wallet in the dark. Whoever has it *must* hand it over to anybody who catches them. If you get caught and don't have it, say so. I *know* I can trust you all not to *cheat*.'

'That sounds like *fun*,' Joan Darling enthused. 'But I'd better warn the rest of you that I'm a poor player and a bad loser.'

'I don't think you could be *bad* at anything, my dear,' Sir Granville claimed gallantly.

'There's one thing worries me, sir,' McCallister asserted. 'Somebody might bump into you while we're moving around in the dark.

'Thank you for your concern,' Sir Granville replied, as a murmur of concurrence arose from the rest of the group. He pointed across the room and towards the well polished planks of the open space where they were gathered before continuing, 'I'll have Brown move me behind the top end of the billiard table and, providing you stay on the wooden part of the floor, I don't think any of you will reach me there. Are you going to join in, Ludwig?'

'I think *not*!' von Helsinore answered stiffly. 'And, as I have some telephone calls I wish to make, I will attend to them while you are playing.'

'I know you don't want to play, Doc,' Sir Granville stated breezily to Dubarry, making no attempt to change the Dane's mind. 'So you can go into the back hall and act as time-keeper as usual.'

During the session of jokes, the footmen had been available for any of the guests who required another drink. Watching them, McCallister was impressed. Despite looking like the kind of men one would not wish to meet in a lonely place on a dark night, they carried out their duties in a satisfactory manner. They might not achieve the ultimate state of a servant – being so inconspicuous that they are no more than a pair of hands carrying out a task, but they were not in any way obtrusive and none of them did more than let their faces take on a barely noticeable smile as they listened to what was being said.

The doctor considered that the butler was probably responsible for getting the footmen into such a condition, and achieving it might have called for more than just moral persuasion. However, remembering what his occupation in the Royal Navy had been and the expression which had come over his face when Wanda had threatened the dismissal of the housekeeper and other members of the staff before dinner, McCallister suspected he was capable of enforcing his will upon others by physical means if necessary. Nevertheless, the doctor wondered why Sir Giles had elected to take such men into his employment instead of the more usual types one saw in similar positions elsewhere.

With the explanation of the game completed and following what was obviously a regular routine, the butler and the footmen withdrew from the library. After Guerney had closed the double doors, the faint glow of light showing under them disappeared as the electric bulbs in the entrance hall were extinguished. The drapes had been drawn across all the windows while the clay pigeon shooting was taking place, excluding any chance of illumination from outside. Crossing towards the rear of the big room, von Helsinore and Dubarry left through a door which was made so that it was almost indistinguishable from the wood panelling of the walls.

While the pair were leaving, Brown moved Sir Granville to the position he had mentioned beyond the billiard table. Having fallen into the spirit of the game, the session of telling jokes having served to keep everyone's spirits light even though they were in the presence of their badly injured and incapacitated host, all the guests looked eagerly about them. However, instead of moving forward to join in, Wanda Gore-Kauphin and Michael Mansfield remained by the wall where – except when he had been called forward to perform the introductions – they had been standing ever since entering.

'Now,' Sir Granville said, after his attendant had left him and had crossed to a light switch near the door through which the Dane and the Frenchman had disappeared. 'We're all ready to start. I think that, being a visitor from overseas, we should allow our friend from Texas to have the wallet first. Come and collect it, Rapido.'

Thanking his host for the privilege and crossing the room in his usual unhurried way, the Texan did as he was requested. Having accepted the wallet, he walked back towards the others in the same unhurried fashion. Waiting until he was near them, Sir Granville waved his right hand and Brown threw the switch to put out all the lights. Instantly, the room was plunged into a stygian blackness. Regardless of this, feet could be heard moving on the wooden floor as the hunt began.

'Not fast enough, Rapido!' Beryl announced, almost immediately. 'I've got it now!'

'No you haven't!' McCallister denied a couple of seconds later.

Although the doctor retained the wallet for a few seconds longer than either of his predecessors, he lost it to Brocklehurst. Nor did it end there. To the accompaniment of exclamations of success when the correct person had been contacted, or denials of being in possession of the wallet and other general indications of amusement, the game continued. As the minutes went by, each of the participants was detected at least once while holding the prize. When the door was opened and Brown switched on the lights to indicate the conclusion of the game, Joan, after having and losing the wallet several times, was still grasping it in her right hand.

'I've got *it*, Sir Gra—!' the red head began, waving the distinctive looking trophy triumphantly as she got her bearings and turned around. Then it dropped from her fingers and she gasped, 'Oh my God!'

Following the direction in which Joan was staring, horror-stricken, the rest of the guests realized there was good cause for her behaviour. No longer was Sir Granville erect in his wheelchair. Instead, his torso was bent forward to a point at which it seemed he would topple from his seat. Like his hooded head, his arms were hanging limply downwards and would not have helped in averting a fall.

Under different circumstances, Roz and McCallister in particular would have understood the reason for the apparent flouting of the laws of gravity. As a precaution against some mishap spilling him out of his seat, there was a stout webbing or leather belt attached to the sides of the wheelchair which passed around his waist. Being the kind of man he was, he had no wish to let it be known he employed such a device thus drawing attention to the fact that his lower limbs were useless appendages

94

incapable of supporting his weight. Therefore, the belt was concealed by having the top of the blanket drawn over it.

To give Doctor Dubarry and Brown their due, regardless of the shock they must have felt, they acted with commendable speed. Before anybody else could move, they were hurrying towards the billiard table. On arrival they both looked down and exchanged glances. Then, while Brown stepped behind the wheelchair and drew his employer into an upright posture, the Frenchman turned around. Having a shorter distance to go, they arrived before the rest of the guests reacted. The transition from enjoying a game which they guessed also gave much pleasure to Sir Granville, to a realization of what was happening, had not come as quickly to the guests. Therefore, the examination was being carried out before any of them responded to the sight.

'Stay *back*!' the Frenchman barked, directing a scowl at the guests who were starting to move in his direction.

'I'm a doctor and this lady is a nursing sister,' McCallister announced, indicating Liz as they alone of the visitors continued to advance. As they moved forward McCallister noticed that Wanda and Mansfield had not reacted in the same way as the guests despite the latter looking strained and perturbed. Both remained standing where they had been when the lights went out. At that time Wanda appeared to have been about to select a book from those in the shelves behind her. 'If we can be of any assistance—?'

'You *can't*,' Dubarry refused bluntly. 'Sir Granville occasionally has these attacks and I can do all that is necessary for him.'

Although McCallister had began to stride forward accompanied by the statuesque young woman, it was purely an instinctive gesture on his part. Like most members of his profession, he had always been ready to offer medical advice and aid at the slightest excuse while a student and shortly after having qualified. That phase had soon passed and, particularly in view of his present

95

specialization, he was now inclined to leave emergency treatment to any other doctor present unless his assistance was specifically requested. However, on this occasion, because the high opinion he already held for his host had been increased by personal acquaintance, he was willing to make an exception, despite the less than friendly or polite refusal of his services.

Before McCallister could go any closer, Billie gave a cry of alarm and collapsed limply to the floor!

'Attend to her, doctor!' Dubarry commanded rather than asked. 'And you, Sister!'

Under other circumstances, McCallister would have resented being addressed by a stranger – even one who also was a doctor – in such a cavalier fashion. However, he had developed an interest in Billie since their meeting in the library which was not professional and he considered it to have been reciprocated. Therefore, he was more than willing to carry out the instructions. Despite being annoyed by the Frenchman's behaviour, Roz also reacted instinctively. The words had been uttered in the manner of a senior member of the hospital staff speaking and the discipline acquired in several years of nursing caused her to obey. What was more, before either she or McCallister could go nearer, Brown was pushing the wheelchair towards the side door and Dubarry was following him. Passing through, the latter closed it behind them with a bang.

'Looks like they don't reckon they need help, Doc,' Rapido commented. 'But, could be the lady does.'

'I think she's only fainted,' Roz assessed, crossing and starting to bend over the prostrate young woman.

Even as the summation was being delivered, Billie showed signs of recovery. Before Roz could commence an examination, she pushed herself into a sitting position.

'Are you all right, Billie?' McCallister asked and there was something more than just professional interest in his voice.

'Y—Yes!' the young woman replied, allowing the

96

doctor to help her to rise and give her support. 'It was the sight of Uncle Granville that gave me such a shock. I know he's been having these attacks occasionally for some months now, but it was the first time I'd seen one.'

Before any more could be said, the door through which Sir Granville had been taken was opened and von Helsinore strode in.

'Ladies and gentlemen,' the Dane barked. 'All is well. Sir Granville has recovered and says you must not worry about him, or stop enjoying yourselves on his account. He will need to be kept in bed for the night, but promises he will be fit enough to join you again in the morning.'

CHAPTER EIGHT

I've Already Signed The Death Certificate

'Wake up, guv!' growled a voice, as the lights in Doctor Andrew McCallister's room were switched on.

Much to the surprise of the guests he had invited, Michael Mansfield had not offered to accompany Doctor Christophe Dubarry and William Brown when Sir Granville Delamont had been removed from the library. Combined with the way they had behaved when they had first seen what had happened, it seemed neither Mansfield nor his fiancée were in the least concerned by the incident. However, this had been partially explained when Flying Officer Allan Morningford had expressed the feelings of the others by asking bluntly why Mansfield did not go with his uncle. The reply had been that Sir Granville had a great dislike of anybody other than his personal physician and attendant seeing the ravaged condition of his face. Therefore, as it was certain that the hood would have to be removed before any treatment could be carried out, he would not want even his next of kin to be present. The excuse had been accepted, but even when Wanda Gore-Kauphin and Mansfield had heard the news brought by Baron Ludwig von Helsinore – and they both seemed relieved to know Mansfield's uncle was well again – he had not offered to go and visit his relative.

After having made the announcement, von Helsinore had picked up the red leather wallet dropped by Joan Darling. On straightening up, he pressed at it as if wishing to form an impression of what it contained. Then, taking a sheet of paper from it, he announced the reward Sir Granville Delamont had arranged for the winner of the game. This proved to be a weekend trip for two in Paris, with first class return travel, a suite of rooms at the best hotel, tickets for one of the most sought after boxes at the Moulin Rouge and a sum of money sufficient to cover most of the incidental expenses. When the beautiful red head was told that she had won, having been in possession of the wallet when the lights came on, her attempt to decline was countered by being assured that their host had said he wanted his gift to be accepted.

Despite the suggestion that Sir Granville had recovered from the stroke which had caused his collapse and wanted the festivities to go on, none of the guests had felt in the mood to continue celebrating. Nor had either von Helsinore nor Wanda and Mansfield done anything to try and revive the party spirit. Left to their own devices, despite the suggestion passed to them by the Baron, they had considered the circumstances were not suitable for further enjoyment. Instead, they had remained in the library for a time, talking quietly amongst themselves. However, there was no longer any of the levity which had enlivened the earlier conversations and, by mutual agreement, they had retired for the night shortly after half past ten.

On reaching his room, McCallister had still felt annoyed at the way Dubarry had responded to his and Rosalind Brampton's attempt to assist with Sir Granville. However, he was never a man to brood over things and, having undressed and got into bed, he had soon fallen into a sleep which lasted until he was disturbed by the arrival of the footman who had escorted him to his quarters.

'What's wrong?' the young doctor asked, having been awakened by hearing the door being opened.

'Sorry to have woke you, sir,' replied the bulky visitor, although his voice did not suggest any special contrition, as he came to a stop by the side of the bed. Because he was not wearing his livery jacket and, in addition to being in his shirt-sleeves, was barefoot, he looked even less like a servant in a high class country house. On the other hand, his informality of attire suggested he was no longer on duty and this could explain his disgruntled attitude. 'But the Jer – *Danish* bloke and Frog – *Doctor* Dubarry want you to come to the Commodore's room straight away.'

'Why?' McCallister asked, sitting up.

'I dunno,' the footman answered in a similarly disinterested fashion. 'I was just getting ready to go to kip when Guerney come in and give me the message for you. He said you should come right away, but you don't need to bring nothing with you.'

'Very well,' the doctor said, but he felt puzzled. Although the request for his presence suggested he was being asked in his professional capacity, the last sentence made him wonder if this was the case. However, he had not brought any of his medical equipment with him and, therefore, had nothing to take. Starting to get out of bed while speaking, he glanced at his wristwatch on the table beside the bed and discovered the time was half past one. 'I'll come.'

Despite McCallister's acceptance, he was surprised by the summons. Dubarry had been most curt in refusing his offer of assistance in the library and he wondered what could have brought about the change of mind. Having concluded that the best way of satisfying his curiosity was to go with the footman, he rose to his feet and decided against taking time to change into more suitable attire. Instead, he slid on his bedroom slippers and donned his dressing-gown over his pyjamas. Then, acting instinctively as the result of a habit acquired during his last couple of years as a medical student – when he was often called from his bed in the quarters allocated to him at St Bartholomew's Hospital to attend to a patient – he picked up the fountain-pen which lay by his watch. Without giving a thought to the special qualities which had precluded its use at the Admiral Cornwallis Inn, he thrust it into the breast pocket of the dressing-gown.

Following the footman, who did not appear to be willing to engage in further conversation, McCallister went along the dimly lit passage and up to the second floor. He was guided to a door which, on being opened, gave access to a larger room than the one he was occupying. Instead of following him in, his guide closed the door behind him. It was luxuriously appointed and a glance around informed him this was only to be expected. The wheelchair, standing unoccupied against the wall, with the black hood hanging from the right side handle, and everything else he saw, suggested that it was part of Sir Granville's living quarters. However, at that moment, he was more interested in the occupants than the details of his surroundings. Still dressed as they had been when he last saw them, von Helsinore, Dubarry, Brown and Guerney were standing in a rough – somehow menacing – half circle in front of him.

The sight which met McCallister's gaze as he looked beyond the four men drove everything else from his head!

Covered by a white silk sheet, something which the young doctor recognized as being a body lay on the big four-poster bed!

'Is that—?' McCallister began, before he could prevent himself asking a question to which the answer was obvious.

'It is,' Dubarry confirmed in his heavily accented English. 'He had another of the strokes and died, quite peacefully and without suffering, half an hour ago.'

'Then why have you sent for me?' McCallister inquired, the instruction not to bring his equipment causing him to doubt whether he was being consulted as a result of his specialization. 'Surely, being Sir Granville's next of kin, Michael Mansfield should have been told.'

'There is no *need* for Mansfield to be here,' von Helsinore stated, taking a sheet of paper from his inside pocket. 'This will explain what is to be done.'

Accepting what proved to be a legal document bearing

the letterhead of a prominent firm of solicitors in London, McCallister read its contents. It was an authorization for 'my personal physician, Doctor Christophe Dubarry, my trusted butler, Edward Samuel Guerney, and loyal nurse-attendant William Brown' to carry out Sir Granville's wishes in the event of his death. Stating his abhorence of letting the injuries to his face be seen by anybody other than the three of them, he required that they prevented this happening by arranging for him to be cremated as soon as possible after he died.

'This seems to be quite in order,' McCallister conceded, folding and returning the document to the Baron. In fact, although he did not say so, he decided that it was in keeping with what he had heard about Sir Granville. What was more, the instructions must be legal or the firm of solicitors would not have acceded to them being put into writing and attesting to their authenticity. 'Do you want me to confirm that his death has occurred?'

'That won't be necessary,' Dubarry asserted with cold finality. 'I've already signed the death certificate.'

'Then why—?' McCallister commenced, but he could guess at the answer.

'Surely you were taught in your medical classes that *two* doctor's signatures are required on a cremation certificate?' von Helsinore barked. 'That is *why* we have sent for you.'

'But surely the local doctor would be more appropriate?' McCallister suggested.

'Sir Granville couldn't stand the local doctor,' Guerney claimed, his tone less bland than previously. 'He always said, "Don't let that gossiping bloody old quack come near me alive or dead".'

'So,' the Baron went on, his attitude indicating he considered the matter was closed. 'As you *are* a qualified medical practitioner, we require you to help us carry out our *friend's* last wishes.'

'But why couldn't you have waited until morning?' McCallister wanted to know.

'I should have thought that was *obvious*, no matter

how recently you qualified,' Dubarry snorted. 'With the weather this warm, the sooner everything is done the better. What is more, because he had no intention of having his wishes ignored by anybody who wanted to have a public funeral, Sir Granville made an arrangement with a nearby crematorium to have the ceremony performed as soon after his death as possible.'

Although he did not care for the way the explanation was given, McCallister guessed what had caused the misapprehension about the length of time he had been a doctor. He looked younger than he was. In fact, since qualifying, he had occasionally been mistaken for a medical student when he visited hospitals where he was not known. What was more, under the circumstances, he could not argue against the validity of the need to avoid delaying the issue. Nevertheless, he felt distinctly uneasy. There seemed to be an urgency in the way his assistance was demanded which went beyond mere considerations of hygiene.

Hints at nepotism by jealous rivals notwithstanding, McCallister had earned the appointment he held at his uncle's assistant. Two of the qualities which had helped him secure it had been his well developed powers of observation, and the ability to reach conclusions from those observations which many a detective would have liked to possess. When he had realized what was being asked of him, he turned his gaze once more towards the sheet-covered body of Sir Granville. Before he could look at it, his attention was attracted by something underneath the bed. Realizing what it was, he discovered that other things, which he might have expected to be available, were missing. Their absence added to the speculations aroused by the object he had seen.

'If it is a question of your fee, doctor—!' von Helsinore began.

'My *fee* doesn't enter into it!' McCallister interrupted angrily, jolted from his train of thought by what he regarded as a most offensive suggestion. As always when

103

he was annoyed, his voice became more noticeably Scottish in timbre. 'I'm a guest in this house—!'

'Then you are willing to sign?' the Baron suggested rather than asked.

'Of course I am,' McCallister confirmed. 'But I would like to see the body first.'

'No!' von Helsinore refused bluntly.

'You've been told of Sir Granville's wishes on that point,' Guerney continued and his hostility was all too obvious. 'Besides, there's no need for you to do it.'

'*I* have already signed the death certificate,' Dubarry supported with asperity. He went into a detailed description of the symptoms which had been manifested before Sir Granville had died. 'And I consider it an *insult* for you to imply you think I would be in error with my diagnosis.'

'I didn't intend any insult, sir,' McCallister corrected mildly, trying successfully to look like a very recently qualified doctor who had inadvertently offended one much senior to himself. Starting to walk forward, he went on, 'Of course I will sign.'

Passing between Dubarry and Guerney, the young doctor went towards the bed. As he approached, despite realizing that all four men were following him, he was able to verify at closer range three of the assumptions he had drawn earlier. Despite his suspicion that something was radically wrong, his every instinct warned that he would be prevented – by force if necessary – from making a visual inspection of the body.

Giving no indication of his misgivings, McCallister contrived to stumble. Flailing with his arms as if trying to recover his equilibrium, he fell on to the bed. His right hand descended upon the thin silk sheet where it covered the body's head and the left alighted, apparently just as inadvertently, upon a leg. However, even if it had been his intention to uncover Sir Granville's face, he was not granted an opportunity to do so. Responding more swiftly than he had at any other time during the evening and accompanying the action with a profanity more suited to a Regulating Chief Petty Officer in the Royal Navy than a butler, Guerney lunged forward. Caught by the shoulders by two powerful hands, the young doctor was hauled upwards and flung across the room.

'I'm *very* sorry. I can't understand how I could be so *clumsy!*' McCallister apologized, having managed to come to a stop without falling. Looking at the scowling and now clearly menacing quartet who were confronting him, he hoped any emotion he showed would be attributed to embarrassment over the mishap or annoyance at his treatment by Guerney. Trying to look like he was eager to make amends, he reached for the pen in the pocket of his dressing-gown and went on, 'Where is the cremation certificate, Doctor Dubarry. I consider it a privilege to carry out Sir Granville's wishes by signing it.'

CHAPTER NINE
There's Something Very Wrong

'Are you all right, Andy?' Jimmy Brocklehurst asked in a concerned tone, gazing at the strained features of his unexpected visitor and starting to get out of bed.

Accepting the already completed cremation certificate produced by Baron Ludwig von Helsinore, Doctor Andrew McCallister had taken it to the bedside table. His hope that he would be allowed to use the pen he had brought with him was fulfilled and there was no objection as he carried out his promise by adding his signature to the scrawl made by Doctor Christophe Dubarry. Handing the document to von Helsinore there had been an interruption, much to McCallister's relief, before any notice could be taken of the somewhat rusty-brown colour of the ink. A thickset man with close cropped blond hair and hard Germanic features, albeit suggestive of a lower stratum of society than that of von Helsinore, entered. Except that he wore shoes, he was dressed as the footman had been.

Swinging around, the Baron had started to snarl something in his native tongue which the young doctor guessed was a demand to be told why the man came in without knocking. Snapping to attention, the newcomer had interrupted with an explanation which brought the words to an end. The news was clearly most disturbing to von Helsinore and, although McCallister could not understand what was said, it had been obvious that Dubarry and the butler *did* understand and were equally perturbed. Looking at the young doctor and reverting to English, the Baron said there was no further reason for them to keep him from his bed.

Apologizing for his clumsiness and receiving a less than amiable acceptance, McCallister had been only too willing to accept the curt dismissal. In fact, he regarded it as a blessing in disguise. Because of the summation he had formed and the measures he had taken to counter it, he had been relieved to see the Baron thrust the cremation certificate away without examining it more closely. He hoped it would remain unscrutinized until he had left the premises, as he intended to do after breakfast in the morning.

On leaving the room, McCallister had been relieved to discover the footman had not waited to escort him back to his quarters. Being left alone had enabled him to do as he intended without any delay occurring. Instead of turning into his room, he had passed both his own room and the one allocated to Rapido. Opening the next door and switching on the lights, as he had anticipated would be the case – particularly in view of Sir Granville Delamont's feelings about the conduct of male and female guests – he had found Brocklehurst present and alone. What was more, like himself, the civil servant was a light sleeper and had not needed to be woken up.

'There's something *very* wrong in this house, Jimmy,' McCallister replied to the question provoked by his appearance, even though he did not know he was showing his feelings. 'I've just been taken to Sir Granville's room and told he was dead.'

'*Dead!*' Brocklehurst repeated. 'But von Helsinore told us he had recovered from the stroke.'

'He had another and it killed him, according to Dubarry,' the young doctor explained. 'But as I said, there's something *very* wrong. For one thing, there was a *chamber pot* under Sir Granville's bed.'

'Unless it was kept in a commode,[1] as my grandmother always insisted was a more genteel place for them,' Brocklehurst answered, wondering why his visitor had

1. '*Commode*': used in this context, a small chair or cabinet enclosing a chamber pot.

employed so much emphasis when referring to a commonplace household utensil. 'Where else would you expect it to be?'

'There of course,' McCallister admitted. 'But *who* would be using it?'

'Sir Granville, of course,' Brocklehurst claimed. 'He could hardly get up in the night and go to the bathroom.'

'I can see Roz hasn't told you much about her work,' the doctor stated. 'And I thought *all* nurses talked incessantly about *bed-pans*.'

'*Of course!*' the civil servant ejaculated, remembering that particular kind of utensil from the period when he had been confined to bed in a hospital and had first met Rosalind Brampton. 'He couldn't get up, or use a chamber pot in bed.'

'There was something else,' McCallister warned. 'There wasn't a bell cord hanging by the bed, or a button for an electric bell, and I couldn't see any sign of Brown sleeping in the room so that he could be called if needed.'

'Good god!' Brocklehurst gasped. 'You can't mean—?'

'That's just what I *mean!*' the doctor confirmed grimly. 'Whoever used the bed either had *remarkable* control over his bodily functions, or must have been able to get out and move around without assistance.'

'But Sir Granville was crippled for life in the *David and Goliath* fight,' Brocklehurst protested.

'So *he* was.'

'*Was!* Are you saying—?'

'When they wouldn't let me see the body, I pretended to trip and fell on to it,' McCallister explained, after having told why he had been summoned to their host's living quarters. 'I didn't get a chance to look under the sheet, but it was thin enough for me to *feel* through it—!'

'And?'

'Sir Granville was left completely *bald*, but there was *stubble* on the head!'

'Perhaps his hair has – had – started to grow again?'

'That's *possible*,' McCallister conceded, in a tone

which implied he considered the contingency most unlikely. 'But the face was *smooth* and *complete*. Not only was there a full nose, I couldn't feel a trace of the deep scars which wouldn't have healed even if the hair had started to grow. And the leg my other hand touched hadn't been unable to move since 1917. It was as firm as my own.'

'Oh my God!' Brocklehurst gasped. 'You *mean*—?'

'Whoever was under the sheet was dead,' McCallister answered. 'I've handled enough corpses since joining Uncle Jamie to be sure of *that*. But it *couldn't* have been Sir Granville Delamont.'

'Then who was it?' the civil servant asked, being aware that Sir James Bannister and his companion were pathologists employed by the Home Office.

'Don't ask *me*!' McCallister answered. 'Although I can guess why a substitution would be made when he died. Dubarry and Guerney have a good thing going here and wouldn't want to lose it, which they would as soon as the news got out and Mansfield took charge. With what they knew about Sir Granville and the way he had chosen to live, they could easily arrange for somebody to take his place.'

'That's true,' Brocklehurst conceded. 'But what I can't understand is, why are they so keen to get rid of the body?'

'To prevent the substitution being found out,' McCallister guessed. 'That document I saw gives them the authority to have the cremation and it will destroy all the evidence of what they've been up to.'

'I know it might have been awkward for you if you'd refused,' the civil servant said. 'But you shouldn't have co-signed the cremation certificate.'

'I thought doing it was the best way out,' the doctor answered. 'But it won't do *them* any good. I picked up the wrong pen when I left home and the one I used came from the Magic Supplies' counter at Selfridges. The ink in it disappears after about ten minutes. Unlike some of them, it won't reappear when the paper is heated and can only be brought back by being soaked in a special chemical. I didn't bring it with me and I doubt if they'll have any either. If we're lucky, they won't find out what's happened until they get to the crematorium. At the worst, it won't happen before breakfast and, even if they have found out, they won't dare cut up rough in front of you and the other guests.'

'They could if they get you alone,' Brocklehurst warned.

'I'll make sure they can't tonight,' McCallister claimed.

'How?' Brocklehurst wanted to know.

'By jamming a chair under the doorknob before I go to bed,' McCallister declared. 'Then, if they try to break in, they'll make enough noise to wake you up and you can get Morningford and Rapido to help us.'

'*Rapido?*' the civil servant queried in a puzzled tone. 'I know he's far more intelligent than he acts and can use a shotgun, but he's such a *small* chap—!'

'On the way here, I saw that *small* chap beat *three* much bigger men who tried to attack him,' the doctor declared. Having described the incident at the Admiral Cornwallis Inn, but not his thoughts about the Texan's way of fighting, he concluded, 'If it came to a choice, I think I'd rather tackle Morningford in a fight.'

Before any more could be said, a strange sound originating from somewhere not too far outside came through the open window!

'What was that?' McCallister inquired, as the noise was repeated from closer by.

'It sounded like a bird of some kind,' Brocklehurst replied. Being a keen ornithologist, he crossed the room. 'But it's not one I've ever heard—Or is it?'

'I can't see anything,' McCallister remarked, having followed his companion to the window and looking down to find there was insufficient light from the waning moon to let him do more than make out the dark surface of the garden below.

'Or me,' Brocklehurst admitted. The sound did not

come again from either point and he went on, 'But I remember hearing a call like that in the Bird House at Regent's Park Zoo. Only I must be wrong.'

'Why?'

'The bird that made it was whip-poor-will and they're only found in America.'

'It's a pity Rapido isn't here, he'd know whether it was one or not,' McCallister remarked. Then he turned from the window and reverted to what he considered was a far more important matter than the identity of a night bird; if that was what had made the sounds. 'I wonder how the chap died?'

'That's a point,' Brocklehurst conceded. 'Von Helsinore said he'd recovered from the stroke he had in the library.'

'And Dubarry claimed he'd had a relapse,' the doctor explained. 'In fact, the symptoms he described were such a classic case, he might have been a specialist lecturing to a class of students on heart diseases.'

'But you think he could have died of something else and not from *natural* causes.'

'I don't know *what* to think, Jimmy. If it *wasn't* from natural causes, how did he die?'

'It *couldn't* have been suicide?'

'I shouldn't think so. Which only leaves *murder*.'

'You mean *they* murdered the chap?'

'Why would they?' McCallister inquired, having considered the possibility. 'That would be like killing the goose that laid the golden egg.'

'He could have been wanting to stop playing the invalid for them. I know I wouldn't want to have to spend hours on end in a wheelchair with a hood over my head,' Brocklehurst said. Being engrossed in their conversation, although the dividing walls were thin enough for the faint sounds to pass through, neither he nor his visitor heard Rapido moving about in the next room. 'Or he could have been getting greedy and demanding more money for doing it.'

'Then why kill him when there were so many witnesses about?'

111

'To have witnesses who'd say he'd already had a stroke.'

'And "Sir Granville Delamont" would be declared dead officially, so they couldn't bring in another substitute.'

'Of course. But who else would want him dead?'

'I can think of *two* who wouldn't exactly be grief stricken if the real Sir Granville died.'

'Good god, *yes*!' Brocklehurst ejaculated. 'Mansfield would inherit the whole estate, lock, stock and barrel. The trouble is he wouldn't get a chance to do in the chap he thought was his uncle after he was taken upstairs. Not that he'd have the nerve, even if they gave him a chance. He was a conchie in the war and I once saw him faint when a chap got a nose bleed in a friendly scuffle after a rugger match.'

'He couldn't have done it in the library, either,' McCallister deduced. 'Even if he had the nerve – and I agree with you that he'd be too spineless to even try – there wasn't a sound. In spite of the noise we were making, we'd have heard if he'd strangled the chap.'

'And there wasn't a shot,' Brocklehurst supported. 'But he could have used a knife.'

'There are ways to kill a man silently with a knife,' the doctor admitted. 'But they all take more skill than he'd have and, what's more, he would have to be *very* lucky, as well as skilful, to have struck exactly the right place in the dark. If he'd missed even by a fraction, the chap would have cried out.'

'Do you know something, old boy?' the civil servant said sombrely. 'We've got a *mystery* on our hands.'

'We have,' McCallister agreed. 'But they can't get the body cremated as quickly as they wanted and we should get some of the answers at the inquest I'm going to insist takes place.'

At that moment, the two young men heard the sound of a car's engine being started. Crossing to the window, they saw the big black limousine which was specially equipped to transport Sir Granville off the estate appear from the garage and, without the headlights being switched on, it went along the drive towards the main entrance.

'What's going on?' Brocklehurst asked.

'I don't know,' McCallister replied. 'But they might be getting the body off the premises, so they can have it cremated tomorrow before I can make a complaint which might have them stopped. Thank heavens I signed the way I did.'

CHAPTER TEN

Make Sure *You Get Away!*

About half an hour after Doctor Andrew McCallister and Jimmy Brocklehurst had finished their discussion and separated, the door of the room between those they occupied was opened. Clad as he had been in the Admiral Cornwallis Inn the previous day, except that he had left behind his hat, Rapido peered with every suggestion of caution in each direction. Satisfied that he was not being observed, he emerged and, his boots making no sound on the carpet covering the floor, he walked much more quickly than was his usual gait along the dimly lit passage. Just as he was approaching the head of the stairs, a sound which could have been made by somebody moving stealthily on the ground floor came to his ears. With his attention diverted in that direction, for a vital few seconds he failed to detect a threat much closer at hand.

Having been descending the stairs leading to the second floor and being concealed by the wall of the next room in the passage, the thickset German – Baron von Helsinore's valet, known only as, 'Hans' to the British servants – who had arrived at a vital moment for McCallister in Sir Granville Delamont's living quarters, lunged forward. Although he did not speak, he stepped just hard enough on to the floor of the passage for Rapido to hear him coming and start to turn. However, he arrived too soon for any defensive measures to be taken. Caught by the shoulders, the Texan was swung around and flung along the passage in the direction from which he had come.

Seeing his assailant following and guessing the attack

114

was to be continued, the small Texan gave the impression he was about to topple over backwards. Showing an agility which implied he had had far greater experience at riding a horse than he had claimed before dinner, despite the thud caused by his landing, he did more than just break his fall so skilfully he was not hurt in any way. Rocking on to his shoulders, he catapulted himself back to his feet with the ease of a trained gymnast. Then, bending at the waist and letting out a ringing yell, 'Yeeagh, Texas Light!', he darted to meet the approaching valet. His lowered head rammed into Hans' chest with a force which elicited a pain-filled grunt and changed the menacing advance to a retreat. However, the valet was in much better physical condition than the burly would-be attacker of the previous day had been and he was not affected as badly. What was more, the impact also caused its deliverer to rebound a few steps.

Coming to a halt and straightening up, Rapido was about to launch another attack when he saw his assailant was not alone. Two of the footmen had been on the stairs behind him and they were now coming into the passage. One had twice acted as McCallister's guide and was called 'Lancer' by the rest of the domestic staff. Although the other had been addressed as 'Henry' by the butler, his origins in Liverpool produced the nickname, 'Scouse',[1] amongst his contemporaries 'downstairs'. Lancer was still dressed as he had been earlier and Scouse was clad in the same fashion even to being barefoot. Neither offered an explanation for the valet's behaviour, nor asked what Rapido was doing out of his room at that hour. Instead, they started to move forward in a threatening fashion.

Showing what many people would have considered to be poor judgement, Rapido repeated the shouted words and darted towards the burly pair. Realizing each had

1. 'Scouse': derived from 'lobscouse', a dish made from ground up hard-tack biscuits, meat and vegetables, much favoured by seamen from Liverpool.

size and weight in his favour, although both looked surprised at what had happened to Hans, they clearly did not believe there was any need to take special precautions before starting to deal with the much smaller Texan. This proved to be a mistake. Moving with a speed which could have been the reason for his nickname, Rapido bounded through the gap between them. In passing, yelling, 'Yeeagh, Texas Light!' for the third time, he lashed a back hand swing on each side.

Swiftly though the blows were struck, coming so unexpectedly and with considerable power, both landed hard enough to send their recipients staggering. Halting about halfway between the footmen and where Hans had come to a stop, the Texan swung around to face the pair. However, showing he too was capable of moving quickly, the valet lunged forward to jerk Rapido around and delivered a round-house punch. It was not sent with a skill matching his own and it caught Rapido on the shoulder to propel him in the direction of the footmen. Showing they were not seriously hurt by his attack, they closed in from his rear to grab him by the arms. Snarling profanities in his native tongue, Hans lumbered towards him to continue the attack.

If the words shouted by the Texan were intended to attract attention to his plight, rather than merely a kind of battle cry, they served their purpose. The doors of three other rooms supplied to the male guests were thrown open and, clad in their pyjamas, the occupants came out. Taking in the sight, Flying Officer Allan Morningford reacted more swiftly than McCallister or Brocklehurst. While he did not know what had caused the incident, the sight of three servants attacking a guest to whom he had taken a liking and who, anyway, was much smaller than them, was sufficient inducement for him to intervene. Hurtling across the passage, he went into the kind of tackle which had made his reputation on the rugby field. Taken around the waist with the full force of a man who was somewhat heavier than himself and very skilled in such tactics, Hans came off worse from the attack. Swept from his feet, he was sent headlong against the wall with his close-cropped skull ramming into it hard enough to stun him.

Despite being diverted by the appearance of the male guests, Lancer and Scouse did not release Rapido. However, before either McCallister or Brocklehurst could come to his assistance, the Texan took action in his own behalf. Raising his right leg, he stamped down hard with it. The high heel of the riding boot descended upon Scouse's bare left foot and, although the heel was intended for the purpose its owner had described in the library, it proved just as efficacious when employed in this present manner. A howl of pain burst from the footman and, releasing his hold, he staggered away with blood gushing from his crushed toenails.

Having liberated one arm, Rapido twisted around and gave a surging heave with the other. Taken unawares by the unexpected strength employed, also being disconcerted at the arrival of assistance for their intended victim, Lancer lost his grip and reeled across the passage to collide with the wall. As he was brought to a halt, he realized the situation had changed drastically and the odds were no longer in his party's favour. Not only were the other two guests joining the Texan, who no longer struck him as being small, but Morningford was rising and Hans was not. Using foul language in a broad and seemingly adenoidal Liverpudlian dialect, which rendered them almost as indecipherable as if they had been spoken in a foreign language, Scouse was hopping on one leg and holding his other foot in both hands. Everything indicated that he too was out of contention.

By now, the female guests were aroused. Looking particularly attractive in her bright blue silk pyjamas, Beryl Snowhill appeared from her room holding something small and black in her right hand. Glancing along the passage, she thrust the object into the front of the loose fitting jacket which she wore tucked into the trousers. Although the insertion caused the neckline to open to an indecorous level, she did not remove the hand as she ran forward. However, before reaching the men, she clearly decided they could handle things without any intervention on her part. As she stopped, extracting her hand – but not the thing it had held – she rebuttoned the jacket. Arriving at the same conclusion with regards to the need for help to their fellow guest, Joan Darling and Rosalind Brampton also came to a halt.

Despite the noise having disturbed the guests, neither Wanda Gore-Kauphin nor Michael Mansfield – who also had rooms on the first floor – put in an appearance. The same did not apply to Baron Ludwig von Helsinore and Doctor Christophe Dubarry. Coming from the second floor it was obvious, if their attire was any guide, that they had not gone to bed since dismissing McCallister from their presence. In fact, apart from having removed their collars and bow ties, they were still fully dressed.

'What is *this*?' von Helsinore bellowed, halting and glaring around.

'I couldn't sleep and figured to take a walk,' Rapido answered, before anybody else could speak. 'So I put on my travelling duds and come out just for that. Only these three jaspers jumped and start rough-handling me without so much as a "Howdy you-all, where at you going?" Which I didn't take none too kind to happening and reckoned I'd get me a mite of help, so I yelled a mite to bring it.'

'You couldn't *sleep*?' the Baron challenged, with more suspicion than the explanation appeared to warrant.

'I *never* can first night in a strange bed,' the Texan replied. 'Anyways, 'cepting maybe the feller lying against the wall, ain't nobody's feathers got more than a mite ruffled and I'm willing to forget the whole damned fool game happen *they* are.'

* * *　　　　　* * *

'I wonder who killed him, sir, and *why*?' commented the man sitting in the front passenger seat of the box-like Singer Junior car, his tone deferential in timbre and indefinable by regional dialect.

118

'So do I,' the driver admitted with a voice indicative of a higher social status. 'And, especially now that's happened, I won't be sorry when they're safely out of it.'

'Nor I, sir,' the first speaker admitted. 'And I wish the lady wasn't there.'

'None of us wanted *that*,' the driver declared. 'Unfortunately, there wasn't any other way.'

At the same time that the fight was taking place on the first floor of Mansfield Manor, the Singer was travelling – at a speed suggesting it had been equipped with a more powerful engine than was fitted by the manufacturers on standard cars, and with accessories to make the most of the modification – along the road serving as a boundary between the estate and an area of fairly dense woodland belonging to Colonel Sir Thorley Besgrove-Woodstole. Even having received the improvements, the vehicle did not compare in price and elegant appointments with the products of Rolls Royce and other models available to the 'luxury' trade in England. Nevertheless, regardless of the way they spoke, the occupants did not look sufficiently well-to-do to be its owners. In fact, their ragged attire and general appearance suggested they were tramps. Neither had shaved, or washed if their faces and hands were any indication, for several days.

Taller of the two by perhaps six inches, with short and uncombed tawny hair, the man behind the wheel looked to be in his late twenties. Despite his unkempt condition and having somewhat outstanding ears, he was good looking in an aquiline way. There was something soldierly in his bearing and he exuded a suggestion of wiry strength.

The second man was perhaps ten years older and black-haired. His nondescript features were set in a politely deferential mask more suited to a well trained 'gentleman's personal gentleman' than the tramp he otherwise looked.

Before any more could be said, the car turned a curve and entered a fairly long, straight stretch which passed the front entrance to the Manor. The glow from its

119

headlights had not yet reached the traditionally open front gates when a big limousine pulled out of them. Instead of turning in one direction or the other, it was brought to a halt in such a way that there would be no room on either side for even the small Singer to go by.

'*Trouble*, sir!' estimated the passenger and, despite the slight emphasis on the first word, he spoke more in the manner of one announcing that dinner was served rather than delivering a warning.

'Yes,' the driver agreed, studying the six men who were springing from the limousine. Dipping his left hand into the outside pocket of his ragged jacket, he brought something out and continued, 'I wish we had the Steyr, we might be able to crash through. As it is, be ready to leave fast and get away through the woods. I'll hold them off as long as I can.'

'As you *wish*, sir,' the passenger assented, with just a trace of reluctance.

'Crouch down now and they might not notice you,' the driver advised. 'And make *sure* you get away!'

'I will, sir,' the passenger promised, carrying out the instruction. 'And please make sure you take *it* in time!'

The precaution suggested by the driver was not taken a moment too soon!

Although the limousine had emerged without having its headlights on, the beam of a powerful spotlight lanced from inside to illuminate the approaching vehicle!

In spite of being partially dazzled, the driver proved to have complete control over the Singer. It was closing the gap between itself and the limousine at such a speed that a collision could not have been averted by one possessed of less ability. By a skilful combination of manipulating the accelerator, clutch, gears, brakes and steering wheel, he slowed, turned in a controlled skid, then brought the Singer to a stop a few feet away and almost parallel to the other vehicle. What was more, the halt was made so that his side was facing the spotlight.

'*Go!*' the driver hissed, then popped the object he was holding into his mouth.

Darting a worried glance at his companion, the other man started to obey. Opening the front passenger door, he slipped out quickly and silently. Then, still in the crouching posture, he darted towards the woodland without a backwards glance. There was a high and practically impenetrable hedge flanking the road elsewhere. However, as he remembered from when he had passed that way earlier, almost opposite the point at which he had alighted the hedge was pierced by a five-barred gate secured with a chain and padlock and bearing a large sign announcing, 'TRESPASSERS WILL BE PROSECUTED'.

Hearing sounds of a struggle as he ran to the gate, but still keeping his gaze to the front, the fleeing man placed his right foot on the second bar. Then, gripping the top with both hands and hauling himself upwards, he rolled over more quickly than would have been possible by conventional climbing. On coming down, he darted into the woodland. However, seeing the spotlight's beam was coming in his direction and hearing noises behind him, he realized that his actions had been observed and he could expect to be pursued.

Paying no attention to the passenger's departure, the driver watched the men from the limousine approaching. He identified them as being employed as footmen at the Manor and knew it was highly unlikely he could escape from them. However, he was determined to give his companion as much of a start as possible. He was helped in this just before the first pair reached the side of the Singer.

'One of them's getting away!' bellowed a voice from inside the limousine and the spotlight was swung around.

Making a biting motion at the thing he had put into his mouth and taking advantage of the footmen looking away, the driver shoved open his door with considerable force. It struck the nearest of them and, diving out, the driver knocked the next closest aside with a very well thrown right cross to the jaw. Having done so, he demonstrated he was as well versed in French *savate* as fist fighting by sending a kick to the jaw which precipated the third backwards against the limousine and knocked the spotlight from its alignment on the fleeing passenger. Unfortunately, competent though he undoubtedly was, the odds were too greatly against him for his success to continue.

The three men who had not yet been subjected to the driver's attentions were already close enough to attack him. What was more, having seen enough to warn them they were up against a skilful antagonist, they behaved in a more cautious fashion then their predecessors. Coming in from either side, although one was knocked backwards, another caught the driver by the shoulder. Jerked around, he took a fist in the face which sent him into the arms of the fourth. Before he could escape from the bear-like hug by which he was enfolded, the rest of the men resumed their attack upon him. However, he might have counted himself fortunate in one respect. Some of them were so eager to get at him and repay the blows he had struck that they tended to get into each other's way. Nevertheless, the punches being rained upon him from all sides appeared to be having an effect and he started to crumple into the arms of his captor.

'Leave off, he's done!' commanded the voice from the limousine, as the beam of the spotlight was swung to illuminate the driver. 'Get after the other one, three of you!'

'We must've got the wrong blokes, Chief,' stated one of the attackers before the command could be carried out, looking down at the unkempt appearance presented by the now limp and unresisting victim. Having served in the Royal Navy until receiving a dishonourable discharge for theft, he still tended, when excited, to address the man who gave the orders in such a fashion, 'He's only a bloody spike[2] and the other one looked the same.'

'Then why'd they act like they did?' the butler

2. 'Spike': British criminals' slang name for a tramp.

122

growled, switching off the spotlight and climbing from the vehicle.

'I bet they've half-inched the *gharri* and thought we was rozzers doing a road block to nab 'em doing it,' offered a second footman, interspersing his suggestion with Cockney rhyming slang for 'pinched' and an Indian term for a vehicle. 'Have we got any flashlights in there, Mr Guerney?'

'What for?' the butler asked, wondering whether he had received the correct solution to his previous question.

'We'll need 'em to go after the other bloke,' the footman explained.

'I don't want you running around in there with flashlights!' Guerney stated. 'that Scotch gamekeeper's who so hot on poachers is liable to be roaming around and I don't want him knowing there's something going on.'

'We'll *never* find the bloke in there without 'em!' the footman protested, waving a hand towards the darkness of the woodland.

'Go and take a look, anyway!' the butler commanded and, after three of the footmen had left to make the search, he went to where the driver had been dropped to the ground. 'Take this one to the gate house and get the cars off the road. We'll find out what his game is as soon as we bring him 'round.'

CHAPTER ELEVEN

Nobody *Is Going To Leave!*

Having gone only a short distance into the woodland, the man who had fled from the Singer Junior car stopped as soon as the spotlight was swung away and looked around. Although the thick hedge through which he had passed combined with the trees and bushes to prevent him seeing the road, he could hear enough to suspect his companion would soon be overpowered. The supposition was quickly verified by the command to stop the attack, and the next words warned him that some of the party from the limousine were being sent in search of him. However, despite the order he had been given to make sure he escaped, his next actions were not those that anybody who had heard his promise to do so would have expected.

Instead of moving deeper into the woodland, the passenger retraced his steps silently until he was able to look through the gate from behind the massive trunk of an old oak tree. Distressed by the sight of his companion lying motionless between the cars, he hoped his reminder to take 'it' in time had been acted upon. However, he was relieved by the suggestion that they were suspected of being tramps who had stolen the Singer, and also relieved on hearing the man who was clearly in charge refuse the request for flashlights to be used in hunting for him. Furthermore, learning how his companion was to be treated, he took added comfort from the realization that – being certain his advice about 'it' had been heeded – the interrogation would not be happening until much later that morning, by which time he hoped help would be available to effect a rescue.

Despite the summations he had reached, the passenger did not move off immediately. Flattening out on the ground behind the oak, he watched three of the men climbing the gate. Once over, acting as he had expected they would, they advanced through the undergrowth in the direction he had been taking when the spotlight's beam was diverted. From the noise they were making and the profanity which came to his ears, he concluded they were unused to moving through such terrain in the night and did not care for the task. The assumption was correct. After about five minutes, they returned to the gate and, discovering the remainder of the party had left the scene, climbed over it to follow.

Satisfied that he had evaded the pursuit, the passenger gave thought as to how he could summon assistance for his companion. Feeling sure a watch was being kept on the road, he ruled it out as a possible means of achieving his ends by going along it to the police station in the village of Little Mansfield. However, before coming to the area, he had familiarized himself with its geography. Although there were a couple of small farmhouses nearby, he considered he would find the residence of Colonel Sir Thorley Besgrove-Woodstole better suited for his needs. Having drawn this conclusion, after he had paused for a moment to get his bearings, he set off through the woods. Regardless of his belief that there would be no further attempts to capture him, he took the precaution of moving as silently as possible in case he should be wrong.

Striding out fast, the passenger covered almost two miles without receiving any suggestion of pursuit. Starting to cross a small clearing, he congratulated himself upon having made good his escape. However, as he was trying to work out how quickly the assistance he would summon would arrive, the beam of a flashlight stabbed between some bushes he was approaching. Taken unawares, he came to a halt. Then he heard movements and, in spite of being dazzled, he managed to make out two masculine shapes moving quickly forward. Although unable to decide how men he assumed had been given the means of illumination and sent to resume the search had got ahead of him, he was on the point of making a dash away from them. Before he could do so, the light was deflected just enough for him to detect a glint of shiny metal buttons and a kind of headgear which filled him with relief.

Coming closer, the man with the flashlight proved to be a tall and burly police sergeant. At his side, holding a double barrelled shotgun in a position of readiness, was an equally tall – albeit more slender – civilian whose attire was topped by a deerstalker hat. Remembering the reason given for refusing to permit the use of flashlights in the search, the passenger guessed the latter was the 'gamekeeper who's so hot on poachers'. However, at that moment, his status was of less interest than the presence of his companion.

'Thank heav—!' the passenger began, starting to walk towards the men.

Before any more could be said, striding forward faster than the sergeant, the civilian swung around the shotgun so its butt crashed against the side of the smaller man's jaw. Bright lights seemed to erupt briefly inside his head as he was pitched sideways by the blow. Then blackness replaced them and he did not feel the impact as his body measured its length on the ground.

'What the—?' the burly sergeant began, shoving back his helmet a little with a gesture indicative of annoyance and swinging to face his companion.

'He was *coming* for us!' the civilian interrupted in the voice of a Scottish Highlander of the dourest kind.

'I'd say it was more he was coming *to* us,' Sergeant Harold Widdercombe corrected, his accent indicating he had been born and raised in rural Hampshire. 'And I've told you afore that you're too handy with that shotgun's butt, or a stick across the head, for my liking, Mr Murdoch.'

'The Colonel's told me to stop anybody poaching,' the gamekeeper asserted.

'He looks more like a tramp than a poacher to me,' the sergeant claimed.

'Poacher or tramp, they're all one and the same to me,' Hamish Murdoch asserted. 'And, no matter which they might be, we don't pamper such vermin in the Highlands.'

'You'll be *killing* one happen you keeps on at it,' Widdercombe warned coldly, bending down and directing his flashlight so he could examine the man at his feet. 'You haven't *this* time and I sooner you didn't in *my* district, and I reckon's the Colonel'll feel the same.'

'Have it your own way,' Murdoch said in a sullen tone and jerked a thumb contemptuously towards his victim. 'What're you doing to do with *it*?'

'*We're* going to take *him* to my house,' the sergeant replied, his manner indicating he would brook no argument. 'I'll have the wife give him something that'll make him sleep for a few hours. Then, when he wakes up, I'll *persuade* him to leave the district without causing trouble over what you done to him.'

'That's good of you,' Murdoch declared, with as near to civility and gratitude as he was capable of coming.

'I'm doing it for the Colonel, not *you*,' Widdercombe asserted and told himself that he would ask the owner of the woodland to ensure the gamekeeper refrained from such behaviour in future. 'Come on, give me a hand with him.'

* * *   * * *

'My uncle died last night,' Michael Mansfield announced, coming into the dining-room. Although both were dressed in black clothing suitable for mourning, neither he nor Wanda Gore-Kauphin – who was by his left side – appeared unduly distressed by the demise of Sir Granville Delamont. 'So the party is over.'

The time was shortly after nine o'clock and, showing few signs of being disturbed earlier that morning by the fight in the first floor passage, the guests were assembled for breakfast.

Despite Baron Ludwig von Helsinore clearly being

willing to let the incident go no further after the statement made by Rapido, Flying Officer Allan Morningford had asked why the three men made the attack. Spending a few seconds which were all too obviously used to think up an excuse, Lancer declared it had been a case of mistaken identity. One of the maids claimed she had heard somebody prowling about downstairs while she was going to the lavatory. Knowing they would get no peace if they did not look into matters, he and the other two were on their way to investigate when they came across the Texan in the passage. Before either footman could stop him, Hans had taken the offensive action and, seeing he was not having much success in quelling the intruder – who they had not recognized in the poor light – they had decided to lend him a hand. Scowling bitterly and still nursing his injured foot, Scouse had supported the story.

Although the explanation had inconsistencies, Rapido had asserted he was satisfied and the matter should be forgotten. Stating agreement, von Helsinore ordered the footmen to help Hans upstairs and had suggested everybody else went back to their beds. Acting upon the Baron's advice, the group had separated.

When aroused by the breakfast gong, having dressed in a suitably casual fashion, the guests had gathered in the dining-room. Although Doctor Andrew McCallister had told the others about the death of their host, he had refrained from mentioning his suspicions. Realizing that to do so might lead to a delay in departing, and knowing that his friend wanted to get away before the deception with the disappearing ink was discovered, Jimmy Brocklehurst had been equally reticent. Being unaware of the doctor's discoveries, but remembering the hospitality they had received and the cheerful attitude of their host, the rest of the party were depressed by the news. Nor was this condition improved by the way Mansfield had delivered the information.

'We all had realized it would be,' Morningford asserted coldly. Having joined the rest of the group after doing his regular morning routine of exercises on the lawn in front of the Manor, he had on a loose fitting grey woollen pullover, rumpled grey flannels tucked into thick socks and the lightweight boots he used when engaged in cross-country running. 'In fact, Joan and I were coming to express our condolences to you and then go back to Town after breakfast.'

'Roz and I had the same idea,' Brocklehurst claimed, also annoyed by the apparently unfeeling way in which Mansfield had spoken.

'And me,' Doctor Andrew McCallister declared from where he had been consoling Billie Oakroyd, who was showing more evidence of sorrow over the loss of her uncle than was displayed by his heir to the estate.

'You are *wrong*!' Baron Ludwig von Helsinore claimed, striding through the main entrance followed by the housekeeper and Hans. He was wearing a shooting jacket, riding breeches and black knee boots so well polished they almost reflected their surroundings. '*Nobody* is going to leave!'

While the second sentence was being uttered, Mrs. Blount closed the double doors and stood in front of them with her arms folded. Although the German directed a scowl from Morningford to Rapido, he came to a stop behind his employer and stood as rigidly as if on guard duty.

'What do you mean, *nobody* is going to leave?' Wanda demanded, when Mansfield did not speak.

'Just what I said,' the Baron replied. '*None* of you are leaving until a certain matter is settled.'

'We'll soon see about *that*!' Wanda claimed and, thrusting the vanity bag which she was carrying into Mansfield's hand, she turned to walk towards the main door. Finding herself confronted by the housekeeper, who showed no sign of moving, she snapped haughtily, 'Get out of my way!'

'Go back with the others,' Mrs Blount commanded, laying a big hand on the actress's almost flat bosom.

Anybody who knew Wanda would have warned that,

regardless of her protestations of Socialistic ideals and high regard for the working class, such an action on the part of a person she considered an underling was ill advised. Always quick tempered and never more so than after she had indulged in her addiction to narcotics, as was the case that morning, she was prone to a violent reaction under such circumstances. Not even the incident which caused the financially embarrassing estrangement with her father had taught her to control her vicious tendencies.[1]

Giving vent to a profanity, the actress stepped back and swung her right hand around viciously. The palm struck the housekeeper on the cheek with a resounding 'thwack!' and snapped her head around. However, in this case, Wanda was not permitted to get away without physical retaliation. Bringing her gaze to the front, Mrs Blount's face took on an expression which had struck fear amongst the inmates of Holloway Prison before she was dismissed for ill-treating prisoners who refused to pay to keep in her good books. Showing no sign of having felt the slap, even though it left a red mark where it landed, she struck back immediately, albeit in a more effective fashion. Brought across with the speed and precision which many a male boxer would not have been ashamed to employ, her left fist caught her assailant on the side of the jaw. Arriving with the weight of the bulky and obviously very strong body behind it, the punch

1. *The estrangement was caused by Michael Gore-Kauphin's anger at having to pay a considerable sum of money to prevent his daughter being arrested for striking a housemaid during a visit to the home of a wealthy Socialist Member of Parliament. Being related to a well placed official in the trade union movement, the servant knew her 'rights' and threatened to take out a summons for assault. Aware of the relationship and having no desire to antagonize the uncle, whose support was vital to his continuance in office, Wanda's host had not offered to intercede on her behalf. Instead, he had taken the housemaid's side and insisted on the payment of reparation.*

flung the actress across the room to crash on to the floor by the table.

'Stand still, *all* of you!' von Helsinore barked.

The words brought almost every eye to the Baron and what they saw acted at once as an inducement to obey. While the others were watching Wanda and Mrs Blount, he had produced a Luger automatic pistol from where it had been concealed beneath his jacket. It was noticeable that, although he moved its barrel in an arc which encompassed the male guests, he did not point it towards Mansfield. Nor, except for letting out a squawk of alarm, did the inheritor of the Manor offer to protest at the treatment received by or go forward to help his fiancée.

'What's the game, damn it?' Morningford demanded, but he halted his involuntary movement forward as the muzzle of the pistol was pointing unerringly at the centre of his chest.

'Something of *great* importance is missing,' the Baron replied.

'Are you saying one of *us* has stolen it?' the Flying Officer asked indignantly, but he continued to stand still.

'One of you has it,' von Helsinore stated and, as if wishing to demonstrate his expertise at handling the Luger, he began to toss it from hand to hand while continuing to speak. 'And I am *determined* to have it back. Until I do, *none* of you will be allowed to leave. What is more, I warn you not to *try*. Even if you should get to the garage, which the servants are ordered to prevent any way they have to, you will find that we have let the air from your cars' tyres.'

'Damn it!' Morningford snapped, tensing and then relaxing as the pistol was directed at him once more. 'What gives *you* the right to take such high-handed action?'

'*This* does, among other things,' the Baron answered, gesturing with the Luger before beginning to toss it back and forward again. 'Doctor, attend to *her* – and you, nurse.'

'*Sister!*' Rosalind Brampton corrected instinctively,

the last three words clearly having been an afterthought, going with McCallister to do as was ordered.

'Do you know what you're doing is against the law in England?' Brocklehurst asked.

'I do,' von Helsinore answered. 'But the thing that was taken is of such *great* importance, I don't care about the laws of England. I will do *whatever* must be done to get it back.'

'What might this "thing" be?' McCallister inquired, from where he and Roz were examining the groaning and stirring actress.

'The one who has it knows,' the Baron replied. 'So I would urge the rest of you to persuade that person to return it. I will leave you for fifteen minutes to do so. If it is not returned at the end of that time, *other* measures to retrieve it will be taken.' Walking towards the door, through which Mrs Blount and Hans had preceded him, he paused before leaving. 'My man will be waiting in the hall if you succeed – And don't bother trying to contact the police. The wires for the telephones have been cut.'

'I can't speak for anybody else,' Brocklehurst remarked, after the trio had left and the doors were closed. 'But neither Roz nor I have got whatever it is he wants.'

'Neither have I,' Joan Darling stated, looking indignant. 'In fact, I'm *sure* none of *us* have. How about *you*, Mansfield?'

'I don't even know what he was talking about,' the recipient of the question asserted with more fear than indignation. 'It *must* have been one of the servants who took it.'

'The working class can kiss my arse, I've got my inheritance at last,' Morningford intoned mockingly, fitting the words to the tune of *The Internationale*. 'And before anybody asks, I haven't got the bloody thing either.'

'Or me,' Beryl Snowhill stated.

'I don't have it, comes to that,' Rapido drawled. 'Which, none of us having it, I conclude that *hombre's*

132

going to be more'n just a mite riled when we tell him.'

'He is,' Morningford agreed, having crossed to the French windows and looked out. 'So I'm not going to wait for *that*!'

'What are you going to do, Allan?' Joan inquired worriedly.

'Go and fetch the police,' the Flying Officer replied.

'How?' the actress queried. 'He said they'd let the air out of all of our tyres.'

'I know,' Morningford admitted. 'But it's only five miles to Lower Mansfield and I'm *certain* I can outrun anybody in this house.'

'They won't have touched their own cars and can use one to come after you,' Brocklehurst warned.

'I'll go across country,' the Flying Officer replied. 'They won't be able to catch me that way.'

'Where have you been, ma'am?' Rapido inquired, looking across the room and causing everybody else to follow the direction of his gaze.

'I thought he might have somebody listening outside,' Billie Oakroyd replied, coming through the door at the rear of the room. 'But it's all right, he hasn't.'

CHAPTER TWELVE

This Isn't The Wild West

'Do you want any of us to come with you, Allan?' Jimmy Brocklehurst inquired, feeling relieved by Billie Oakroyd's assurance that nobody was eavesdropping.

'No thanks, old boy. All you chaps had better stay here and take care of the girls,' Flying Officer Allan Morningford answered, then noticing the way in which another of the party was looking at him, he asked, 'Is something wrong, Rapido?'

'Are you *sure* you're doing the right thing, *amigo*?' the small Texan asked. 'That Baron jasper looked like he meant what he was saying about nobody trying to sneak off while he was showing us how handy he is with a gun.'

'He might be handy with it, but he won't dare use it,' Morningford claimed. 'People don't shoot at other people in England, old boy. This isn't the Wild West, or even the Continent.'

'*He* might not know *that*,' Rapido warned sombrely. 'And 'most every one of the fellers I've seen working around the place look like they've been, or should be, making hair bridles in some penitentiary for doing bad meanness to folks, or whatever you do with convicts over here.'

'I can't argue with you about the staff, old boy, I wouldn't want to come up against any of them in a dark alley,' the Flying Officer admitted. 'But British criminals don't go in for using guns and, under these conditions, I'm sure I can show them a clean pair of heels given the start I expect to have.'

'How're you figuring on getting out to start running?'

the Texan inquired, deciding against taking up any more time in attempting to bring about a change of mind.

'Through here,' Morningford replied, gesturing to the French windows. Then, opening the bolts at the top and bottom, he gave a jerk which caused the two segments to part without much noise even though the lock was fastened. 'I thought I could do it. See you shortly, with all the help you'll need.'

Giving a cheerful wave, the Flying Officer stepped quietly across the marble surface of the porch and vaulted its balustrade to alight in the garden. Without looking behind him, he started to run towards the front gates. However, shortly after he had covered half the distance, four men came from the lodge beside it. Although he had hoped to reach the road, which would offer an easier surface for running, he realized this would not be possible unless he could fight his way past them and he doubted his ability to do so. Accepting the inevitable, he swerved aside and went across the lawn with long, raking strides which suggested he had not over-estimated his chances of outdistancing any pursuers on foot.

'How will he get out of the grounds?' Joan Darling gasped, watching from just outside the dining-room, as were all the other guests.

'Over the fence,' Doctor Andrew McCallister guessed, he and Rosalind Brampton having left Wanda Gore-Kauphin sitting up looking very sorry for herself and nursing her swollen and bruised jaw with both hands. 'I saw him go over one that was higher to win the All England Cross Country Championship last year and he's got an even breater inducement for doing it tod—!'

The words were halted by the crack of a shot from somewhere above the guests!

To the accompaniment of horror filled gasps from the spectators, Morningford staggered and sprawled face down on the springy turf!

'They've *killed* him!' Joan shrieked and started to go across the porch.

'He's still alive!' Rapido contradicted, catching the actress by the shoulder and pulling her back. 'Stay put. You watch out for them, Jimmy. Doc and I'll go!'

The less than gentle way in which she was handled served to bring Joan to her senses. Glancing over her shoulder as Brocklehurst took hold of her arm in a prohibitive fashion, she said she was all right and would behave. Then she turned her gaze back to the garden. Relief flooded through her as she saw the Flying Officer was forcing himself on to his hands and knees. Although his attempt to stand up failed and he toppled to the ground once more, she knew Rapido was correct. However, led by the butler, the men from the lodge ran up. Hauling him erect, two of them supported him in that position while Guerney started to search him. For a moment, she was incensed by the way in which Rapido and McCallister were behaving. On reaching the lawn, instead of running, they began walking backwards with their hands raised above their heads. Just as she was about to scream at them to hurry, she realized why this was being done.

'Don't shoot, *hombre*!' the Texan called, looking upwards and confirming the beautiful red head's summations. 'We're only going to help Mr Morningford.'

There was no response from above, nor could the two young men see whoever had shot the Flying Officer. However, as he did not open fire at either of them, they turned and, lowering their arms, they walked without haste along the drive. This was done on Rapido's advice. He had warned McCallister that to do otherwise might cause the gunman they had failed to locate to start shooting again, with them as the targets. Because of the slow pace he set, before they arrived, Guerney had completed a thorough search and Morningford was allowed to sink into a sitting position on the ground. The butler and his companions drew back a short distance, but formed a half circle indicating they were ready to stop either guest trying to dart past and escape.

'The blasted Hun shot me!' the Flying Officer gasped

in a disbelieving manner, clasping both hands around his left thigh about three inches above his knee in an attempt to staunch the blood which flowed over his fingers.

'No he didn't,' Rapido denied, as McCallister knelt down and gently drew away Morningford's hands. While the doctor was taking out and opening a pocket-knife to slit along the seam of the flannel trousers' left leg and expose the wound to their view, he continued, 'I've seen some pretty fair hands with a short gun back to home in the "Wild West", but there wasn't *any* of them could have hit you on the run from where you was throwed down on. That sort of shooting took a feller with a rifle and a 'scope sight, 'less I miss my guess. Top of which he's way better than average, just *nicking* you like he did instead doing anything *worse*.'

'I must remember to *thank* him for being so *lenient* when we meet,' Morningford said grimly, despite realizing the Texan was talking to help take his mind off the wound and the pain being inflicted by McCallister's examination despite the care he was taking.

'Did you find *it*?' Rapido inquired, turning his gaze towards the butler.

'No,' Guerney replied, before he could stop himself. He was about to tell his men to search the Texan and the doctor, but remembered how well the former could fight. Guessing any attempt to carry out his order would be strenuously resisted, taking a lot of time, he kept in mind that there could be people passing along the road who would investigate the cause of any disturbance. Deciding to leave the location of the missing object until a more suitable moment, he scowled and went on in a sneering tone, 'But I hope the rest of you have learned your lesson from what's happened.'

'You've made your point, 'far as I'm concerned,' Rapido asserted, sounding almost mild and gentle. 'You won't catch me doing anything like it.' Then he looked down and inquired, 'How bad is it, Doc?'

'It could have been a *lot* worse,' McCallister reported,

showing relief. 'The bullet went through the fleshy part and didn't hit anything that matters.'

'Will I be able to ballet dance when its better?' Morningford inquired through gritted teeth.

'Of course,' the doctor confirmed, taking out a large white handkerchief to serve as an extemporized bandage.

'That's *good*,' the Flying Officer said. 'Because I *couldn't* before I was shot.'

'With the jokes you tell, I'm surprised you haven't been shot before now,' McCallister asserted in his most dour Scottish fashion, wrapping up the wound with deft hands although he had not been required to carry out such a task since becoming a pathologist. Then he looked at Guerney and asked, 'How about two of your men helping to carry Mr Morningford to the house?'

'He can crawl there for all I care,' the butler replied, still retaining a dislike for officers which he had always sought to conceal while in the Royal Navy. What was more, having lost a night's sleep, his temper was not improved by the man from the car still being unconscious. 'It's his own bloody fault he got shot.'

'Times like this a man finds out who his *friends* are, *amigo*,' Rapido drawled and turned his attention to McCallister. 'Looks like it's up to *us*, Doc.'

'That it does,' the doctor agreed, then directed a baleful glare at the butler. 'And I can't wait to be able to do *something* for you.'

Swinging away from Guerney, who clearly had not learned of his speciality, McCallister helped Rapido to raise Morningford from the ground. While doing so, he confirmed his supposition that the small Texan was exceptionally strong. Supporting the Flying Officer with his arms across their shoulders, their task was made easier by him being in such superb physical condition. Despite the shock and pain caused by the wound, he was able to keep the injured leg bent clear of the ground and hop with his other foot. In that way, they made a steady progress to the front of the house. Assuring Joan that he

138

was only suffering a 'scratch', which she clearly did not believe even though she made no comment, Morningford was taken into the dining-room. On entering, the three young men discovered that Roz had made preparations in case they should be needed by tearing a white table cloth she had found into strips suitable for serving as bandages. Sitting the wounded man in the chair she had placed ready for him, McCallister turned to where Hans was standing inside the main entrance.

'Do you speak English?' the doctor replied.

'Little bit,' the German replied.

'Then go and *tell* Doctor Dubarry to bring everything we'll need to attend to a bullet wound,' McCallister demanded rather than merely requested.

Before the order could be acted upon, or refused, Baron Ludwig von Helsinore stalked through the main entrance with the Luger dangling by his right side. Barking a command which caused Hans to close the doors, he strode towards Rapido, McCallister and Morningford and halted a short distance in front of them.

'So!' the Dane said, snapping the word out as 'Zo!'. 'You had to try and be a hero. I warned you that anybody who made an attempt to escape would be *stopped* by whatever means were required.'

'You've gone *too* far, damn it!' Jimmy Brocklehurst stated, ranging himself alongside the other three male guests. 'I don't care what influence you might have with your Embassy, you'll not get away with what you've done!'

'If I was you,' von Helsinore countered in a voice charged with menace, starting to toss the Luger from hand to hand once more. 'I'd be more concerned with what is going to happen to *all of you* if I don't get what I'm after.'

'You're pretty fair at doing that,' Rapido drawled, speaking even more slowly than usual and stepping forward in what seemed to be a leisurely fashion. His words brought the Baron's attention to him, but not quickly enough to have his next actions prevented. Speeding up his movements, he shot out his right hand to catch the Luger in mid-flight and went on, 'Now let's see happen you can do *this*!'

Shock came to the faces of von Helsinore and Hans as they realized the former had been disarmed and one of their captives was now in possession of a fully loaded and cocked weapon. However, before either could decide upon a line of action, what happened next came as such a surprise it caused them to stand immobile and do nothing more positive than stare.

While saying the second sentence, the small Texan pushed back the safety catch with his thumb and prevented the weapon from being discharged. Having done this, without even the owner of the weapon noticing his action, he slid his forefinger through the triggerguard. After a couple of experimental movements to get the feel of its balance, he started to twirl the Luger around at a high speed. Still spinning like a catherine wheel, it was thown from his right hand to the left and the twirling continued without interruption. Next it was tossed upwards behind his back and his right hand caught it as it passed over his shoulder. Taking it down, still whirling, he raised his right leg to flip it beneath his knee into the other hand.

There was an almost deathly silence in the dining-room. Everybody present, even Michael Mansfield and Wanda Gore-Kauphin, realized they were witnessing a display of fancy gun handling none would ever see equalled, much less bettered. That it was being performed with an unfamiliar weapon made the feat even more noteworthy. However, what happened at the conclusion came as much of a surprise to everyone as had been its appropriation. Bringing the Luger to a halt, Rapido pressed the stud on the right side of the frame and shook free the magazine. Then he pulled at the knurled cocking knobs on top of the frame to operate the action and eject the bullet from the chamber.

'My daddy always told me *never* to hand a loaded gun

to *anybody*,' the Texan remarked, as if merely passing the time of day. Then, to everyone present's amazement, he offered the magazine and the unloaded pistol, the latter butt first, to their owner. 'Which I reckon's real good advice to follow.'

Such was the amazement at Rapido's latest unexpected behaviour that, for a good thirty seconds, nobody moved or spoke. Then von Helsinore let out a long breath and started to slide the magazine into the butt of the Luger. As if his employer's activity broke the spell for Hans, he snarled a profanity in German and lunged forward. On this occasion, he did not meet with even the partial success which had crowned his first attack on the Texan earlier in the morning. Springing to meet him, Rapido took advantage of the surprise he was given to lash up a kick. It was not, McCallister realized, the painful yet comparatively harmless kind employed against the first would-be assailant at the Admiral Cornwallis Inn. Rising between the German's thighs, the sharp toe of the right boot made its contact upon the most vulnerable point of the masculine anatomy. It arrived with great force and the adverse effect upon the soft flesh it encountered was increased by the silver toe cap.

Just how efficiacious the small Texan's attack proved showed in the reaction it elicited. Shock and agony came to Hans' previously savage face. His eyes rolled back until only showing the whites, his arms flopped limply to his sides and the rest of his body went rigid for a moment. Then his legs buckled and he dropped on to his knees. He would have flopped either face downwards or over backwards to the floor, but was not given the opportunity. Rapido's right hand shot out to catch him by the throat. However, as the doctor observed, the Texan did not grip it to the fullest extent of his span. Instead, he sank his fingers and thumb in so they were around the windpipe. The result of the hold he obtained quickly made itself apparent as gurgles indicative of breath being cut off burst from the German.

For a few seconds, von Helsinore stood as if turned to stone, staring as if unable to believe the evidence of his eyes. Then, so amazed by what he was seeing that he did not think of shouting to summon assistance, he jerked back the cocking mechanism of the Luger. Having done so, he bellowed 'Let go!'

'Say "please",' Rapido answered, keeping his thumb and fingers buried into the burly man's throat with such strength they pierced the skin and began to draw blood.

'Let go, damn you!' the Dane roared above the sounds of strangulation, as he waved the reloaded pistol in a threatening fashion.

'Say "*please*",' the Texan repeated and the two onlookers with medical training realized his captive was in very real danger of being choked to death.

'*Gott in himmel!*' von Helsinore thundered. The Luger was shaking with barely controlled fury as he raised it to eye level and took aim. 'Let go, or I'll shoot you!'

'Had such been your intent', you'd've done it 'stead of talking,' Rapido asserted calmly and without relaxing the grip. 'Only I conclude you'll all fired up to know how come a lil ole Texas boy like me can handle his-self so good. Happen I'm wrong, cut loose and *make* me leave go. Should I be right, say "*please*".'

'*Please!*' the Baron snarled.

'Folks're always more obliging when they're asked *nice*,' Rapido stated and released his hold. Then, as Hans collapsed face forward, his voice hardened and a change seemed to come over him. Such was the strength of his personality, he appeared to have grown in height and bulk until he towered over everybody else in the room. Thinking about the metamorphosis, McCallister realized it must have happened at the Admiral Cornwallis Inn and was the cause of the consternation shown by his three victims. '*Hombre*, you tell every one of those mule-headed yacks of yours I won't be lied to, mean-mouthed, nor 'specially laid hands on. I don't do none of those things to others, 'less I'm pushed first, and I won't stand for them being done to me.'

'I will tell them,' von Helsinore promised coldly. 'But first I want to talk with you in private!'

'Something told me you just *might*,' Rapido drawled sardonically, bending to wipe the blood from his fingers on his victim's shirt. 'Where at shall we do it?'

'In the lounge there, if that suits you,' the Baron suggested, pointing to a small alcove at the end of the dining-room.

'It'll do,' the Texan confirmed. 'And we'll go as soon as you've had that tame French sawbones of yours bring everything Doc McCallister needs to fix up Mr Morningford's leg.'

CHAPTER THIRTEEN

They Call Me 'Rapido Clint'

'Let me out of here!'

On the point of putting through a telephone call to Colonel Sir Thorley Besgrove-Woodstole – accepted as the well liked and respected squire by most people around Little Mansfield – Sergeant Harold Widdercombe heard the shouted words, accompanied by a surprisingly vigorous banging on the door, from the block of cells at the rear of the house he occupied and known locally, albeit a touch grandiloquently, as the 'police station'. He realized the man he had brought in some hours earlier had returned to consciousness and seemed more robust than he would have believed possible. A frown came to his rugged and yet amiable features as the demand and banging were repeated. Such a response suggested the prisoner was in a state of righteous indignation and, remembering what had happened in the woods, might not be amenable to the way he intended to deal with the matter.

Having brought the man to the police station and dismissed Murdoch, Widdercombe had called upon the services of his wife. Although she had retired from being a nursing matron shortly after they married, she had a reputation as a healer which caused many of the local population to visit her and not the local doctor when sick or injured. After satisfying herself that the prisoner's jaw had not been broken by the blow from the gamekeeper's shotgun, and sharing her husband's high regard for the peppery yet good-hearted Colonel, she had done as requested without hesitation. Giving the man a sleeping potion of her own concoction in a glass of milk as he was

144

regaining consciousness, she had ensured he would sleep heavily for several hours.

As soon as the prisoner lapsed into somnolence, Widdercombe had carried him into the cell and, having removed his battered footwear, had placed him on the bed. In preparation for what was to come when he recovered from the draught, his threadbare jacket was doused with some of the raw and potent locally brewed cider. On recovering, he was to be given the choice of leaving the district without complaining about his treatment by Murdoch, or face the magistrate's court on a charge of being drunk and disorderly. If he accepted the former alternative, which the sergeant had considered likely, he would be reimbursed with a couple of pounds and sent on his way. The money would be repaid by the Colonel on hearing what had happened, although not the whole story as – being a magistrate and an honest man – he would not have approved of the means taken to ensure compliance with the instructions.

'Now then, now *then*!' the sergeant boomed in his most authoritative manner, striding into the cells and opening the barred grill in the door. 'You're mak—!'

'Let me out!' the ragged man demanded, swaying and clearly needing to employ all his will power to keep on his feet. 'I have to use your telephone.'

'Would that be to call your solicitor?' Widdercombe inquired dryly, despite realizing the prisoner's voice had a more cultured timbre than might have been expected from his unkempt appearance.

'Let me *out*, damn it!' the man repeated with a violence which the police officer felt boded ill for achieving the required peaceable settlement.

'You sound as if you're still full of scrumpy,' Widdercombe declared. 'Like you was when I—!'

'I was *sober* when we met and you know it!' the man asserted, aware that 'scrumpy' was the name given to the raw cider much favoured by many in the area. He was struggling to hold down the nausea caused by the smell of it permeating the cell. 'And, if you value your rank and your pension, you had better do as I ask straight away.'

'Oh had I now?' the sergeant inquired, then became aware that his wife was standing behind him.

'*Harold!*' Mrs Widdercombe said urgently. Almost matching her husband in height and bulk, she had a face capable of being friendly or *very* stern as circumstances required. 'I'd listen to him if I was you. I didn't think there was anything to it at the time, but I remember noticing his hands and feet didn't look like he was a tramp.'

'Why should I let you out?' the sergeant inquired and, as he had a great respect for his wife's judgement, he spoke in a less officious tone.

'So I can make an urgent telephone call to Mr J.G. Reeder,' the man replied. 'You can put it through yourself. The number is listed in your S.B. 120.'

'What do *you* know about *that*?' Widdercombe demanded in a puzzled voice. The existence of the Home Office's Secret Book 120 – which contained much confidential information of use to police officers, including telephone numbers for various important officials – was what a later generation would term 'restricted information' and not available to the general public.

'It's a book about this size, bound in red Morocco leather and fitted with a lock,' the man replied, gesturing with his grubby hands. 'You'll keep it in your safe, I should imagine. My name is Parker and I work for Captain John Gray. Now let me out so that I can contact Mr Reeder— And I hope I am not going to be too *late*.'

* * *   * * *

'Firstly,' Baron Ludwig von Helsinore said holding his voice down so what he said could only be heard by the man he was addressing. 'Who—? You are *armed*!'

Having complied with the small Texan's requirements, the Dane had accompanied him to the alcove at the far end of the big dining-room and gestured for him to enter first. Showing what all except one of the other guests who were watching considered to be an untypical lack of caution, Rapido had done so. However, when he turned around, von Helsinore discovered that his intention of regaining control of the situation would not be as easy to implement as he had imagined. He had not attached any significance to the Texan reaching into the right side pocket of the unusual looking trousers. Now he realized he had made an error in his judgement, so his question was ended before completion and the substitution was made.

'I wouldn't feel dressed happen I wasn't packing iron, even if it's only this lil ole stingy gun,' Rapido drawled, making a gesture with superposed twin 'barrels of the small black Remington Double Derringer he had taken from the pocket of his Levi pants. 'But don't let her size fool you. She's not as big as that old Luger of yours and won't throw a slug near as far, but she's .41 against nine millimetre and sure hell on wheels this close.'

'You have been armed *all* the time!' von Helsinore said pensively.

'Why sure,' the Texan agreed. 'Which being, don't start getting any notions that it was *me* who gunned down the gent in the wheelchair last night—!'

'You know about *that*?' the Baron growled, so startled that he did not continue to ask his interrupted question.

'I smelled fresh' burned powder while the lights were out, but hadn't heard any shots,' Rapido explained. 'So I looked 'round for where the lead'd gone. That Brown *hombre* moved real fast, but I saw there were *three* holes in the back of the chair afore he pulled the feller up straight again and hid them. Stingy here only takes two shells at a time and there's *no* way of fixing a silencer on her. Which being, the noise she makes when she cuts loose, I'd've *had* to use one. Top of which, those holes wouldn't be more than .38 at most. Fact being, I'd say they came from a .32 of some kind.'

'You are a most perceptive young man,' von Helsinore said speculatively 'May I ask who you think killed him?'

'There's some would say that Mansfield *hombre's* got the best reason.'

147

'He wouldn't have the *nerve*, even if he knew how to use a gun, which I doubt.'

'That's how I read the sign myself,' Rapido admitted, but he did not take the matter any further. 'You still haven't found whatever it is you're hunting, huh?'

'I have *not*!' the Baron answered and accepted the change of subject so easily it seemed he regarded the loss as more important than the murder.

'Well I don't have it,' the Texan declare. 'Only, happen it should come to mind, I won't stand for being searched. *Nobody* puts their hands through Rapido Clint.'

'*Rapido Clint,*' von Helsinore repeated with a frown. 'I thought your name was Edward Marsden?'

'That's nothing but a summer name, what you'd call an alias. Back home to Texas, they call me "Rapido Clint".'

'You took a *very* grave risk out there, Mr *Clint*,' the Baron claimed, concluding that any attempt to learn why an alias was required by the Texan – who he no longer regarded as small and insignificant – would be resented and deciding that he had no desire to lose face by being rebuffed again, even though there would be no witnesses on this occasion. 'I might have shot you.'

'Like I said, I reckoned you was too interested in finding out about me to do it,' Rapido replied. 'Which, seeing's how you didn't cut me down, I called the play right. So get to asking.'

'Why are you in England?'

'I was over on vacation, but got kind of close to the blanket where money's concerned. So I hired out to ride shotgun on Miss Snowhill while she's over in the US of A looking to buy some racehorses for her folks.'

'Ride *shotgun*?'

'Likely you'd call it being her bodyguard. Which's how come I took the chance when your man *tried* to jump me. Hell, how'd it look when we get back to her place did she have to tell her folks I'd let myself be hoorawed and buffaloed without doing *anything* back?'

'I see your point,' von Helsinore admitted. 'And I can also see you are a man to be reckoned with. Would you care to "ride shotgun" for *me*?'

'I'll think on it when I've finished the chore for Miss Snowhill,' Rapido replied.

'I mean for you to start straight away.'

'I can't do that. Ole Jubal Branch, who taught me *everything* I know about this game, always said I should stick to one rule. "Once you're hired, stay hired until the job's through," Jubal told me. "'Cause, happen you quit on a boss, he'll spread the word and other's'll think more than twice afore they offer to take you on. Top of which, the jasper you've let hire you away'll always figure you've quit one boss and'll likely do it again, so he'll not trust you." That's what Jubal told me and I conclude he was right. What I will do, though, is try to help you get back whatever it is as's gone missing.'

'That is generous of you,' von Helsinore said, but there was little gratitude in his harsh voice. He nodded towards the people in the dining-room, none of whom were taking any obvious interest in what was taking place in the alcove. 'Which one of them do you think has it?'

'None of them,' Rapido replied with complete assurance. 'I don't know what you've lost, nor *want* to, but it *must* be real valuable to you. Which I don't see any of the gents I've been getting on so well with having taken it. They're not thieves and I don't reckon any of them's so short of cash they'd turn bad. How about your men. 'Least, the bunch who work here. Every one of them wears the owlhoot brand, which means they wouldn't stick too close to the straight and narrow path where anything *real* valuable's concerned, or I can't read the signs.'

'It wasn't one of *them*,' the Baron stated, but his voice did not express complete conviction. Then he shook his head and went on, 'No, it *has* to be one of those three.'

'Any special reason why?'

'I questioned Mansfield about them before I told him

of his uncle's death. According to him, although they aren't his friends, every one of them went out of his way to get invited here.'

'Could be they'd heard about these house-parties and wanted to come and try for the prize in that game we played. Or maybe, not knowing the rules here, they wanted to take their lady friends some place for something *more* than just holding hands and cuddling. I've heard tell such doings come off at house-parties.'

'There is *that*, I suppose.'

'Do you reckon any of them would be smart enough to take it?' Rapido asked. 'Or have any reason?'

'Regardless of how they look and act, they all have the intelligence to have done it,' von Helsinore declared. 'A man does not win the Sword Of Honour as top cadet of his year at Cranwell, as Morningford did, if he is stupid, and an aspiring young officer will take many chances if he thinks there may be promotion in it. Brocklehurst is private secretary to an important official at the Home Office and said to be most competent at *all* his duties, some of which are of a most confidential nature. And I found out just before I came down that, far from being newly qualified, McCallister has been a pathologist at the Home Office for three years. Every one of them could have been sent for it.'

'Would any of them bring his lady friend here, happen he was planning to steal something he'd know you prized so high?' Rapido queried, drawing a conclusion from the last sentence in particular.

'Whoever it is might have assumed we would think that way,' von Helsinore replied. 'Or believed we would not *dare* take any really *strenuous* measures to recover it should we find it had been giv— it had gone before they left.'

Before any more could be said, a tal , slim man who Rapido had not seen before came hurrying through the dining-room. Instead of wearing the livery of a footman to indicate he was a member of the household staff, he wore the trousers and waistcoat of a brown pin-striped suit which had come 'off the peg' at a reasonably priced store and there was nothing of the toughness shown by the male domestic employees in his appearance. Although there was a suggestion of military training about his bearing, he looked like a technician of some sort, rather than a combat soldier. Entering the alcove, his attempt to address the Baron was forestalled.

'There's a mess—!' the man began, his accent indicative of birth in Birmingham.

'*Sprechen sie Deutsch*, Mr Mars—*Clint*?' von Helsinore inquired, without looking at the newcomer, his voice having a casualness which suggested the question was not particularly important.

'Whatever you said,' Rapido drawled looking puzzled, 'you'll have to run it by me again so's I can understand it happen you want an answer.'

'It was nothing *important*,' the Baron declared, then turned his gaze to the newcomer. '*Was ist verkehrt?*'

On starting to answer the demand to be told what was wrong, the man proved to be one of those who believed he would make himself understood far better in a foreign language if he spoke loudly. Scowling as he listened, von Helsinore watched Rapido for a moment and was met by a look implying a total lack of comprehension. Then he turned his gaze to the occupants of the dining-room and found that all of them appeared to be engrossed in their own affairs. Satisfied by the discoveries, he allowed the man to continue talking in the same fashion.

'I must bring our talk to an end, Mr M—Clint,' the Baron stated at the conclusion of the information. 'There is an important matter demanding my immediate attention. Think of my offer. Perhaps *something* may happen to change your mind.'

Swinging around without giving Rapido a chance to reply, von Helsinore accompanied the man from the alcove. They crossed the dining-room and left without paying any attention to its occupants. While the conversation had been taking place, Dubarry had called in two of the footmen and they had carried away the still

151

unconscious Hans. It seemed the Baron was confident that he had blocked every avenue of escape and no guard was necessary. When he closed the door, there were only the people who had been at the party left behind. However, as Rapido strolled forward, he noticed that McCallister was no longer present. Their number was further decreased before the Texan could rejoin them by Billie Oakroyd saying she had to go to the lavatory and then leaving the room.

'I hope you had an interesting talk, Rapido,' Brocklehurst said and there was just a tinge of mistrust in his attitude.

'I played the fool with his gun and his man to get him talking,' the Texan answered. 'Which he fell for, I'd say. Do any of you speak German?'

'I know a *little*,' the civil servant understated, being fluent in that language.

'And me,' Morningford seconded.

'Does "*schiessen mannschafft*" mean what I reckon it does?' Rapido inquired.

'It means "shooting team", if that's what you thought,' Brocklehurst confirmed. 'Did you understand the rest of what was being said?'

'Not *all* of it,' the Texan confessed. 'The German they were speaking's some different to the kind I learned back to home, like the Spanish over here's different from Border-Mex. But there's one thing I have got figured out.'

'What's that?' Morningford asked.

'Seeing's they've fixed the cars so there's no way we can get the hell out of here fast enough to be any good,' Rapido drawled quietly – but something in his voice sent a cold shiver through almost every member of his audience – 'We're going to have to make a stand, root, hog, or die, right where we are.'

Even as Joan opened her mouth to ask a question, the double doors were thrown open and McCallister returned. One glance told the other guests something was very wrong. His now flushed face had an expression of anger, his clothing was dishevelled and his collar had come away from the rest of his shirt.

'They've got *Billie*!' the doctor gasped and, as further indication of his agitated state of mind, his accent was again noticeably Scottish. 'The biggest of the footmen was forcing her to go upstairs as I came into the hall. I went after them, but he shoved her into a room and grabbed me by the throat. I was like a baby in his hands and, before I could do anything, he threw me down the stairs then went in after her. Who's going to help me rescue her?'

CHAPTER FOURTEEN

Shoot To Kill

'I'll come, Doc,' Rapido Clint offered. 'Just so long as you and everybody else *know* what it means once we start things going.'

'What does it mean, old boy?' Flying Officer Allan Morningford inquired and Joan Darling moved nearer to him although her eyes never left the grimly cold expression which had removed all the amiability from the *big* Texan's face.

'We're not locking horns with your usual bunch of English owlhoo – criminals here,' Rapido assessed, and his gentle drawl held a note of ice cold warning. 'Sure, the hired help around the house likely are. But the men at the top, von Helsinore and that butler jasper in particular, won't draw the line at *anything* – up to and including torture or *murder* – to get their way. Which, once we stir them up, it'll be the last unless they're stopped – and I mean *stopped*!'

'You paint a *grim* picture, old boy,' Morningford said quietly, placing his right hand upon that of the beautiful red head.

'And a *very* real one, I'd say,' Jimmy Brocklehurst declared.

'We still have to try and rescue Billie,' Doctor Andrew McCallister claimed. 'They can use her as a hostage to make us do as they want as long she's in their power.'

'That's why she's with them,' Rapido pointed out. 'And I'm willing to go help you pry her loose, just so long as you *know* what's going to be turned loose back. 'Cause what we could have to do to get her back won't

154

be sporting, nor even pretty to watch. Fact being, somebody's right likely to get hurt real *bad*.'

'Very well,' the doctor said, despite feeling a chill of apprehension at the prospect conjured up by the Texan. 'We'll do what we have to.'

'Will you go with Beryl so's she can fetch *the bag* from my room, Jimmy?' Rapido inquired, glancing at Beryl Snowhill as he put a slight emphasis upon the item he wanted collecting.

'Well yes,' Jimmy Brocklehurst began hesitantly, glancing at Rosalind Brampton. 'But—!'

'Beryl's got a stingy gun, happen you want to borrow it,' the Texan drawled, and the beautiful little blonde produced from the pocket of her jodphurs the Remington Double Derringer she had concealed in her pyjama jacket earlier that morning.

'I've got something a bit more substantial of my own, thank you,' the civil servant answered, and reached under the pullover he wore to draw out a Webley & Scott .455 automatic pistol. Having done so, he worked its cocking mechanism and applied the safety catch. If the expression which came to his fiancée's face was any guide, she was as surprised as the other guests to learn he was armed. 'Sorry, darling. I hoped you wouldn't need to see this.'

'Can you use a short gun as good as you use a scatter, Allan?' Rapido asked, before Roz could reply, and he took out the pistol which had come as such a surprise to von Helsinore.

'Not quite,' Morningford admitted. 'But I have fired one.'

'At Bisley, representing the RAF, in fact,' Joan supplemented with more than a touch of pride.

'You'd best have this,' Rapido stated and held out the Remington to be accepted by the Flying Officer. 'It's not much, but it's better than no gun at all.'

'He could have had a *Luger*,' McCallister said, eyeing the Texan in a way which implied criticism.

'If you mean the one I took from von Helsinore,'

Rapido replied without looking in the least abashed by the suggestion that he had acted in a most ill-advised fashion. 'I didn't figure any of you were set for the kind of trouble keeping it would've cut loose, which's why I gave it back to him.'

'You might bring my guns down too, if there's time,' Morningford requested, directing a prohibitive glance at the doctor. 'They could be *useful* if trouble starts.'

'Why sure,' the Texan agreed. 'Soon's we're gone, fasten all the doors and those French windows and try to block them with something that'll hold a while should those jaspers try to bust 'em in. Don't open up until you know it's *us*.'

'I wish we had more guns,' Joan said.

'They'd be real handy, but seeing as we don't, we'll just have to do with what we've got,' Rapido drawled and, reaching behind his back beneath the leather jacket, he brought a Colt Government Model of 1911 automatic pistol into view and made it ready for use. Then his voice took on a chilling note and, once again, the sheer force of his personality dominated the room. 'Now this game's getting started, keep one thing in mind. I've always been taught that any time things are bad enough for you to have to point a gun at somebody, they're bad enough for you to have to shoot. It gets to there, don't try to scare the feller off, *do it* – And, if you have to shoot, don't try anything fancy like figuring just to wound. Shoot to *kill*. It's a damned good rule and, happen you're wanting to stay alive, you'd best set yourselves to follow it.'

Watching and listening as the Texan pressed down the pistol's safety catch and inserted his forefinger through the triggerguard – which he did not do until the barrel was pointing away from him[1] – Morningford noticed that, unlike Brocklehurst, he did not cock the action. As he was obviously most competent in such matters, this

---

1. *How dangerous a failure to take such a precaution could be when drawing a firearm is described in:* THE FAST GUN.

implied he had been carrying the weapon with a round in the chamber and the safety catch applied; a most imprudent habit, the Flying Officer had often been told, and the reason why many people considered a revolver was a more reliable proposition.

'Do you really think things might be that *bad*?' Morningford inquired, more impressed by the quietly spoken words than he had been with anything he had ever heard.

'Things are *certain* to get that *bad*, there's no *might* about it!' the Texan affirmed. Then he glanced to where Wanda Gore-Kauphin and Michael Mansfield stood a short distance away. They were listening intently, but had not offered to move closer nor speak. His gaze went to the vanity bag she had retrieved from her fiancé and he went on, 'Happen you two want to live long enough to take over this place, you'd best both start helping the ladies do as I said.'

Without offering the obviously disturbed and frightened couple a chance to reply, Rapido signalled for Beryl, Brocklehurst and McCallister to accompany him. Opening the double doors, he made sure the hall was empty. Having done so, he led the way upstairs. On arriving at the first floor, the civil servant looked at the Texan and seemed on the point of speaking. However, he did not, and he was left with the blonde to perform the tasks they had been assigned. Carrying on with the doctor to the second floor and being informed where Billie Oakroyd had been taken, Rapido gave whispered instructions. Nodding concurrence, McCallister walked quietly forward with him.

'Billie!' the doctor hissed and continued to follow his instructions by tapping gently on the door. 'It's me, *Andrew*. Can you come out?'

Although the door was drawn open, it was not the young woman who emerged!

Muttering an imprecation, the largest of the footmen loomed into view!

Before McCallister could decide upon what action to

take, the matter was resolved without any need for intervention on his part!

Despite holding the big automatic in his right hand, Rapido did not attempt to use it as a deterrent or for a more deadly means of ending the danger posed by the enormous man. Instead, rotating himself at the waist to give an added impetus and put the full weight of his exceptionally powerful body behind it, he thrust out his left hand. It was not clenched into a fist. However, the effect it produced was far more efficacious than any conventional punch would have been. Extended like twin steel spikes, his first and second fingers – which had pierced the skin on Hans' throat in the library – were driven at an upwards angle into the man's eyes. Instantly, all the aggression left the recipient of the attack. A screech of sheer agony burst from his lips and he blundered backwards into the room with his hands rising to his face.

'My eyes!' the man screamed and McCallister saw blood flowing between his fingers. 'Holy Mother, my *eyes*!'

Before the doctor could even think of the grim warning given by the Texan about the means which might be needed to effect Billie's rescue, there was a response he had not anticipated. A feminine scream of horror came from inside the room. Then, shrieking in a hysterical fashion, Billie dashed through the door to throw herself into his arms.

'Hell!' Rapido growled, as the young woman continued to scream at the top of her voice. 'Now the powder's going to hit the fan!'

* * *   * * *

'What the devil?' Mrs Blount ejaculated, looking through the window alongside the front entrance to Mansfield Manor at a large dark brown car which was coming to a halt in front of it. 'Who let them through?'

Although she was not aware of the fact, the house-keeper had come into the main hall just after the party

158

from the library had gone upstairs. She was accompanied by Lancer and a man whose surname, Palmer, led to him being called 'Pedlar' – a traditional sobriquet of the armed forces given in honour of a famous boxer – by the other servants. Each had a Webley service revolver tucked into his waistband, but she was not armed.

'Guern—*Mr* Guerney must have let 'em through,' Lancer suggested, belatedly applying the honorific as he knew the woman shared the butler's insistence upon it being used at all times. 'There's only him and Chalky down at the gate-house. The rest are in their rooms.'

For once, Mrs Blount did not offer to rebuke the lapse on Lancer's part. Her full attention was occupied with the vehicle which had arrived so unexpectedly. It was not one, such as the tradesmen's or post office van, which could call without prior notice and be accepted as innocuous. If she had been better informed about such matters, she would have recognized it as an Austrian-built 1928 Steyr Type XX. Designed originally for operating over mountainous terrain, it was large and rugged. However, its white walled tyres and glossy paintwork implied it had also been given a certain amount of luxurious appendages. None of this interested her. At that moment, she was more concerned with studying the couple who were emerging from it.

Proving to be a good six foot three in height on straightening up, with golden blond hair and exceptionally handsome features, the driver was in his early twenties and had a muscular development which was well beyond the average. There was a tremendously wide spread to his shoulders and his torso trimmed down to a slender waist set on long and clearly powerful legs. Nevertheless, despite his size and obvious strength, he carried himself lightly and looked capable of moving very fast should the need arise. He was bare headed and the white silk shirt, a yellow cravat of the same material, and the grey flannels – supported by a very broad brown belt – he wore were obviously tailored for him. However, although the same applied to the black blazer he was wearing, it seemed a little baggy on his giant frame. A suggestion of his origins came from his heeled and sharp toed tan boots looking similar to the pair worn by the guest from Texas.

The only passenger was a girl not long past her twenty-fifth birthday. Five foot six in height and pretty without being excessively beautiful, she too did not wear a hat and her reddish-brown hair was cut in a shortish, tousled, curly 'wind blown bob'. Although the current fashion called for a slim boyish figure, her shapely body only just fell short of the Junoesque 'hourglass' contours which had been all the rage of a few decades earlier. The swell of her full and firm bosom, her trim mid-section and well rounded hips were exhibited to their best advantage by an unfastened waist-long brown leather jacket, a dark blue satin blouse and matching bell-bottomed slacks. Like the jacket, her footwear was of the same kind worn by the small Texan.

'What do they want?' Lancer inquired.

'How the devil should I know!' Mrs Blount demanded, watching the visitors coming towards the porch. 'Go and get rid of them!'

'I'll do it, Lancer,' the other servant offered.

Having the least unprepossessing appearance of all the footmen, Palmer had actually served in such a capacity at another country mansion before being discharged for theft and taking the appointment at Mansfield Manor. Therefore, he considered he was the better qualified to carry out the task without arousing suspicion. Waiting until the bell was sounded, he drew open the door and looked out.

'Howdy, you-all,' the blond giant greeted. His voice was a pleasant baritone with an accent much the same as that of the small Texan. 'I'm Ranse Smith and this's Rita Yarborough—!'

'There's been a death in the house, so we're not receiving,' Palmer stated, using a speech he had heard made by the butler at his previous place of employment. However, he was not sufficiently perceptive to draw any

160

conclusions from the way in which he had been addressed. 'You'll have to come back later.'

Having delivered the message, instead of waiting for a reply, the footman closed the door. Exchanging a glance with the girl, the blond giant set his weight on his right leg. Then, swinging up and around with the left, he drove it forward. There was a crash as the sole of the boot struck the door and, such was the power of the kick, it burst inwards to slam against Palmer's still upraised hand. A yelp of pain left him and he staggered back clasping his stinging fingers in his other fist.

'We're *back*!' Ranse stated, striding through the door with Rita close on his heels and moving to his left on reaching the hall.

While making the announcement, the blond giant sent his right hand beneath his jacket and the reason for the tailor having made it somewhat baggy became apparent. Carried in an open fronted spring retention holster on the wide belt was, although none of the English trio could have given it a name, a Burgess Folding Riot Gun. Having proved its capability for comparative ease of concealment when worn by a man of his size, he demonstrated how swiftly it could be made ready for use. When first coming into view, the barrel was turned beneath the operating section and butt in the manner which supplied its name. However, after it was slid free from the holster's springs and swung forward, it pivoted on a hinge until it snapped home and automatically locked with the receiver.

An important feature of the Burgess's design was that the tubular magazine beneath the barrel could be filled to its six shot capacity and be ready for use when the weapon was folded for carrying, and Ranse at once set about utilizing this quality. Deftly catching the foregrip in his left hand as it rose and was secured in the operating position, he continued to tilt the barrel upwards. While doing this, his right hand was manipulating the longitudinally sliding pistol grip and triggerguard assembly. This served the same purpose as the 'trombone' type of foregrip fitted to similar, albeit more conventional, weapons of the same category manufactured by other companies. Such was the excellence of the design and his skill in handling it, that the weapon was ready for use before he had taken his second step over the threshold.

Caught unawares, Lancer started to grab for the Webley in his waistband. Neither as a soldier – despite having served in a cavalry regiment – nor since taking to a life of crime, had he acquired any familiarity with handguns.[2] Therefore, he did not exhibit any of the speed and dexterity displayed by the blond giant. Before his fingers could close upon the butt, he found himself confronted by a type of weapon he had never seen before. However, the size of the yawning muzzle pointing at him with disconcerting steadiness suggested it was a shotgun of some kind. What was more, it had been produced and handled with a rapidity he could barely believe was possible and indicated the possession of considerable skill in its use.

'Take it out real *slow* and drop it on the floor!' Ranse commanded, then glanced quickly at Palmer. 'You do the same, *hombre*!'

'You'd best go back to the kitch—!' Rita began as the order was being obeyed, her accent indicating she came from that part of America known as New England.

Watching the girl walking towards her while speaking,

2. According to King's, later Queen's, Regulations, *an 'other rank' – private up to sergeant – in the British Army who was armed with a handgun was allocated sixty rounds per annum for training purposes. Throughout all the twelve and a half years I spent as a dog trainer in the Royal Army Veterinary Corps, although having a revolver issued as a personal weapon, neither I nor any of my contemporaries ever received the allocation even when we were engaged in anti-terrorist patrol duties. Nor, despite the fact that our lives might depend upon being able to use it in action, were we ever given any instruction whatsoever in handling the revolver.*

Mrs Blount reacted as anybody who knew her would have expected. Knotting her right hand into a fist, she set about using it with the speed she had showed when felling Wanda Gore-Kauphin. However, on this occasion, she failed to achieve a similar success. Reacting with a speed which the actress had lacked, the girl brought up her hands. Catching the approaching wrist in a surprisingly strong grip, she forced it upwards. Pivoting underneath the raised arm, she brought it down again in a way which caused the big woman's balance to be destroyed. Before she could try to resist, her feet left the floor. Turning an involuntary somersault, she alighted on the polished wooden parquetry blocks with a resounding thud which would have gladdened the heart of many a female convict at Holloway Prison, or those members of her sex in the domestic staff who had incurred her displeasure.

Seeking to take advantage of what he believed to be a distraction, instead of trying to retrieve the revolver he had dropped, Lancer lunged at the blond giant. An instant later, wanting to repay the pain inflicted when the door had been kicked open, Palmer duplicated the action, but also made no attempt to rearm himself. However, despite having flickered a glance at the women, Ranse proved to be alert to the danger. Making a thrust as if using a rifle and bayonet, he rammed the muzzle of the Burgess into his first would-be assailant's *solar plexus*. An explosive belch of suffering burst from Lancer. Folding at the middle, he staggered backwards and was in no condition to see how his companion fared. Not that Palmer came off any better. In what appeared to be a continuation of the thrust, Ranse swung around and used the butt with a speed and precision Gamekepper Murdoch might have envied. Smashed at the side of the head, the second footman was pitched sideways and crashed unconscious to the floor.

'Stay there!' Rita ordered, releasing the wrist and moving around until alongside her victim's head. 'Or do you want to try for a new face?'

Despite the surprise she had received, Mrs Blount had managed to reduce some of the force with which she landed. However, in addition to being particularly winded by the descent, there was another factor which contributed to making her take notice of what was said. The girl was standing on one leg and the high heel of the other boot was hovering a couple of inches above her nose. She could imagine just how painful and damaging the result would be if it was brought down and, as she expected would happen if she resisted, be ground into her face.

Before the housekeeper could decide upon a course of action which would allow her to escape without suffering the painful and damaging consequences she envisaged, there was the sound of gun fire from somewhere upstairs.

CHAPTER FIFTEEN

There's A Feller With A Rifle Out Here

Making the declaration, although Doctor Andrew McCallister was too occupied by trying to cope with Billie Oakroyd's hysterical behaviour to pay much attention, Rapido Clint gave him yet another surprise. While the small Texan was speaking, doors began to open in both directions along the passage. Before anybody could leave the rooms, he tossed the Colt Government Model of 1911 automatic pistol to his left hand. Immediately the right was empty, it disappeared under the left side of the open leather jacket to make a twisting motion and then returned to view holding another of the big black weapons. What happened next exceeded the display of gun juggling he had given in the library.

Despite the precautions to avoid injury in the event of an accidental discharge being taken, the latest weapon to be brought out was lined to the right at shoulder height and crashed in less than a second from the start of its withdrawal. Swiftly though the movements were made, the bullet narrowly missed a footman who was coming out of a room on the other side of the passage. Yelping in alarm, he hurriedly retreated and jerked the door closed. An instant later, the Colt in Rapido's left hand performed a similar function against another of the servants who tried to step from his quarters in that direction.

The pair were only the first to receive the small Texan's attentions. Before the second ejected cartridge case struck the floor, the right hand pistol thundered to dissuade a third footman from appearing. A fourth was

165

about to enter the passage beyond the third, but the left hand weapon was extended beneath it's owner's right arm and drove him back. Almost as if wishing to repay the favour, seeming to be responding of its own volition, the off side Colt swung to the left and performed a similar service. Then each was turned outwards in their original directions to speak practically simultaneously and deter another pair of men from appearing despite the fact they were in different positions.

'Get going, Doc!' Rapido commanded, evidence of his deadly marksmanship having produced a hiatus so far as any attempts to come into the passage were concerned.

Eager though McCallister was to do so, he realized obeying the command was not going to be easy. Instead of taking comfort from his presence and the way in which the Texan was holding any would-be captors at bay, Billie continued to scream and struggle furiously in McCallister's arms. In fact, at one point, it had seemed her wildly flailing right hand would catch hold of Rapido and distract him from his task. Some considerable time had elapsed since the doctor had needed to cope with a hysterical woman and, despite knowing one way which frequently brought success, he hesitated to use it on a person for whom he had formed a warm affection. Nor was he compelled to take that action.

After having fired and driven back a man who allowed himself to be goaded by Baron Ludwig von Helsinore's bellowed demand for something to be done, Rapido glanced around. Showing no hesitation, he swung his right hand so the butt of the pistol caught Billie on the back of the head. Instantly, she went limp and would have fallen to the floor if McCallister had not been able to support her.

'Get her downstairs!' the Texan snapped, as the doctor glared furiously at him. 'It's life, or *death* for *all* of us from here on in!' Then, firing once more to end another attempt to intervene, he raised his voice. 'Listen, you Limey sons-of-bitches. I've not *hit* any of you yet, but only 'cause I *wasn't* aiming to. Now I'm getting quick sick of being a nice feller. The next to show's going to get *hurt* – and *bad*!'

For a moment, as he was scooping the young woman up in his arms, McCallister thought the threat was going to pay dividends. Then the door of the room into which he had been taken to sign the cremation certificate was jerked open and, snarling incoherent words, Hans came out. There were indications of suffering added to the rage which suffused his face. A bandage was around his throat and he was limping, but he had a Luger in his right hand. Even as he was bringing it into alignment, Rapido turned the right hand Colt his way. The big pistol roared an instant before the Luger was levelled at its owner. With a sensation of shock, despite the warnings he had received, the doctor saw a hole appear between the German's eyes. Hans's head snapped back, his raised arm flopped limply down and, with the weapon dropping from his hand, he went backwards out of sight to crash to the floor.

'I've took that one out *dead*!' Rapido shouted, gesturing with the left hand Colt in a sweeping motion towards the head of the stairs. 'And anybody else who shows'll join him in *hell*!'

Until that moment, in spite of the specialization he followed, McCallister had never seen anybody meet with violent death at the hands of another person. However, shaken though he was, he did not let the experience freeze him into immobility. Acting on the signal he had been given, he lifted Billie in his arms and started to carry her down the stairs. Glancing over his shoulder, he found Rapido was following him walking backwards. Arriving at the first floor without any attempt having been made to stop them, they were met by Beryl Snowhill and Jimmy Brocklehurst. It was obvious they had been able to carry out the tasks assigned to them. Both were still holding the weapons they had produced in the dining-room. In addition, the beautiful little blonde had a brown pigskin bag with a combination lock in her left hand and the civil servant was carrying Flying Officer Allan Morningford's gun-case.

'What happened to Billie?' Brocklehurst inquired.

'Hysterics!' McCallister replied, but was not allowed to elaborate.

'Get down to the hall as fast as you can!' Rapido ordered, without taking his eyes off the stairs he had just finished descending. 'Open her up and get me two full'n's when you're there, Beryl. All hell's going to pop even *worse* than already!'

* * *   * * *

Seeing both of the newcomers glance towards the stairs, Mrs Blount made the most of the opportunity with which she was presented. Grabbing the foot hovering over her face, she gave a twisting thrust with all her not inconsiderable strength. As the girl was sent away in a staggering run, the housekeeper showed surprising agility for one of her bulk by coming to her feet and darting towards the rear of the hall. Still clasping at his midsection, Lancer took advantage of the blond giant's attention being diverted still further from him by Mrs Blount's actions. Despite realizing Pedlar Palmer had been knocked unconscious by the blow from the shot-gun's butt and would be unable to join the flight, he did not hesitate before turning to run after her.

Contriving to regain control of her movements without falling, Rita Yarborough came to a stop. Passing behind her back and beneath the jacket, her right hand reappeared grasping the butt of a short barrelled Colt Detective Special revolver. Bringing it to shoulder height at arms' length in a double handed grip with a speed which suggested considerable practice, she took aim. However, although her command for the fleeing woman to halt was ignored, she did not open fire. Nor, sharing her disinclination to be hampered by prisoners, did Ranse Smith attempt to prevent Lancer from following the housekeeper.

'Yeeagh! Texas Light!' the blond giant bellowed, looking anxiously towards the stairs as the door through which the pair had disappeared was closed behind them.

'Thank *God*!' Rita breathed when the shout was

168

answered in kind, and she allowed the revolver to sink until it dangled in her right hand by her side.

'I'm right *pleasured* to see you both,' Rapido Clint declared with genuine warmth as he followed his party down the stairs.

'Something told me you just *might* be,' Ranse drawled sardonically, but there was an undertone of relief in his voice. 'They likely to be coming after you?'

'There's a fair chance they will, once their boss can spur 'em up to doing it,' the smaller Texan admitted. 'Keep the stairs covered, *amigo*. Soon's I've loaded up again, I'm going to get the gals out of here.'

'Go to it,' the blond giant authorized, looking up the staircase and holding his Burgess Folding Riot Gun in a position of readiness. 'They're covered.'

'Twice,' Rita supplemented, ranging herself alongside Ranse with the Colt once more in both hands.

While the conversation was taking place, Beryl had placed the case on an old oak chest by the stairs. Manipulating the combination lock, she raised the lid. Inside were two boxes of rimless .45 calibre ammunition and half a dozen magazines for the Colt automatics, one of which was intended for a specialized purpose. Removing a couple which were fully charged, she took them to Rapido and he exchanged them for the pair in his weapons.

Having replenished the Colts and returned them to their respective holsters, and leaving his friends to carry out the duties he had assigned to them, Rapido followed Beryl, McCallister and Brocklehurst into the dining-room. The others had already announced themselves and the double doors were drawn open by Joan Darling. Following them in, the Texan discovered much had been done to secure the big room as well as possible with the means at hand. Chairs had been jammed under the handles of the other doors and the big table had been overturned and pushed back to block the now closed and bolted French windows.

'I'm pleased to see you're all right after all the

169

shooting from upstairs, old boy,' Flying Officer Allan Morningford declared from where he was standing behind the table and looking across the lawn towards the gate-house. 'Did they hit Billie?'

'Nope, that was me,' Rapido answered, the words having been directed to him. 'She got hysterical and it was the only way to quieten her so's Doc could tote down here.'

'I'm sure she'll forgive you when she comes round,' Joan Darling guessed.

'Likely,' the Texan drawled in what seemed an almost disinterested fashion. His eyes went to Rosalind Brampton, who was going to where McCallister still cradled the unconscious young woman in his arms. 'Save 'tending to her until you're in the car, ma'am. You ladies are all getting out of here as fast as we can load you up.'

'As I didn't hear any hostile noises outside, old boy,' the Flying Officer put in, 'I presume those people who drove up are your friends?'

'You've never presumed presumier,' Rapido replied. 'Happen there's time, I'll present you to Ranse all proper-like as we go through and you can say, "Howdy, you-all", or whichever you fly-boys say it, to Rita while she's driving you off.'

'Just *me*?' Morningford asked. 'What about the rest of you chaps?'

'Jimmy and Doc can go along,' the Texan answered. 'Happen they can squeeze in.'

'I'm not leaving you!' Brocklehurst declared and McCallister stated his agreement.

'If they don't go,' the Flying Officer said. 'Neither do I!'

'You're not spry enough on your feet right now to stay,' Rapido pointed out. 'Which being, you'll be a whole heap more useful riding shotgun on the gals.'

'*I'm* not stopping behind!' Michael Mansfield screeched, before Morningford could make any response.

'You'll do as you're damned well told, else you'll find

170

out how it feels to get busted on the jaw like your *lady* already knows,' the Texan stated bluntly. 'Who-all's out there, Allan?'

'Just Guerney and one of the footmen,' the Flying Officer reported. 'At least, that's all I've seen at the gate-house. They're still looking up here, but they haven't offered to come.'

'Watch 'em, Jimmy,' the Texan instructed. 'And, happen Allan says, "Why sure", fire up those fancy scatterguns and keep one for yourself.'

'Why sure, as we Texans say,' Morningford authorized.

'Take the lady out to the front door, Doc,' Rapido said, glancing to where Billie was showing signs of recovery. 'And you other ladies go with him. You help Mr Morningford, *hombre*.'

'I'd sooner hobble!' the Flying Officer asserted, eyeing the obviously reluctant Mansfield with distaste.

'Lean on me, Allan,' Roz offered, striding purposefully over.

'Thank you,' Morningford assented and did as was suggested.

'You can stay right where you are!' Brocklehurst ordered, as Mansfield made a movement indicating he intended to go with the others who were leaving.

'But—!' the new owner of the property croaked, his face showing terror.

'But me no buts, or I'll make sop of you!' the civil servant snapped, misquoting William Shakespeare and gesturing menacingly with the shotgun borrowed from Morningford. 'Or as near as I can by beating you over the head with Jemina. Or is she Hortense?'

Staring at the grim expression which came to Brocklehurst's face, Mansfield stood cowering instead of carrying out his intention of demanding he be taken to safety.

'Damn it!' McCallister ejaculated, as Rapido drew open the front door. Although Billie had recovered sufficiently for him to set her on her feet, he was still supporting her. 'We've forgotten that chap with the rifle upstairs.'

171

'Huh huh!' the small Texan drawled and raising his voice, he directed the words through the door. 'Hey, Comanch'. There's a feller with a rifle up above us someplace.'

'There's a feller with a rifle out here!'

The voice which replied came from somewhere in the grounds and suggested it belonged to another denizen of Texas. However, it possessed a ventriloquial quality which made locating its exact place of origin impossible. Nor, judging from appearances, was it only the doctor who found this to be the case. By the gate-house, Guerney and the footmen drew revolvers and gazed about them in a mixture of surprise and alarm. Then, obviously perturbed by their inability to ascertain the whereabouts of the speaker, they retreated hurriedly into the building.

'Let's go!' Rapido ordered.

'But if there's another man with a rifle—!' McCallister began, drawing no conclusions from the pair's behaviour in his still disturbed frame of mind.

'It's that cowhand humour I told you about,' Rapido explained with a grin. 'That damned fool *amigo* of mine means *himself*. One thing you can count on sure as night follows day. Did they have another rifleman out there, he won't be feeling like doing *anything* at all after Comanch's said, "Howdy, you-all" to him. Get set to follow me as soon's that *hombre* with the long gun up there gets sort of discouraged, happen he tries to spoil things.'

As he finished speaking, Rapido stepped out of the door. However, despite the threat posed from one of the upper floors by the man with a rifle, he seemed to have reverted to his earlier close to lethargic behaviour. In fact, the way he sauntered towards the Steyr Type XX car was more as if he was on his way to a function he did not particularly wish to attend instead of paving the way for an escape from the clutches of ruthless enemies.

The English members of the party watched Rapido with a mixture of amazement, concern and even a little resentment over his dawdling gait. Being so engrossed in his behaviour, none of them noticed the way in which Ranse Smith and Rita Yarborough – the latter once more gripping her Colt revolver with an easy familiarity implying a knowledge of handling weapons almost the equal of her male companions – kept a watch on the stairs, instead of looking to see how the small Texan fared. Their vigilance paid off when, holding a Webley service revolver, one of the footmen came cautiously into view. Despite seeing him, the blond giant took no action. However, drawing the required conclusion from her companion's lack of response, Rita lined her Colt doubled handed and squeezed its trigger. Alarmed by the girl's rapid movement, and hearing the bullet hissing by his head, it being only his second taste of gun fighting, the man hurriedly withdrew. Nor did any more of them attempt to take his place.

Outside, there was a crack of a shot from upstairs. However, Rapido was not hit. Although no further sound had come from the grounds, the detonation was preceded by a cry of pain. Then there was a clatter as a rifle equipped with a telescopic sight fell to the ground. Changing his gait to a swift dart, the Texan reached the vehicle. Turning as he arrived, he brought the Colt from beneath the left side of his jacket with the same kind of speed he had employed upstairs. Grasping the butt in both hands and supporting them on the roof of the Steyr, he fired twice in an upwards direction.

'Start getting over here *fastern'n* just *fast!*' the small Texan barked, continuing to keep the weapon pointing towards the windows above him.

Before the order could be obeyed, a big pantechnicon bearing the name of a well known furniture removal company came through the open gates. Halting just inside, it started to disgorge men carrying weapons of various kinds. Looking around, Rapido let out a profanity. Then he swung on his heel and ran towards the house.

'It's too *late!*' the small Texan growled bitterly, coming

173

through the door. 'The god damned Shooting Team's arrived. Now we'll have to fort up in here, root, hog, or *die*. There isn't any other way.'

'Why not give von Helsinore what he wants?' Billie suggested.

'He'd still gun all of us down,' Rapido replied. 'We've seen and done too much for him to handle it any other way.'

'Look!' McCallister snapped, pointing along the drive.

Guerney and the footman who had remained with him at the gate-house came out from it. They were supporting a man whose unkempt appearance suggested he was a tramp and who appeared to be unconscious.

'Oh my god!' Beryl gasped. 'They've got *Johnny Gray*!'

'You at the house!' Guerney bellowed, before anything more could be said. 'We've got one of your crowd here. Unless you come out and surrender, we'll kill him in front of you!'

CHAPTER SIXTEEN

Shoot Him, He's Not One Of Us

'*Now* what do we do?' Doctor Andrew McCallister asked, looking at Rapido Clint.

'Give them what they want!' Billie Oakroyd demanded rather than suggested.

'I *wouldn't*, even if I'd got it,' the small Texan declared bluntly, turning from the open door. 'Hey, Ranse, do you recall reading what Belle Boyd told Grandpappy Dusty one time?'[1]

'She told him a heap of things on and off,' the blond giant drawled, remaining at his position for covering the staircase. 'Which was it?'

'If you can't lick 'em, *trick* 'em!' Rapido obliged. 'Which last's the only way out for Johnny and us.'

'How're you figuring on doing it?' Ranse Smith asked.

Instead of starting to explain his scheme in a way everybody could understand, the small Texan said something in the kind of Spanish employed along the Rio Grande. Although the English members of his audience looked uncomprehending, the blond giant and Rita Yarborough glanced at Billie. However, their attention returned to Rapido as he reverted to English

---

1. *Information about Belle Boyd, known as the Rebel Spy, is given in*: THE COLT AND THE SABRE, THE REBEL SPY, THE BLOODY BORDER, BACK TO THE BLOODY BORDER, THE REMITTANCE KID, THE WHIP AND THE WAR LANCE *and various volumes of the* Floating Outfit *series in which she makes a 'guest' appearance.*
1a. *The identity of 'Grandpappy Dusty' can be found in the* APPENDIX.

and began to say how he hoped to effect the rescue of Captain John Gray. Nothing showed on Ranse's face, but Rita and the others looked perturbed as they realized the implications of what they were hearing.

'It's *dangerous*!' Flying Officer Allan Morningford warned.

'So's *everything* else hereabouts,' Rapido answered.

'Rita will be more use than me in here,' Beryl Snowhill commented. 'Let her stay and I'll do *it*!'

'It's no job for a woman,' McCallister protested. 'Let *me*—!'

'Happen you can use that hawg-leg,' Rapido countered, glancing at the Webley service revolver discarded by Lancer and which the doctor had picked up. 'You'll be more use in here. There's few enough of us to cover all the ways they could get in.'

'I've never fired one,' McCallister admitted. 'A shotgun's more in my line.'

'Take Hortense in that case,' Morningford asserted, holding out the Purdey he had retained and a box of shells. 'I think you can count on me to hit a running villain with the Webley, especially if he's running *at* me.'

'I can't *stand* it!' Billie screamed and, showing signs of the hysterics which had affected her earlier, she began to run towards the stairs.

The outburst and action was so unexpected that the young woman had gone before anybody at the door could prevent her departure. However, as she passed, Rita inserted a foot between her legs. Tripping, she sprawled face down on to the bottom step. Almost as soon as she landed, the American girl had followed her and bent to ram a knee into the centre of her back.

'You make just *one* shout and I'll blow your brains out!' Rita warned savagely, thrusting the muzzle of the Colt Detective Special revolver against the back of Billie's head and, despite the mechanism operating on the double action principle, drawing its hammer to fully cocked with her thumb.

'What the *devil*—!' McCallister roared, having turned to watch and being incensed by what he saw.

'Hold hard!' Rapido commanded, catching the doctor's arm in a grip like iron and preventing him from starting to move forward. 'She's in cahoots with *them*!'

'Wha—?' McCallister gasped, turning a face showing shock and more than a trace of disbelief towards his captor.

Then the doctor remembered various incidents which suggested he was being told the truth. During dinner the previous evening, in addition to questioning him about his reason for attending the party, Billie had shown considerable interest in discovering what he knew about the other British male guests and whether he had heard what had made them accept Michael Mansfield's invitation. By pretending to faint in the library, she had helped to prevent Rosalind Brampton and himself going over to examine the man in the wheelchair. That morning, she had left the dining-room after hearing Morningford planned to go for help and he could envisage how her reason differed from the one she had given. She had warned somebody in the back hall that the attempt was to be made thus allowing the man with the rifle to be ready to counter it. More recently, if she had not made so much noise, her 'rescue' might have been achieved without alerting the men in the other rooms. What was more, while struggling and screaming in what seemed to be blind panic, she had had to be restrained from grabbing hold of Rapido. If she had succeeded, time would have been granted for the men to enter the passage and deal with the small Texan and himself.

'Sorry, Doc!' Rapido said quietly.

'Can you keep her *quiet*, Roz?' Rita inquired retaining her position, having paid no attention to McCallister's outburst.

'I *can*!' the nursing sister declared with confidence and went forward.

'Don't take any chances,' the American girl advised,

straightening up when the nursing sister arrived. 'Knock her down and jump feet first on her face if she so much as *breathes* extra loud.'

'I *will*!' Roz assured and bent to jerk the dazed, bewildered young woman upright by the scruff of the neck. Deftly twisting an arm around in a hammerlock, she hustled her captive away from the stairs saying, 'Don't you even *think* I *won't*!'

Satisfied she could leave controlling Billie in the nursing sister's obviously capable hands, Rita turned her attention once more to covering the first floor.

'Hey, you in the house!' Guerney bellowed, diverting the attention of the group at the door from what was happening across the hall. 'What about it?'

'You're trying a bluff, *hombre*!' Rapido replied just as loudly, walking on to the porch with his empty hands raised. 'He looks like a god-damned hobo – what you call a tramp – to me. I want to know for *sure* who he is afore we hand *anything* over.'

'Then come and take a closer look,' the butler offered.

'Do I have your *word's* you'll let me come back no matter which way she goes?' the small Texan asked, seeing the captive stirring as if just regaining consciousness.

'You have,' Guerney confirmed.

'Then I'm coming right now,' Rapido claimed and spoke *sotto voce* over his shoulder as he walked forward. 'Lordy lord. I sure hope there's nobody from west of the Big Muddy among those yahoos!'

'Guerney doesn't mean to keep his word!' McCallister breathed, remembering from his visit to the United States that the 'Big Muddy' was a colloquial name for the Mississippi River.

'Rapido doesn't expect him to,' Beryl replied. 'That's why I'm going after him.'

Saying the words, the beautiful little blonde slipped out of the house. Darting to the Steyr Type XX car, endeavouring to keep the Texan between herself and the men along the drive, she slipped into the front seat without being challenged by them or anybody upstairs. Having done so, she operated the ignition key and, much to her relief – such items not being in general use – it caused the engine to start immediately.

'*Hell!*' Morningford ejaculated, after Beryl had achieved the first part of her assignment successfully. 'We've forgotten to have somebody watching in the *library!*'

'Go, Rita!' Ranse barked urgently. 'I can 'tend to the stairs!'

'I'll come!' McCallister stated, wanting to make up for his mistake where Billie was concerned.

On entering the library, Rita and the doctor discovered that Morningford's recollection of danger had not come a moment too soon!

Carrying a Thompson submachine gun with a fifty round drum magazine and followed by Lancer, who had acquired another revolver, Mrs Blount was coming through the door by which the body had been removed the previous evening!

On arriving in the back hall, the housekeeper had learned enough from the frightened female servants who were present to realize things were going even worse than she envisaged. Hurrying up the rear stairs, she discovered that none of the footmen were willing to face the guns in the hands of the people on the ground floor. Nor had the production by Baron Ludwig von Helsinore of a weapon much more potent than the Webley revolvers served to boost their courage. Still furious at the way she had been treated by the American girl, she had announced her intention of showing them what a set of cowards they were. Ordering a reluctant Lancer to go with her, his acceptance being caused by the realization that to do otherwise could be *very* dangerous in her present mood, she had taken the submachine gun and led the way to the rear entrance of the library in the belief that their arrival would not be detected by the intended victims until too late.

Seeing the American girl coming through the double

doors, Mrs Blount snarled a profanity and began to raise the Thompson so as to start shooting. At that instant, the difference between the backgrounds of Rita and McCallister made itself apparent. Skilful though he was at using a shotgun for sporting purposes, and despite appreciating the danger, his mind did not conceive it as being a weapon to be employed against another human being. On the other hand, the girl's life for some time past had been such as to prepare her mentally and physically to meet the threat to her existence.

Coming to a halt on spread apart feet, Rita went into a crouching posture similar to that Rapido had employed when shooting at the clay pigeons. With her left hand flashing over to join the right on the butt, she thrust out the Colt to arms' length and opened fire in a single blur of motion. Three .38 Special bullets in very rapid succession sped through the air, each striking the big woman in the body. However, although hurt, she kept her feet and tried to turn the involuntarily deflected Thompson towards her assailant.

Realizing what must be done, the girl did not hesitate. Sighting along the short barrel and changing its alignment, she sent off the next piece of lead in a vitally different direction. Flying as was intended, it entered the centre of the housekeeper's forehead. Killed instantaneously, as Rita had known was the only way to stop her, she spun sideways and the submachinegun chattered briefly, but harmlessly, before being released. As it and she went down, seeing what was happening and McCallister belatedly starting to raise the shotgun, Lancer sprang backwards and ran to tell the others that the attempt at a surprise attack had been thwarted.

*　*　*　　　　　　*　*　*

'This's as close as I'm coming,' Rapido Clint announced. 'You two bring that jasper out from those other *hombres* a ways so I can see him better.'

Having forced himself to ignore the sound of shooting from his rear, although he drew some solace from its briefness, the small Texan had strolled with seeming nonchalance along the drive. However, he had come to a stop while still about fifty yards from the menacing group who were awaiting his arrival. He ran his gaze over the members of the 'Shooting Team', as he had been informed was the name given to the party from the pantechnicon. They were a mixture suggestive of Germanic, Gallic and Slavonic blood. The only thing they had in common was a military and disciplined bearing regardless of their respective origins. However, much to his relief, none of them had the appearance of having adopted an American life-style; especially one west of the Mississippi River.

'Very well,' Guerney assented, feeling sure he and the footman could throw down their slightly moving burden and overpower the small and absurdly trusting young American without difficulty once they were closer.

'Hell!' Rapido snorted, before the pair were near enough to put into operation the treachery he suspected was intended. He made what appeared to be a nervous gesture by jerking his head back and forward quickly then continued, 'Happen you're so minded, shoot him, he's not one of *us*!'

Fortune had favoured Captain John Gray that morning. On his recovery from the effects of the capsule charged with chloral hydrate he had bitten open during the attack, his captors had all been occupied with other matters during the potentially dangerous period of returning to sentience when he might have spoken or acted in an unwise manner. By the time one of them had come to examine him, he had recovered sufficiently to be able to pretend to be still unconscious. Having continued the deception even on being brought from the gate-house and, listening to what was said, he had drawn an accurate conclusion. Seeing the Steyr Type XX car start moving and being aware of its special qualities, his suggestion of starting to recover had been made with the contingency he hoped was planned in mind. Guessing the movement Rapido's head had made before denying their connection was a signal, he also deduced what was expected from him.

181

'You damned *liar*!' Gray yelled, giving a wrench which dragged him free from the two men and plunging forward with outstretched hands. 'I'll teach—!'

The rest of the threat went unsaid!

Grabbing the approaching man by the right wrist, Rapido spun around and gave a surging swing which precipitated him onwards. Continuing to turn on releasing the hold, the Texan's left hand grasped and drew open the side of his jacket. Working in smooth coordination, the right flashed beneath it to where one of his Colt Government Model of 1911 automatics was suspended in an open fronted, spring-retention shoulder holster. Drawn free, it was clear of the jacket and ready for use by the time he was facing the startled pair once more.

'Tell them to stand still, Guerney!' the Texan commanded, lining his weapon with unerring accuracy at a portion of the anatomy which he suspected would be an especially effective inducement to compliance. 'Happen they might get me, but *you'll* be *gut-shot* afore I hit the ground!'

Even before the threat was completed, the butler was aware that the large calibre automatic was being aimed at the centre of his stomach. Although he had contrived to spend most of his career in the Royal Navy as a 'barrack stanchion' on shore duties and never saw active service, he was aware of just how agonizingly painful a wound there would be before inevitable death brought what might be considered a merciful release. Nor did he doubt that the *big* Texan would be able to do as was intimated. Faced with such a prospect, he knew there was only one course open to him.

'Don't *anybody* make a move!' Guerney bellowed, glaring prohibitively to his rear.

Having expected something of the sort, Gray was prepared and did not lose his balance as he was flung onwards with considerable force. Recognizing the girl who was driving the Steyr, he deduced what was required of him from the way she pointed over her shoulder with her left hand. Continuing to run until he reached the vehicle, he snatched open the rear door and dived inside without her needing to stop.

Kept subjected to discipline even more severe than that enforced in the French Foreigh Legion, all but one member of the Shooting Team refrained from taking action on hearing the command given by a man they had been informed was high in the hierarchy of their organization. Being at the rear and shorter than the others, the exception drew a Mauser automatic from the wooden holster – which could be converted into a butt stock – on his waist belt. Having done so, he crouched and started to move behind his companions with the intention of reaching a position from which he could start shooting. Before he could achieve his purpose, although there was no sound of a shot, he felt the shock of something hot striking his right thigh and passing onwards to impale the left. Letting out a cry of pain, he collapsed with blood spurting from the holes which had appeared.

'I won't *wound* the next bastard to move!' warned the ventriloquial tones of the concealed Texan. 'I'll send him straight to hell and some more of you to boot.'

'I told you *all* to stand still!' Guerney thundered, glaring over his shoulder and trying not to let the alarm he was experiencing tinge his voice. He had forgotten the unseen marksman, but was aware that his own life had been placed in even greater jeopardy by an ill-advised act by one of the Shooting Team. 'I didn't know—!'

'I'll buy that,' Rapido replied.

By the time the acceptance was delivered, Beryl Snowhill had brought the Steyr to a stop alongside the small Texan. While she was making an adjustment to the gears and keeping her feet on the clutch and brake, Gray carried out the instructions she had given during the approach. Leaning over, he opened the front passenger's door. Moving sideways without taking the Colt from its alignment, Rapido made a dive through the opening.

The moment he was inside, Beryl raised her feet and the car began to reverse.

'Now we'll see if she's as good as you J.G. boys reckoned,' the Texan drawled, closing the door and watching Guerney diving to the ground with surprising agility for one of his bulk.

Concluding they were at liberty to do so, while the remainder tried to locate the unseen rifleman, several members of the Shooting Team opened fire at the departing vehicle with a variety of weapons. However, although a number of hits were made, they did not have any effect on the occupants. Even those which struck the windshield only left scars on the outside and could not penetrate it.

'Well?' Gray inquired in a challenging tone.

'She's as good,' Rapido conceded, having been informed the car was made completely bullet-proof in addition to having other features added since coming into the possession of Mr J.G. Reeder. 'Seeing as they didn't bring him out with you to help them dicker, I reckon Parker got away.'

'He did,' Gray affirmed. 'Or, at least I hope he did.'

'You got cause to reckon he didn't?' the Texan inquired.

'No,' Gray admitted. 'But, if he had, I'd have expected help to be here by now.'

'I hope it's not too long coming,' Rapido drawled. ''Cause we're in for one hell of a fight until it does.'

CHAPTER SEVENTEEN

Go Arson Around With Matches

'Go tell your *amigos* we've got a *plenty* of help on its way, Miss Oakroyd,' Rapido Clint ordered. 'And take this knobhead with you.'

Showing skill in handling the heavy Steyr Type XX, which was far less manoeuvrable than her 1925 MG Super Sports two-seater tourer and other vehicles to which she was accustomed, Beryl Snowhill had contrived to turn it around while her passengers were talking. Having done so, realizing the danger as bullets from the upper floors of the Manor joined those sent after them by the Shooting Team, she had not halted on the drive. Instead, taking advantage of the car's power and superb suspension, she had driven it up the steps into the shelter of the porch to shield them from the weapons overhead. What was more, she halted at an angle in front of the main entrance and they were able to disembark while still given its protection from the men outside the gate-house. Before leaving, the small Texan had taken a grip, similar to the one she had fetched downstairs, from the back seat and carried it in with him.

Although none of the trio realized it, there had been no danger from above after the first bullets came their way. Still without betraying his location, the unseen Texan had shot one of the men at the windows with his silenced weapon. Having received this second example of his marksmanship, the first being when he had crippled Scouse and caused the loss of the telescope sighted rifle used to halt the first attempt to fetch assistance, they all refused to put themselves in a position to become another victim.

185

Entering the main hall, as he had expected, Rapido found that Ranse Smith had organized the defence of the building in a satisfactory manner. The blond giant and Rita Yarborough, the latter now holding the Thompson submachine gun taken from Mrs Blount, were still covering the staircase. Armed with the two Webley service revolvers captured from Lancer and Palmer, Flying Officer Allan Morningford had been helped by Joan Darling to return to his post by the French windows in the dining-room. She was with him and was holding, in a determined manner, the Purdey used earlier by Jimmy Brocklehurst to threaten Michael Mansfield. The library was under the protection of the civil servant with his Webley & Scott .45 automatic pistol, supported by Doctor Andrew McCallister and the second shotgun. Having declined a weapon, Rosalind Brampton was standing guard over Billie and keeping a watch on the still groggy looking footman also sitting with his back against the wall. However, as the small Texan had expected, the new owner of the property and his fiancée stood well back and were showing no sign of being involved in its defense.

'You can get up,' Roz authorized, when the woman who had been made her special responsibility made no attempt to move in spite of Rapido's orders.

Directing a scowl filled with hatred from the Junoesque nursing sister to Rita, Billie did as she was told. Having needed no further permission, the male captive was already on his feet and making for the door at the rear of the hall. On pulling it open, he had a narrow escape as the footman who was keeping watch on it fired without waiting to see who was doing so.

'It's me, *Pedlar*, you stupid bastard!' Palmer yelled. 'They've turned me and Brownie's bit of stuff loose!'

Having delivered his information, the way she was described bringing Billie's baleful glare his way, the footman advanced cautiously. Allowing her to pass through, he jerked the door closed as if expecting to be

186

shot by the occupants of the hall, in spite of having been told he could rejoin his companions.

'Well, that saves us watching them,' Rapido drawled and looked around. 'Take some real *fighting* fodder to Joan and Doc to use in their scatterguns, please, Beryl. Tell them it's way past time for bird-shot to do the job.'

Accepting and taking the grip which was offered to her, the beautiful little blonde carried it to the oak chest where she had put the other. On being opened, it proved to hold several boxes of twelve gauge shells. Selecting two each, containing respectively buckshot and solid ball, she set off to deliver them.

'Is Comanche all right, Rapido?' Rita inquired, having adopted the habit of always using the aliases most frequently employed by two of her companions to reduce the chance of making a mistake when it could have disastrous results.

'What I saw of him,' replied the small Texan, whose real name – which he only rarely used in the line of duty as a sergeant in the Texas Rangers' elite, yet little known, even in its home State, Company 'Z'[1] – was Alvin Dustine Fog.

'Happen you'd seen him, he wouldn't be,' drawled Ranse, who held the same rank and appointment; as did Mark 'Comanche Blood' Scrapton, the man they were discussing. In fact, explaining the error in identity made by Morningford when describing the trick he had played on a group of Royal Air Force officers, he had been posing as Alvin Fog on the assignment which brought them to England.[2] 'What's doing out there?'

'Looks like they're going to use the truck to come up here,' Rapido assessed. 'Reckon that folded up pump of yours can do anything about it?'

'I'll put some solid ball in her and give it a whirl,' the

1. *Information regarding Company 'Z' of the Texas Rangers is given in the* APPENDIX.
2. *What the assignment was is described in:* THE RETURN OF RAPIDO CLINT AND MR J.G. REEDER.

blond giant asserted. 'Happen Momma here can 'tend to the stairs, that is.'

'I'll 'tend to *you*, you knobhead, once we're through with them!' Rita threatened. 'So far, I've had to do all the 'tending that was needed without *your* help.'

'Lordy lord!' Ranse drawled as he was passing the other Texan after having collected a box of solid ball shells from the grip. 'Whoever gets that gal's sure going to have him a wife to step aside from.'

'Why sure,' Rapido answered. However, although the relationship between Rita and himself was very close, he did not sound unduly perturbed by the prospect. Turning his attention to the business at hand, he looked to where the little blonde was returning after carrying out her task. 'Stoke up Long Lou for me, please, Beryl, I've a notion she could be needed before this shivaree's over.'

* * *   * * *

'Things go *badly*!' Doctor Christophe Dubarry stated in a worried voice. 'Those damned cowards will run away if anything else happens!'

'I *know*!' Baron Ludwig von Helsinore admitted, also ignoring the cause of the reluctance to take chances which was shown by the footmen.

Selected for their toughness, and being competent in that style of fighting, the male domestic staff would have been willing to take on the most vicious members of any race course gang or other violent criminals of their own kind. However, even those who had seen active service before being discharged with ignominy from the Army or Navy, had never come up against such deadly and efficient enemies. Having discovered their own ability with firearms was minimal compared with the skill which the party downstairs displayed, they had become demoralized by the kind of opposition they were meeting. Nor, having seen the rescue of Captain John Gray, had the arrival of the Shooting Team changed their attitude. The killing of one of their number by the unseen rifleman in the grounds had been yet a further deterrent and the message brought by Billie Oakroyd and Pedlar Palmer

188

threatened to be the last straw where they were concerned.

'It's *happened*!' William Brown stated, turning from the window at which he was standing with the young woman at his side.

Going over, the Baron and the doctor saw the cause of the exclamation. The members of the Shooting Team had stopped boarding the pantechnicon and the reason for this was not difficult to ascertain. Three large lorries and a sizeable car, all painted in the olive drab colouration of the Army, had stopped on the road outside the main gates. Soldiers wearing steel helmets and having two Lewis guns to supplement their rifles and bayonets were springing from the former vehicles. An officer, whose uniform's peaked cap bore an encircling red band and with the epaulettes on his jacket displaying the insignia of a Brigadier, left the car followed by two civilians.

Although any of the footmen could probably have identified the taller of the civilians, neither Billie nor her three companions recognized Mr J. G. Reeder. They were equally unaware that the man with the appearance of being a tramp was Captain John Gray's 'gentleman's personal gentleman', Parker. Nor did they give any thought to the matter as something else happened. With a shattering roar from their engines, three obvious Royal Air Force fighter aircraft in a 'V' formation swept over the building and dived towards the pantechnicon.

'*Gott in himmel!*' von Helsinore barked, taking in the sight. Then, he went to the bed and picked up a Luger. Equipped with a 'snail' drum magazine offering a capacity of thirty-two rounds and having a longer barrel than the one he had had in the library, it was a 'Naval' Model. 'We must get away. You and Brown go down to the garage and start a fire to keep them occupied, Doctor. I'll get my car ready for us.'

'Get a gun from one of the blokes and go with him, Billie,' the medical attendant ordered. 'I'm not saying I don't *trust* you, Baron, but I'd hate to do that job and find you'd *had* to leave without us.'

189

If the scowl darted at Brown by von Helsinore was any indication, the precaution was not without justification!

* * *   * * *

'What was *that*?' Ranse Smith asked as the V of fighters passed overhead, pausing as he was about to change the buckshot shells in the Burgess for solid ball loads.

'Our borrowing neighbours have got here, with good old J.G. and Parker to boot,' Rapido Clint answered from his place at the door, but he continued to carry out the alterations to the way one of his Colts was loaded by using the device he had asked Beryl Snowhill to prepare for him. 'And when J.G. promises help, I'll tell you *help* is what you get.'

'Sounded that way,' the blond giant drawled.

'Reckon things're settling down out front,' the small Texan assessed and glanced at the stairs. 'Shall we join the *ladies*?'

'I was wondering when you'd ask,' Ranse declared. 'I'll take the high road and you take the low road, huh?'

'Whichever you want,' Rapido assented, studying the consternation shown by the Shooting Team as they watched the soldiers taking up positions along the fence and across the entrance to the grounds. 'Likely you'll not need it, Rita, but fetch that chopper over here in case any of those yahoos try to make a run for the house.'

'Yo!' the attractive American girl responded, using the traditional US Cavalry assent to an order. Walking across the hall, she went on, 'Take care, both of you!'

'We'll do our living best, honey,' Ranse promised and Rapido nodded concurrence.

Going from door to door and informing the occupants of the library and dining-room what was intended, the small Texan joined the blond giant. Neither spoke, but the glances they exchanged showed each was aware that the task upon which they were about to embark might prove dangerous.

Moving quietly up the stairs, Ranse arrived on the first floor without incident. However, as he began to climb onwards, one of the footmen appeared in the opening which gave access to the next passage. Seeing he was holding a Webley service revolver, the blond giant did not wait to find if he intended to put it to use. The barrel of the Burgess was tilted upwards, held at waist level and, aimed by instinctive alignment, boomed loudly in the confined area. The method of firing proved fortunate for the footman in one respect. Only two of the nine buckshot balls spreading outwards on leaving the barrel found their mark. Nevertheless, they proved all that was necessary. Hit in each leg, he howled and flopped to the floor with the weapon dropping unheeded from his grasp.

Flipping back and forwards the action of the Burgess, causing the empty case to be ejected and another shell fed from the magazine tube into the chamber, Ranse was satisfied with his effort. Striding onwards even more swiftly, he halted where he could see along the passage around the edge of the room on either side. He had arrived just too late to catch the leaders of the party taking their departure down the stairs leading to the rear. Nor were any more of the footmen in sight.

'Hey, you knobheads!' the blond giant thundered, after having had his order obeyed for the wounded man to throw the revolver down the stairs. 'The game's *up*. You've got the count of ten to come out, with *empty* hands held *high* and surrender. After that, I'll *kill* every one of you who shows. One! Two!'

Before the count had reached five, doors were being opened and the footmen came out in the required manner. Nor, despite discovering only one adversary was present, did any of them change his mind about surrendering. Instead, they obeyed the command to sit on the floor and await further instructions.

* * *   * * *

'It's lucky we'd got everything ready,' William Brown remarked as he and Doctor Dubarry entered the roomy garage.

The condition of the building gave a suggestion of the fate which had awaited the guests if the property for

191

which von Helsinore was seeking had been handed over. In addition to having their tyres deflated, the cars belonging to the visitors had had the tanks drained and the petrol was in buckets. A coffin was standing on a bench near where the big black limousine – which was behind the gate-house with the Singer Junior car – was normally parked. It had been brought to the Manor ready to cope with the situation which had unexpectedly arisen.

For some reason, it had not been previously discovered that Sir Granville Delamont had agreed to resume his association with friends in the Royal Navy twelve years after going into voluntary retirement. The time would soon be up and it was decided by the leaders of the International Attainers to close down the base they had established with the aid of the deception. The arrangements stipulated by the Commodore for the disposal of his body had helped to make this possible. It had been intended that a corpse would be supplied for the cremation. Discovering their man had been murdered, von Helsinore – a senior European member of the organization's hierarchy – had elected to take advantage of what was believed to be a young and recently qualified doctor being on the premises to obtain the requisite second signature on the cremation certificate.[3]

Although the main doors of the building were closed, the smaller one for use by pedestrians stood open. Through it, the two men could see the Shooting Team

3. *Mr J.G. Reeder's 'criminal mind' had suggested the substitution had taken place and, learning of the stipulation made by Sir Granville Delamont and deducing what it would mean, he concluded the replacement was afraid his embezzlement of a considerable sum from the money which passed through his hands would come to light when the base was closed. Therefore, being aware of how painful the repercussions would be when his defalcations were discovered, he had decided upon the betrayal instead of waiting for this to happen.*

discarding their weapons and raising their hands to indicate surrender. Despite realizing it would have been fatal to do so under the circumstances, the pair wished their supposed reinforcements had fought for at least long enough to let them carry out their task and make good their escape.

'Come on!' Brown snapped, collecting a bucket and starting to throw its contents over the open sports car in which Joan Darling and Morningford had arrived.

Goaded into motion by the words, Dubarry set about dousing the coffin. Then they continued making the preparations for the fire they were going to start. Both were so engrossed with the task that they failed to keep watch through the door. Therefore, the arrival of a bucket which was thrown from that direction and landed to spread its highly inflammatory contents over their feet came as a complete surprise.

'Happen you fellers are pleasured to go arson around with matches,' said a voice with the accent of a Texan. 'You're likely to touch off and burn real *good* soon as I get you started!'

About six foot tall, with a slender build which suggested the possession of whipcord strength, the speaker had reddish-brown hair and was in his late twenties. Deeply tanned, his handsome features – which normally had a deceptive aura of almost babyish innocence, except for the reckless glint in his curious red-hazel eyes – gave an indication of his mixed blood ancestry. With the exception of three items, he was clad after the fashion of an English farm worker. On his feet were what a knowledgeable person from the United States would have identified as moccasins of Comanche manufacture. Hanging in a sheath from the left side of a belt which bore the 'medicine' symbols of the same tribe, was a long ivory handled hunting knife. Most noticeable difference, however, was a Western style gunbelt which slanted down to his right thigh. Butt forward in an open topped holster was a Webley-Fosbery automatic revolver.

Possessing inherited and well developed skills at concealment which Captain John Gray lacked, Sergeant Mark 'Comanche Blood' Scrapton had been hidden in the grounds of the manor from just after sundown the previous evening. His joint task was to receive the item which Rapido Clint was to be given by whoever supplied the requisite password and to offer support should it become necessary. In accordance with the plan, he had crossed to the vicinity of the house at the appointed time, when it had been assumed everybody else would be asleep. On giving the call of a whip-poor-will to let his *amigo* know he was there, he had it answered in kind. Along with the red leather wallet that had been thrown through the bars of the open window, he received a written record of the information which the small Texan had overheard – using a glass tumbler placed against the adjoining wall of the rooms to act as an aid – being given to Brocklehurst by Doctor McCallister.

Delivering the fancy wallet and note to Gray, for onwards transmission to Mr J.G. Reeder, Comanche had returned to his hiding place amongst a clump of bushes to await whatever might happen next. As a precaution – thankfully, in the light of the unanticipated development – he had taken along the Short Magazine Lee Enfield Rifle equipped with a telescopic sight and silencer carried in the Singer to supplement his knife and handgun, and he was thankful he had fired it on a target range sufficiently often to acquire the proficiency he possessed when using his own long range weapon.

Such was Comanche's ability at hiding and as a marksman, he had remained undetected when firing at Scouse and, later, the member of the Shooting Team and another of the footmen. Knowing his companions were likely to be attacked by the surviving occupants of the Manor, he had been devoting some of his attention to searching for any who might try to get at them from outside. It had been his intention to join the others when the reinforcements arrived. However, seeing the pair moving about in the garage, he had changed his intentions.

Hoping he would not be mistaken for one of the enemy, Comanche had set off towards the building. Although he did not learn it until later, one of the soldiers had pointed him out and he was identified as a friend by Mr Reeder. Having seen and heard enough to know what was happening before he arrived at the open door of the garage, he had decided on what he considered was the best counter-measure. Leaning the rifle against the wall, he had taken a book of paper matches from his pocket. Then, stepping with the silence his footwear made possible, he had entered undetected and thrown the bucket filled with petrol.

Swinging around with startled exclamations, Brown and Dubarry stared at the newcomer. The former started his right hand moving towards the butt of the Webley revolver tucked into his waistbelt. However, he halted the movement as he saw what was held in the upraised left hand of the tall young man. He realized that, should the trick have been mastered – which he felt sure was the case – the thumbnail resting just below the heads of the matches could ignite them as effectively as the more usual method. There were sufficient fumes from the petrol already splashed around to ensure a fire would be started when he lit and tossed the matches at them.

Sharing his companion's appreciation of the danger, Dubarry lacked self control. Letting out a yell of terror, he set off in a lumbering run towards the connecting door through which they had come from the house. Seeing the newcomer look after the fleeing Frenchman, Brown resumed the attempt to arm himself. It proved to be a fatal mistake.

Turning palm outwards and moving at a speed his opponent could not equal, Comanche's right hand enfolded the butt of the Webley-Fosbery. It was carried in a manner permitting greater ease of removal than was presented by Brown's weapon. Twisted from the holster in a deft move indicative of long training, the unconventional weapon – arguably the only type ever to use such a mechanism – was lined at waist height and crashed twice.

195

Caught in the chest by two .455 calibre bullets, just as his own revolver was drawn free from the clutches of the waistbelt, Brown spun around and dropped it while falling face down on to the petrol soaked floor.

'You're *next* 'less you stop *now*!' Comanche shouted, raising the Webley-Fosbery to allow him to use its sights and send a third bullet whistling by the fleeing Frenchman's head.

'Don't *shoot*. I *surrender*!' Dubarry screeched; he was not in such a panic that he didn't understand the warning. Skidding to a stop and raising his hands over his head while speaking, he decided he would have revenge upon the man he blamed for his capture and continued, 'Von Helsinore is going to escape in a car he has waiting at the back gate!'

CHAPTER EIGHTEEN

You *Made The Mistake*

Although Guerney had given the order for the Shooting Team to discard their weapons and surrender, he had no desire to be arrested. What was more, knowing the kind of men they were and that they all had a good reason to share his disinclination, he believed there was a way by which he might avoid capture. Carrying their rifles at the 'high port' position, the soldiers advancing through the main entrance to take them prisoner were coming between them and the Lewis guns beyond the fence. Not only were they shielded from the automatic weapons, but the three fighter aircraft – whose appearance had been a strong inducement for them to give up – still circling overhead would not be able to attack with everybody at such close quarters.

'Attack them!' the butler yelled.

Even as Guerney spoke, he discovered similar conclusions had been reached by some members of the Shooting Team. Bellowing the same advice in his native tongue, a burly Parisian deserter from the French Foreign Legion sprang towards the soldiers. Others followed his example and soon the hand to hand melee sought by the butler was commenced. However, it did not prove to be the comparatively easy task the reinforcements supplied by the International Attainers envisaged. Being battle hardened fighting men who had frequently been employed in insurrections organized by their employers, they believed they would be in contention against raw recruits without combat experience and would have the advantage. The assumption was incorrect. Every soldier had only recently returned from

197

disembarkation leave after a tour of duty on the Northwest Frontier of India. While there they had frequently been engaged on active service against the savage hill tribes of an area justifiably renowned for producing competent and ruthlessly efficient warriors. Therefore, they were well equipped mentally and even better physically to cope with the attack launched at them. What was more, their task was made easier at first by the men with whom they were dealing being over confident.

Having had no intention of joining in the fight he helped to start, Guerney swung around and started to run across the lawn. His plan was to reach and make his escape in the powerful car belonging to Baron Ludwig von Helsinore which was at the back gate. Despite the Shooting Team playing their part in a satisfactory manner, his scheme failed. Imbued by a hatred for him in his present and previous capacity, 'Chalky' White — the footman who had helped bring Captain John Gray from the gate-house – had guessed what was planned and also stayed clear of the action so he could take the same means of effecting an escape. Snatching up a revolver, he aimed and fired twice. Struck in the back by the heavy bullets, the butler plunged face forward and dying on to the ground.

With his revenge taken against Guerney, White returned his attention to the fighting before setting out for the car. He did so just an instant too late. Having passed around the edge of the melee, a medium sized man who looked like a tramp and was armed in the same way as the soldiers was rushing towards him. Startled by an expression of fury he had never seen equalled, he hesitated instead of responding immediately to the sight. He was not given time to recover from the surprise.

Thrust out with the skill and precision which made Parker in demand by various Territorial Army units in London as an instructor for that style of fighting, and to the accompaniment of the awesome kind of yell he always insisted upon being employed at such a moment, the bayonet sank into White's torso just below the breast bone. Shock, pain, and the force of the blow caused him to be swept off his feet. Losing his hold on the revolver, he crashed backwards. Even as he landed supine, a foot descended on his chest and, adding to his suffering, he felt the blade being twisted in the wound.

'Where is *he*?' Parker demanded and nobody who knew him would have recognized him as the invariably quiet spoken, polite and inconspicuous 'gentleman's personal gentleman' met in the rooms at the Albany occupied by Captain Gray.

'*Strewth*!' ejaculated a burly sergeant who, having wrenched free his weapon and felled the man who tried to take it from him with a butt stroke, came up. 'Take it easy, mate!'

'Where is he?' Parker repeated, without giving any indication of having heard the words. Nor had he. At that moment, he was oblivious to everything except getting the information he was seeking. Continuing to twist the bayonet with the savagery born out of concern for an employer who he also considered a very good friend, he elaborated, 'The man you captured last night, is he *dead*?'

'N—*No*—!' White screamed and, despite his suffering, contrived to wave a hand weakly in the direction of the Manor. 'The—They res—rescued him!'

'Thank god for *that*!' Parker hissed with relief.

Jerking the weapon from the wound, the valet looked around to find out if his assistance was needed by the soldiers. Deciding from the way in which the resistance of the Shooting Team was being overcome that it was not, he went to deliver the good news to Mr J.G. Reeder.

* * *   * * *

Passing through the rear wall without any interruption, the man who had shot at Pedlar Palmer having gone upstairs with him, Rapido Clint thrust open the kitchen door. Screams of alarm arose from the female members of the domestic staff who were gathered there as they saw the grim expression on his face and the Colt Government Model of 1911 automatic pistols in his hands. Glancing around, he discovered somebody else was present. However, he realized there would be no danger of intervention from that source. Billie Oakroyd was sprawled limply on the floor with blood from a cut on the top of her head dribbling down the side of her face.

'It wasn't none of us who done her, mister!' declared the massive cook, having a record at Scotland Yard for violent behaviour which made her determined to avoid being blamed for the condition of the young woman. 'That bloody Jerry bashed her with his gun as soon as they come in here!'

'Where's he at now?' the Texan demanded, realizing who was meant despite the inaccurate ethnic designation.

'Gone out the back door,' the cook replied and waved a massive hand to make sure there could be no mistake about the means of departure. 'We didn't—'

'Then *don't*!' Rapido interrupted, concluding the male servants were not alone in having had criminal backgrounds. 'Do what you can for her, a couple of you. The rest stay right where you are!'

'He's got her gun as well as his own, mister!' warned a skinny and unprepossessing housemaid, wanting to be able to claim she had acted in a co-operative fashion if the need arose.

'Who-all's with him?' the Texan inquired.

'Nobody *now*!' the cook supplied and the other women murmured agreement.

'*Gracias!*' Rapido thanked instinctively in Spanish, and started to stride swiftly across the kitchen.

However, the Texan did not make for the door at the rear. Instead, he went to one of the windows which flanked it and looked through. The precaution proved justified. Although walking quickly and having almost reached the shooting stands of the clay pigeon range, Baron Ludwig von Helsinore, in addition to carrying a

200

weapon with a much greater potential than the Webley service revolver he had taken from Billie, was constantly looking behind him.

Satisfied with his inspection, Rapido climbed on to the sturdy wooden work bench which ran the length of the wall. Moving along until in front of the window, he covered his head with his arms and plunged through it. Taking the shattered panes and wooden framework with him, he contrived to alight on his feet and avoid being cut by the broken glass. As he anticipated, the sound of his departure from the kitchen caused von Helsinore to turn around. Going into a rolling dive, he avoided the pair of bullets from the heavy revolver which came his way. However, as he returned to his knees and retaliated with three shots from the left hand Colt, he too failed to make a hit. Nevertheless, the third bullet he fired passed very close to its objective and produced a fairly satisfied result.

Startled by the near miss, it having been the first time he had come under hostile fire since the end of the Great War, the Baron acted without thinking. Instead of going around, he dived through the open door of a cabin employed for dispatching the targets used when skeet shooting was taking place. While it would offer protection against the Texan's bullets, there was no other way out. Despite this disadvantage, by making use of the slits through which the clay pigeons were dispatched, he would be able to prevent his attacker coming after him.

Having rapidly drawn this conclusion, von Helsinore darted to the right side slot. Nor, he concluded, was he any too soon. Already the Texan had risen and was commencing a swerving run forward. Trying to get the Webley into alignment, he touched off three more shots. Sensing each was getting nearer to their intended mark, he squeezed the trigger once more. Only a dry click rewarded his efforts. Billie had taken the gun from the footman who fired at Pedlar Palmer when he was set at liberty by the defenders and the spent cartridge had not been replaced. Snarling a curse, he watched his antagonist disappear behind the 'down the line' trap-house which he knew to be as well protected as his own hiding place.

'Give it up, *hombre*!' Rapido suggested, after thrusting himself erect sufficiently to allow him to fire four shots in rapid succession from each automatic at the front of the skeet hut and disappearing again before he could be subjected to retaliation. 'You can't get away. When I threw *it* out of the window to my *amigo* with the rifle last night, I sent word for him to go and fix that car you've got stashed by the back gate, so it won't go any place.'

'You said you didn't have *it*!' von Helsinore shouted with something close to indignation, not realizing the Texan was only guessing the vehicle was available, and aware that a man who had the same kind of accent and was armed with a rifle was in the grounds. Trying to prevent his consternation being noticeable, he continued with the distraction he was seeking to cause, 'You gave your *word* you didn't!'

'I said I *hadn't* got it,' the Texan corrected. 'Which I *didn't* have when you asked. If you'd asked *had I had it*, I'd have had to say, "Yes". As it was, I told the truthful *truth*. Now, are you coming out, or do I have to come in and fetch you?'

'You can *try*,' the Baron offered and, remembering what Billie had told him about the way his adversary reacted to a certain name, decided to put it to use. 'If you *dare*, you damned *Yankee*!'

'Don't you go calling me no *Yankee*!' Rapido bellowed furiously and reared up long enough to send another three bullets which splattered around the firing slot.

Having been changing positions, von Helsinore was not able to shoot back before the Texan disappeared behind the trap-house again. Watching for a chance to open fire, he gave his attention to thinking how he might escape from the building before any more of the defenders, or their military reinforcements, arrived on the scene.

Although he was Danish by birth, the Baron had served Germany during the Great War. However, the suggestion of him having held a commission aboard the *Osnabrucken* during the *David and Goliath* battle had been made to offer a reason for his presence at the party. In fact, he had risen to the rank of colonel and commanded a crack regiment of Uhlans which had seen much action all through the conflict. Nor had he ever forgotten the training he had received to prepare him for his duties. One thing he had been taught, and contrived to keep up practising, was counting how many shots an antagonist had fired at him. It was a trait which had saved his life on two occasions and he felt certain it would prove just as efficacious in his present situation. Up to that moment, the Texan had fired seven bullets from each of the Colt automatics. Allowing for him having had a round in the chamber when he inserted full magazines, that meant the weapons had only one more apiece.

Gambling on his judgement, seeking to give the impression that he meant to emerge, von Helsinore let himself be seen briefly in the doorway. From all appearances, the Texan took the bait and, by doing so, gave what appeared to be confirmation of the estimate reached by the Baron. Firing the left hand Colt without effect, Rapido tried to do so again. Then, discovering the weapon was empty, he sought to use the other pistol and once more there was no explosion of detonating powder. Such was his consternation at discovering he had emptied both Colts, he let out what sounded like a yell of alarm and dropped to cover once more.

A flood of elation swept through the Baron. He possessed a savage and ruthless nature which, in addition to establishing his reputation of being a brutal martinet second to none – in an army which had many very strict and punishing disciplinarians – had made him hated and feared by the men under his command in the Uhlans. This character trait would not allow him to adopt the sensible course of taking flight immediately. Although unaware if he had been told the truth about his car being rendered inoperative, he wanted to kill the small and insignificant looking young American who had played such havoc with his plans. He told himself that, even if he was left without the vehicle, he could still evade pursuit – by employing the skills he had acquired hunting big game around the world – once he reached the woodland beyond the grounds, until he could obtain some other form of transport. Then he set about putting his scheme for vengeance into effect.

'*Always* count how many shots you fire, *Yankee*!' the Baron shouted, leaping from the hut and grasping the Luger's butt in both hands as he started to run towards the trap-house. 'You've made a mis—!'

The triumphant words came to an end as the Texan suddenly rolled from behind his place of concealment!

For an instant, despite the other still holding the Colt in his right hand, von Helsinore felt no concern. He was confident that, especially while in such a restrictive position, there had not been sufficient time for his adversary to have changed even one empty magazine for a loaded replacement. Satisfied that all was going his way, he skidded to a halt and began to bring up the Luger.

At which point, everything went wrong for the Baron!

Just too late, von Helsinore realized the Texan was not behaving as he would have expected from one who, until a few seconds ago, had displayed such competence and skill at handling firearms. Everything he had done up to then had indicated he was not involved in his first fight with handguns. Yet apparently he had failed to take the precaution of counting how many shots he fired. In fact, his behaviour had suddenly become more suited to a rank amateur and nothing until then had even remotely suggested such was the case.

Even as the appreciation began to strike home, the Baron saw flame spurt from the muzzle of the big automatic he had assumed to be empty!

Extending the Colt at arm's length as he rolled from

behind the trap-house, Rapido sighted and squeezed the trigger while on his back, and there was the crash of a shot. Continuing to turn over and over, he discharged the powerful weapon three times more. Despite the awkward position from which they were fired, every bullet flew true. Swept backwards by the hail of lead which tore into the vital organs of his body, von Helsinore fired the Luger several times. However, it was the involuntary action of a man stricken mortally and the bullets winged off haphazardly instead of being directed at his enemy. Going down, he died without learning where his plan had gone wrong.

'No, *hombre*,' Rapido said quietly, coming to his feet. He was gratified that his apparently ill-advised behaviour in the latter stages of the fighting had produced the desired effect. 'For all you'd got one of those snail drum magazines on your Luger, *you* made a mistake when you didn't take Long Lou here into account.'

While speaking, the small Texan glanced at the device which had brought about the Baron's downfall. Long Lou was a magazine with a capacity of twenty rounds of a kind originally designed to offer extra fire power for the crew of aircraft before machine guns were put into service.[1] Having heard about them and realized how such a modification might be of use to him in his often dangerous duties with Company 'Z' of the Texas Rangers, he had had it made. Looking at the man sprawling ahead of him, he concluded its purchase had been money well spent.

1. Colt Government Model of 1911 automatic pistols intended for use with the long magazine in aircraft were fitted a wire cage to catch the ejected empty cartridge cases and prevent them from possibly damaging the fabric covering the fuselage, or any fragile instruments.

CHAPTER NINETEEN

It Isn't Over *Yet*

'All in – um – all,' Mr J.G. Reeder said with a hesitancy which did not appear in accord with such a positive statement. 'A *most* successful operation. While some quite important and high ranking officials of the – um – International Attainers died, something I for one do not regard as a subject for – um – mourning, every surviving member of their Shooting Team is either under – um – arrest, or hospitalized under guard. I am reasonably – um – sanguine that requests for their extraditions to stand trial in various countries will soon be forthcoming. Regrettably, we suffered four soldiers injured, one seriously, in the fighting.'

An hour had elapsed since Rapido Clint had killed Baron Ludwig von Helsinore. He had just been changing magazines on his left hand Colt automatic when the elderly looking detective had arrived accompanied by Captain John Gray – whose rarely used surname was Reeder – Parker, Jimmy Brocklehurst and half a dozen soldiers. Told that the situation was in hand, he had returned with them to the Manor. With all the routine matters completed, including various of the prisoners being subjected to interrogation, all those who had attended the house-party were gathered in the library and most of them heard the full story for the first time.

The reasons why the male guests who had aroused Baron Ludwig von Helsinore's suspicions, on account of their respective official status, had sought out Michael Mansfield and obtained invitations to the house-party had been explained.

There had been an ulterior motive behind Doctor

Andrew McCallister's eagerness to be asked to attend, but it was nothing to do with the International Attainers. In fact, he had not even known of their existence. The desire to get away from London and remain incommunicado until Tuesday had arisen because Sir James Bannister was on vacation and it was the turn of his other assistant to be on stand-by duty for the weekend. A notorious shirker of responsibility, Doctor Kinnock had developed the habit of calling upon McCallister to help with any problems, no matter how slight, which arose whenever their superior was absent, and he had been determined to avoid such unwanted attentions for a few days.

Having told the truth about the reason for his decision to seek an invitation, Flying Officer Allan Morningford's presence was equally innocent. Wanting to spend some time together in greater privacy than would have been possible in London, or anywhere else they knew of, Joan Darling and he had seen the solution on hearing Mansfield was having difficulty obtaining guests for the house-party. Therefore, each had contacted him and hinted at their availability and this had produced the result they wanted. There was nothing significant about him having his shotguns with him. He had heard of the clay pigeon range installed at Mansfield Manor and intended to use them to help pass the time during the day.

By the kind of coincidence no author of fiction would dare include in the plot of a novel, Rosalind Brampton and Jimmy Brocklehurst had had a similar motivation. However, on Sir Howard Houghton-Rand having learned of his destination, the latter was asked to act as support for the collector of the information should this prove necessary. Therefore, with the possibility of trouble should anything go amiss, he had decided to be armed during the visit.

Probably the greatest good fortune of the whole affair – despite involving another of the coincidences so common in real life, but generally shied away from by fiction writers – had been the means by which it was possible for Rapido Clint to attend. Beryl Snowhill's family had been seeking to negotiate the purchase of a piece of property belonging to Sir Granville Delamont which adjoined their racing stable in Wiltshire. This was used as an excuse for her to visit the Manor and have the small Texan accompany her.

While Mr Reeder had expressed qualms over the advisability of Beryl and Roz attending – he was unaware that Joan would be another guest – he had realized their presence was necessary and had taken every precaution he could envisage to ensure their safety. Their first meeting had proved that, young as she was, the beautiful little blonde had courage and the nerve to face danger without panic.[1] She also possessed sufficient skill in the use of firearms, plus a willingness to use them if necessary, which would stand her in good stead if some emergency should arise. What was more, he had had the fullest confidence in Rapido's ability to cope with any unforeseen eventuality until the support he had arranged could arrive. His faith had been justified, as had been proved by the fact that they had all emerged unscathed from the desperate situation caused by the murder of Sir Granville's substitute.

According to what Mr Reeder had learned from Doctor Christophe Dubarry, who was particularly forthcoming in the hope of obtaining lenient treatment, Sir Granville Delamont had died of a stroke when confronted by his substitute and had been buried in the grounds. The man who replaced him had been put under observation when it was realized that considerable sums of the organization's ill-gotten gains which passed through his hands never reached their destination. Mr Reeder had been correct in the assumption that, in the event of a betrayal by the substitute, preceding a departure with the money skimmed – to use a term of a

1. *A description of the meeting is given in:* CAP FOG, TEXAS RANGER, MEET MR J.G. REEDER.

later generation – from their coffers, Mr Reeder would be regarded as the most likely recipient of any information which could be used to obtain a secure future for the substitute wherever he decided to make a new life. This had explained the scrutiny to which he and his organization was subjected and why he had elected to meet with his superior and the Home Secretary in such a clandestine fashion.

Concluding that the betrayal had been planned and might soon take place, the leadership of the Attainers had sent von Helsinore to conduct an investigation and, if necessary, deal with the situation. After the man was murdered, he had decided to close down the base at Mansfield Manor immediately and dispose of the body by cremation in accordance with the Commodore's wishes. However, the plan had not proved so easy to put into execution as he had envisaged. The operator of a powerful radio set installed in the attic had brought disturbing news just after Doctor McCallister was coerced into supplying the requisite second signature for the cremation certificate. Information had been received that, as was feared would be the case, the substitute had arranged to give to the authorities details which would bring disaster to the higher echelons of the Attainers, but which would facilitate the substitute's intended defection.[2] He was to deliver these to a guest at the house-party and, after a thorough search had failed to reveal anything of such a nature on his person or in his living quarters, it was assumed the transfer had taken place.

Acting with Teutonic thoroughness, von Helsinore had instituted measures intended to prevent the information leaving the premises. He had instructed his man-

2. *Subsequent investigation by Mr J.G. Reeder established that the operation had been betrayed by a civil servant at the Home Office. He had Bolshevik persuasions and, having been duped by the International Attainers, believed he was helping to prevent the arrest of a group of Russian anarchists using Mansfield Manor as a base for their operations.*

servant and the two footmen to patrol the house and prevent any of the guests leaving, which led to the confrontation with Rapido. The watch kept by Guerney's party on the road, with orders to halt any vehicle passing along it – using a supposed burglary as an excuse should the occupants prove to be harmless travellers – had come closer to success. However, Captain Gray had hidden the wallet – which subsequently proved to contain the key to a safe deposit box and authorization for 'the bearer' to open it – delivered to him by Comanche Blood in the Singer and it was not searched.

The situation was regarded as being of such gravity by the leaders of the Attainers that the Baron had been given the support of the so called 'Shooting Team'. They were flown to England in two Farman F.60 Goliath airliners, owned by one of the organization's seemingly legitimate companies, from their secret headquarters in France and landed at a clandestine airfield they operated in a poorly populated area of Suffolk.[3] However, having learned of their impending arrival, the criminal who had previously refused to talk about the Attainers to Mr Reeder had warned him of it. This had supplied an additional reason for obtaining the kind of support – including the covert authorization for a modified state of martial law permitting the use of the Armed forces – he requested to ensure the safety of the guests at the Manor.

'You don't look too happy, Allan,' Roz remarked. 'Is your leg hurting you?'

'Not too much,' replied Morningford, who was sitting

3. *Younger readers who know only modern jet aeroplanes might doubt the possibility of a comparatively large passenger aircraft being able to use the limited facilities offered by such an airfield. We would point out that, even in the mid-1930s, pilots of airliners like the Armstrong Whitworth Argosy developed the habit of studying the terrain ahead to select suitable ordinary fields in which to land should there be an emergency. What is more, such descents were not infrequently carried out in safety.*

in an armchair and resting the injured limb on a stool. 'I was thinking about those kites which rescued us.'

'I thought the licentious soldiery did most of the rescuing,' Gray protested, being an ex-Army man himself. 'Are you sorry those smelly and noisy *devices* of yours couldn't spray everywhere in sight with their machine guns?'

'It's not *that*!' the Flying Officer corrected as soberly as if the conversation was in earnest. 'They came from *Seventeen Squadron* at Hawkinge.'

'What's wrong with that?' Gray inquired, although he could guess.

'Good heavens, old boy,' Morningford replied. 'I'm with the *magnificent* Twenty-Three and if the lesser souls of Seventeen find out it was *me* they'd been sent to rescue, I'll *never* hear the end of it.'

'Talking of never hearing the end of something,' Joan put in from her place by the Flying Officer's side. 'Now we're engaged, there'll be no more popping off to give low flying displays to impressionable young females, regardless of who their daddies might be.'

'I'll remem—!' Morningford began, then a realization of what the beautiful red head had said struck him and he swivelled around to stare up at her at the cost of some pain for the wounded leg. '*Engaged?*'

'In every melodrama I ever saw, or appeared in, the heroine was compromised when she was taken un-chaperoned to a house-party and the hero had to marry her,' Joan explained and sought verification. 'Isn't that correct, Mr Reeder?'

'That has always been my – um – experience with such edifying and – um – uplifting forms of entertainment,' the elderly looking detective confirmed sombrely, hav-ing a penchant for melodramas when in search of relaxation.

'There now,' Joan said, with the air of one who had had a point supported by a noted authority on the subject. 'And, anyway, I wouldn't think of going to Paris for the weekend with anybody other than my fiancé.'

'I always did want to see Paris,' Morningford claimed. 'You're on, old girl. We'll pop up to Town this afternoon and get the jolly old ring.'

'Now *that* is what I call a really *romantic* proposal,' Rita Yarborough asserted. 'And, if I'm *lucky* enough to get one like it, I'll stay a *spinster* for the rest of my days.'

'I'll keep *that* in mind,' Rapido declared before he could stop himself. Then, to cover his confusion, he went on quickly, 'How about you, *amigos*?'

'And me,' Ranse Smith supported with a grin.

'Now me,' drawled Comanche Blood, also showing amusement at his usually self-controlled *amigo's* discomfiture. 'I don't *ever* aim to let myself get caught where it'll make any never-mind.'

'Well, I'll say one thing, Jimmy,' Roz remarked, amused by the way in which the tone of the conversation had become lighter. 'You did warn me we'd probably be *bored* by the party.'

'It isn't *over* yet,' Rapido stated before Brocklehurst could reply and something in his voice caused every eye to go to him. A grim expression had come to his face and he continued, 'Leave us not forget the feller we thought to be Sir Granville Delamont was *murdered* last night.'

'Von Helsinore or one of the others did it,' Michael Mansfield claimed, making his first contribution to the meeting.

'Why?' the small Texan queried almost mildly.

'They knew he was going to betray them,' the new owner of Mansfield Manor claimed with the air of one who was pointing out a fact which should be obvious to everybody and failing to notice his fiancée was glaring at him with angry disapproval.

'Not *then*,' Rapido corrected. 'They didn't find out until early this morning. Until that happened, they wanted him alive and able to talk.'

'Then if *they* didn't kill him,' Morningford said in a puzzled tone. 'Who *did*?'

'I'll take the gun you've got in your vanity bag,

ma'am,' the small Texan said quietly, but his demeanour was charged with menace.

'*Gun?*' Wanda Gore-Kauphin repeated, but her attempt to appear uncomprehending was far from successful.

Until that moment, the actress was convinced the death of the man she had believed to be Sir Granville Delamont was to be forgotten or passed off as having been the work of the men who were with him.

The only reason Wanda had practically forced Mansfield to become engaged to her was so she could become the mistress of the property he would inherit. Her intention on taking possession was to turn it into a safe haven for Bolshevik agents and a training ground for anarchists of like persuasion. The latter were to serve as the nucleus of a force to overthrow the Government in a revolution which would establish her as the leader of the Socialist Soviet Republic of the British Isles. However, she had realized the terms in Lady Anne Delamont's will would prevent her from doing so as long as the present incumbent was alive.

There was, Wanda had concluded, an obvious solution to the dilemma. Delamont must be removed. The problem she faced was how to bring this about. Of one thing she was certain. Mansfield was too cowardly to make the attempt personally. However, it seemed fortune was favouring her. Pavlo Gorbochev, an especially ruthless Bolshevik assassin currently operating in England, was expecting to be arrested for having killed a family of prominent Russian exiles. She had offered to supply him with what would amount to an unshakable alibi in return for his assistance. However, on being released from the custody into which he had surrendered himself as the result of the story she told, he had refused to carry out the killing personally. Instead, he had provided the means and, based upon what she told him about the game invariably played at the house-parties, he had suggested the method by which it could be done.

As the actress had anticipated, not even being primed

with cocaine had given Mansfield the courage to perform the deed himself. Being made of sterner stuff, particularly as she too had made use of the narcotic, she had done it. She knew where 'Delamont' would be placed while the lights were out and had practised finding her way there, then away, in the darkness. When the game had been commenced, keeping clear of the participants, she had made her way across the room. Locating the wheelchair with the aid of the billiard table, she had fired three shots through its back from the silenced and otherwise lethally equipped revolver presented to her by Gorbochev.

Having carried out the shooting without being detected, Wanda had returned to where Mansfield was waiting and had placed the weapon behind some books she had selected as offering an ideal place of concealment. When the lights had come on, she had discovered that – despite being of such a light calibre, .32, she would have had qualms about using it if she had been more experienced with firearms – the Russian had been correct about the lethal qualities of the bullets he supplied. In addition to being made on the principle known as 'dum-dum', the head of each contained a dose of curare. On entering the body, the deadly poison was released by the rupturing of the thin coating holding it in place. Therefore, her victim had suffered more than just the wounds and had been killed without making a sound.

Being possessed of the kind of mentality which led her to assume everybody else was of a far lower intelligence than herself, Wanda had had no qualms over what would happen when the discovery was made that 'Delamont' had been shot. Such was her ego that she was sure she would not be suspected, or no proof would be forthcoming even if she should be. Nor, despite being grateful –albeit puzzled – that it happened, had she given any thought to why the body was removed so secretively by Dubarry and William Brown and there had been no attempt made to discover who had killed him. It had been her intention to retrieve and dispose of the revolver by throwing it into the woodland beyond the boundary fence. However, there had been a commotion on the first floor while she was in the library and she had decided to do it later and so had returned to her room undetected. With footmen patrolling the house for the rest of the night, there was no chance for her to get rid of the gun and, in the light of subsequent developments, she was not sorry she still had it in her possession.

There had been no need for Wanda to defend herself with the revolver and, having been confident nobody suspected her of being armed, she suddenly realized this was not the case. Despite the expected attack having failed to materialize and the servants all being taken into custody, she had remembered how she had not been allowed to leave the rest of the party after the rescuers came on the scene. Her suggestion of taking a walk to 'clear her head' was countered by a proposal that the American girl should accompany her in case any of the enemy were still at liberty. A similar insistence upon her having an escort had prevented her from going alone to her room and hiding the revolver there until it could be disposed of as she originally intended.

'*Gun,*' Rapido confirmed. 'I found out there was one in that bag of yours when the housekeeper knocked you cold and it hit the floor.'

'I must – um – *request* that you hand the firearm over, Miss Gore-Kauphin,' Mr Reeder stated in an almost apologetic sounding voice. 'There is nothing to be gained by you trying to –um – protect Mr Mansfield.'

'It wasn't *me*—!' the new owner of the Manor yelled, responding to the assumption that he was guilty of the murder as had been anticipated.

'Shut your damned mouth!' Wanda screeched.

'Proving *you* did it will present no – um – difficulties,' the elderly looking detective asserted as if the interruption had not taken place, still apparently addressing Mansfield. 'When we have the ballistics experts make a – um – comparison, they will *prove* the bullets in the body of your victim came from your gun.'

'Gorbochev said that couldn't hap—!' Wanda began to remind her fiancé, then realized she too had fallen into a trap.

'I've been hoping to see the famous – um – firearm of Mr Gorbochev for some considerable – um – time,' Mr Reeder exclaimed, knowing the statement he had partially elicited was in all probability true.

'You'll do *more* than just *see* it!' the actress shrieked, thrusting her hand into the vanity bag.

'If you *try* to bring it out,' Rita warned, having moved around until standing in a position which allowed her to thrust the muzzle of her Colt Detective Special revolver into the other woman's back, 'I'll save your country the cost of a hanging!'

However, seeing Wanda had no intention of yielding to the threat, the girl did not carry it out. Instead, before the revolver could be brought from the vanity bag, she swung up her own weapon and snapped it down. Struck on the head with the butt of the Colt, the actress buckled at the knees and collapsed like a rag doll from which the stuffing had suddenly been jerked.

'It was all *her* doing!' Mansfield screamed. 'She insisted on killing Dela—*Uncle Granville* and *nothing* I said stopped her going through with it.'

'I'm *sure* the jury at the Old Bailey will take *that* into – um – account,' Mr Reeder said dryly, picking up and studying the revolver. Of European manufacture, it was compact and had a silencer attached to the muzzle; qualities which, when combined with the poison-loaded bullets, made it the ideal weapon for an assassin. It was, he suspected, one of the arms sold to the Russians – who as yet lacked the technical skill to produce anything so sophisticated – by the International Attainers and he hoped the information he was promised would allow the supply to be cut off permanently. He mentioned none of this, but continued in what seemed to be an apologetic fashion, 'However, regrettable though I find the – um – necessity, I have no other course than to put you on trial as a – um – accessory before, during and after the fact.'

'Would you say it's over *now*, Rapido?' Roz inquired, as the elderly looking detective took out handcuffs and deftly fixed them upon Mansfield's wrists.

'Well, yes,' agreed the small Texan, without whose competent behaviour the nursing sister and the other guests knew they would in all probability have been killed. 'I reckon we can say it's over now.'

APPENDIX

In every democracy, the laws framed for the protection of the innocent have loopholes which can be exploited for the benefit of the undeniably guilty – and frequently are!

Although accepting that such a state of affairs must exist in a free society, the serving Governor of Texas grew very concerned over the ever increasing wave of lawlessness which had followed in the wake of the well meant – albeit unpopular, ill advised and difficult to enforce – ratification of the so called 'Volstead Act'.[1] He concluded that only unconventional methods could cope with malefactors who slipped through the meshes of the legal system. Ordinary peace officers, being severely restricted by Federal, State, county and municipal

1. 'Volstead Act', the colloquial name for the Eighteenth (Prohibition) Amendment to the Constitution of the United States of America. This defined intoxicating liquors as those containing more than one half of one per cent alcohol and made illegal the manufacture, transportation and sale of such liquors for beverage purposes. Introduced by Representative Andrew J. Volstead of Minnesota, the act was ratified – over the veto of President Woodrow Wilson – on 18 October 1919. By the time it was repealed in 1933, it had inadvertantly helped finance and pave the way for the rise of 'organized crime'.

regulations, were unable to take the necessary action in circumstances of this nature.[2]

While pondering upon the problem, the Governor met three prominent European criminologists who were touring the United States and giving a series of lectures on this subject to the heads of major law enforcement agencies. Acting upon the unconventional suggestions of George Manfred, Leon Gonzales and Raymond

2. *The jurisdictional authority of a town marshal or police department was restricted to the municipality by whom they were hired and a sheriff's office only had jurisdiction within the boundaries of the county to which its personnel were elected. As was suggested by the title of the latter, Arizona and Texas Rangers and State Police were restricted to their specific States. United States' Marshals, their deputies, the Federal Bureau of Investigation and Prohibition agents had country-wide jurisdiction. However, the first three were responsible only for handling 'Federal' crimes such as robbery of the mails and kidnapping. Except for Company 'Z' when on 'official unofficial' assignments, Texas Rangers were expected to wait until invited by the county or municipal agencies before being able to participate in either's investigations.*

2b. During the late 1870s, the Governor of Arizona formed a similar force to Company 'Z', Texas Rangers, to cope with law breaking in his State. The same decision was taken by a later Governor and the Arizona Rangers were brought back into being. Why it was considered necessary to organize the first force, how it operated and was finally disbanded is recorded in the Waco *series.*

2c. The Texas Rangers were to all practical intents and purposes abolished – their functions being taken over by the more prosaic Department Of Public Safety at Austin and the Highway Patrol – on 17 October 1935. This was almost one hundred years to the day after their formation. Although their first purpose was to act as militia, or what in present day terms would be called a 'paramilitary' organization, to help fend off marauding Indians, they became increasingly responsible for supporting the local authorities in the enforcement of law and order.

Poiccart,[3] he had instructed the State Attorney General to select a special group of Texas Rangers who would form – without any mention of it being made public – a new Company given the identifying letter 'Z' and put under the command of Major Benson Tragg. Every man was picked for his courage, skill with weapons, and bare handed combat, integrity, specialized knowledge and devotion to the cause of justice. Their purpose was to deal with such criminals as could not be touched by conventional methods, even if the means they employed to do so might be considered as stepping beyond the legal boundaries of the law.

Aware that his men were well known to the underworld, Major Tragg had enrolled Alvin Dustine Fog, Mark Scrapton and Ranse Smith, who he knew possessed all the requisite qualities and one other. Although all had served as local peace officers, none of them had previously been connected with the Texas Rangers. Despite this, after a probationary period during which each had proven himself capable of carrying out the duties required of him, they were appointed to the rank of sergeant to give them the necessary authority when on an assignment.

Having met members of Company 'Z' while they were engaged in trapping a crooked financier who could not be extradited from Mexico when she was trying to take revenge upon him for causing the death of her parents, Rita Yarborough was made an 'official unofficial' member of the group.[4] She proved herself very useful,

3. George Manfred, Leon Gonzales and Raymond Poiccart were the surving members of the 'Four Just Men' crime fighting organization, the fourth having been killed before their first recorded adventure was published. Although none of the folllowing volumes cover their lecture tour of the United States, see chronologically: THE FOUR JUST MEN, THE COUNCIL OF JUSTICE, THE LAW OF THE FOUR JUST MEN, AGAIN THE THREE and THE THREE JUST MEN by Edgar Wallace.

4. Told in: RAPIDO CLINT.

particularly when there was a need to deal with other women in the course of Company 'Z's' specialized type of duties.[5]

When producing the manuscript of 'CAP' FOG, TEXAS RANGER, MEET MR J.G. REEDER, we were under the impression that Cap had already acquired his sobriquet by becoming the youngest man ever to be promoted to captain in the Texas Rangers. As we explained in THE RETURN OF RAPIDO CLINT AND MR J.G. REEDER, he was still a sergeant and, in fact, his promotion came about as a result of the events we recorded in the latter volume. We first selected KILL MR J.G. REEDER as title for the former volume, but the executors of Edgar Wallace – biographer for the famous British detective – said they would prefer a reference to our character as well and we substituted, MR J.G. REEDER, MEET 'CAP' FOG. For some reason which was never explained, Corgi Books changed this to the one which now appears in our list of titles in chronological order on the advice of their Sales Department.

One of the points raised by members of the J.T. EDSON APPRECIATION SOCIETY since we were allowed to start producing the Alvin Dustine 'Cap' Fog series is to question the very close physical resemblance he had with his paternal grandfather, Captain Dustine Edward Marsden 'Dusty' Fog – for whom we also have the honour to serve as official biographer[6] – except that

5. *Examples of how Rita Yarborough dealt with another woman in the course of an assignment are given in:* Part Two, 'Behind A Locked And Bolted Door', MORE J.T.'S LADIES; Part Three, 'The Deady Dreams', J.T.'S LADIES RIDE AGAIN *and* THE RETURN OF RAPIDO CLINT AND MR J.G. REEDER.

6. *Details of the family background, career and special qualifications of Captain Dustine Edward Marsden 'Dusty' Fog are given in various volumes of the* Civil War *and* Floating Outfit *series.*

his hair was black instead of dusty blond.[7] The similarity was increased by Cap having received much the same education where gun handling, law enforcement duties and certain Japanese martial arts were concerned.[8] Furthermore, he had always revered the memory of his grandfather and sought to model himself in Dusty's image. However, due to having served as a peace officer after graduating from college – first as a deputy under his father, Sheriff Jackson Fog of Rio Hondo County[9] – Cap acquired only a minimal knowledge of the cattle raising

7. *Alvin Dustine 'Cap' Fog's black hair was inherited from his paternal grandmother. Prior to her marriage to Dusty Fog, she was Lady Winifred Amelia 'Freddie Woods' Besgrove-Woodstole. How she and her husband met and their romance progressed is told in:* THE MAKING OF A LAWMAN, THE TROUBLE BUSTERS, THE GENTLE GIANT, DECISION FOR DUSTY FOG, THE CODE OF DUSTY FOG, BUFFALO ARE COMING! *and* THE FORTUNE HUNTERS.

7a. *Freddie Woods makes 'guest' appearances in:* WHITE STALLION, RED MARE; THE WHIP AND THE WAR LANCE; *Part Five,* 'The Butcher's Fiery End', J.T.'S LADIES *and, under her married name,* 'Mrs Freddie Fog' *in:* NO FINGER ON THE TRIGGER *and* CURE THE TEXAS FEVER.

8. *Alvin Dustine 'Cap' Fog's instructor in the employment of, among other aspects of Japanese martial arts, ju-jitsu, karate and the yawara stick, was a nephew of Tommy Osaki, a samurai warrior who acted as valet for General Jackson Baines 'Ole Devil' Hardin, C.S.A.*

8a. *Details of the special qualifications of the General and Tommy are given mainly in the* Ole Devil Hardin *series.*

9. *Although as yet no details have been forthcoming with regards to the activities of Jackson Marsden Fog in his capacity of sheriff of Rio Hondo County, Texas, he makes a 'guest' appearance – based upon an incident when he was serving with the American Expeditionary Force in France towards the end of the First World War – in:* Case Two; 'Jubal Branch's Lucky B.A.R.', YOU'RE A TEXAS RANGER, ALVIN FOG.

business. Therefore, although equally competent as a gun fighter and, arguably, the finest combat pistol shot of his day,[10] he never excelled as a cowhand as did his grandfather.[11] On the other hand, circumstances had never compelled Dusty to adopt the kind of unconventional measures employed by Cap and Company 'Z' during those periods when he had been required to serve as a lawman in the Old West.[12]

As a tribute to the memories of their paternal grandfathers, Cap and Mark adopted the aliases, '*Rapido* Clint'[13] and 'Comanche Blood' when seeking to establish themselves as desperate criminals, as these had been used on similar occasions by Dusty Fog and the Ysabel Kid.[14] Ranse had inherited the looks and

10. *Some authorities give pride of place as the best combat pistol shot of the period to Ed McGivern of Montana, author of among other works* – FAST AND FANCY REVOLVER SHOOTING AND POLICE TRAINING

11. *One occasion when Dusty Fog proved his excellence as a cowhand in competition with his peers is recorded in:* GOOD-NIGHT'S DREAM

11a. *Despite there already being an entirely different English volume with the same name, in the USA, Bantam Books Inc. re-titled their 1974 edition,* THE FLOATING OUTFIT.

12. *In addition to the first five titles listed in* Footnote 8, *which refer to the early association between Lady Winifred Besgrove-Woodstole and Dusty Fog, further information pertaining to his activities as a peace officer is given in:* QUIET TOWN; DIAMONDS, EMERALDS, CARDS AND COLTS; THE SMALL TEXAN *and* THE TOWN TAMERS.

13. *Why Dusty Fog used the alias,* Rapido Clint *in told in:* BEGUINAGE *and* BEGUINAGE IS DEAD!

14. *Information regarding the family background and career of Mark Scrapton's grandfather, the Ysabel Kid, can be found in the* Floating Outfit *series.*

14a. *Occasions when the Ysabel Kid employed the alias, 'Comanche Blood' are given in:* HELL IN THE PALO DURO, GO BACK TO HELL *and* Part Three, 'Comanche Blood', THE HARD RIDERS.

physique of his maternal grandfather, Mark Counter who had been a good friend of Dusty and the Kid.[15]

15. *Details of the career and family background of Ranse Smith's grandfather, Mark Counter, are given in the* Floating Outfit *series.*

15a. *As is told in the* Rockabye County *series — which covers the organization and duties of a present day Sheriff's Office in Texas — Ranse's activities with Company 'Z' induced another member of the family, Bradford 'Brad' Counter, to become a peace officer.*

THE END